THE FATAL BELLMAN

GUY JENKIN

The Book Social Ltd, 51 Gower Street, London, WC1E 6HJ
info@legendtimesgroup.co.uk | www.legendpress.co.uk

 British Library Cataloguing in Publication Data available.

Print ISBN 9781918291865
Ebook ISBN 9781918291872
Set in Times.
Cover design by Rose Cooper | www.rosecooper.com

Praise for *The Fatal Bellman*

'A delicious and intelligent tour de force. I loved it. Truly engaging characters with whom to travel into the dark alleys, playhouses and rogue-inhabited streets of the edgy London of James I. Unputdownable.'

Carol McGrath, author of the *She-Wolf Queens* trilogy

'A gripping tale, buzzing with dark comedy and set in a dangerous Jacobean world of assassins, spies, witch-hunters and temperamental actors.'

Andy Hamilton

'A brilliant sequel to *Murder Most Foul*. We are back in world of Will Shakespeare as he and his darling Ann run the gauntlet of killers, shady pretenders, mad aristocrats and a witch-obsessed king as they seek to uncover the killer of a much-loved actor. Our favourite characters are back with a bang in this rollicking adventure combining dark undertones and belly-laughs.'

G J Williams, author of *The Tudor Rose Murders* series

'Riotous, subversive and completely bloody brilliant. William Shakespeare and Ann Marlowe take on criminals, plotters and spymasters in a clever, funny and illuminating tale set amid the affluence and effluence of James VI and I's reign.'

Chris Lloyd, author of the *Occupation* series

Praise for the *Quill and Dagger* series

'A delightful cross between *Wolf Hall* and *Blackadder*.'
The Express

'Clever, funny, ingenious and endearing.'
Lissa Evans

'Funny, thrilling and full of wonderful Easter eggs for Shakespearean theatre fans.'
David Greig

Guy Jenkin is a multi BAFTA, RTS and Emmy award-winning writer, director and producer. His television series include *Outnumbered*, *Kate & Koji* and *Drop The Dead Donkey*, all co-written with Andy Hamilton. He also wrote and directed a number of TV films including *A Very Open Prison* and *Crossing The Floor*, and two feature films, *The Sleeping Dictionary* and, with Andy Hamilton, *What We Did On Our Holidays*. His first novel, *Murder Most Foul*, was published in 2025 and was shortlisted for the Bollinger Everyman Wodehouse Prize for Comic Fiction.

To Bernadette… again

ACT ONE

THURSDAY

ANN

The moon was behind Ann, and her shadow stretched and climbed the walls as Duck Lane twisted ahead of her. It must have been seven o'clock because the cathedral's boy sopranos began their nightly practice and their sweet voices wove through the alleys of Canterbury. As usual, that set off the dogs and the choir's psalms were accompanied by a rising racket of barking and howling.

Her father had died three days ago with the name of Jesus on his lips. 'Christ, get me some claret,' he'd said, but pegged out then and there before they could tell him he'd drunk it all long ago. It was Ann and Dot who stripped and cleaned him with a rag and some rubbing alcohol. Ann had held up the bottle.

'Don't know how he missed this one.'

Her sister had snorted bitterly. The body still lay on the kitchen table, wrapped in the sheet he died in. Every undertaker in Canterbury refused to take him without a deposit, they knew the Marlowes too well. They died often but paid seldom.

Ann carried a half-guinea she'd prised from her husband, John, at the price of a lecture on her family's failures – long and sanctimonious, but to be fair, spot on. The choirboys were singing 'The Lord is My Shepherd', and she joined in as she jumped a frozen Angel Brook, turned the corner into a bitter wind and headed up the hill to her father's cottage to meet the coffin maker.

The front garden was a mess. She clambered over the stumps of a fence, hitched her gown up so as not to catch on the brambles and opened the door. She lit a candle. There was her father's body on the table and – Sweet Jesus – another body lay on the floor with its throat cut. It was Hal Dove, the coffin maker, still holding his measuring rod.

She clutched for something to steady herself but scrabbled at thin air for a moment until she found the wall. She realised she was still singing along with the distant voices of the choir.

'He leadeth me beside the still waters. He restoreth my soul.'

It helped to steady her, so she kept going. She put the candle on the table, knelt down and put a thumb on Hal's wrist. His pulse was racing crazily. She had a half-second of hope before she realised it was her own. Hal was dead.

She must give her body a moment to return to her, to think clearly, work out what to do and in what order.

But as she paused, the door to the kitchen opened with a scrape and a large man filled the gap. He wore a black cloak and a scarf covered the lower half of his face. His eyes were neither brown nor blue nor green nor grey but strangely colourless and not quite human. In one hand he held a long knife. He stepped between Ann and the front door. Ann stopped singing.

WILL

The young woman's neck was so slim and the blade so huge. The instant her head extended from the block, the black-cloaked figure swung the axe. There was a bang and a puff of smoke and her severed head tumbled into a basket. The crowd seemed to breathe in all together in one long gasp.

Will had worked out how the conjurer and his assistant did this. It was the next bit that stumped him and kept bringing him back again and again to the performances.

It was the climax of their act, the execution of Mary, Queen of Scots. It was surely unwise to keep performing this now Mary's son James was England's thin-skinned king, who'd throw you in the Tower for the slightest hint of ridicule. Still this mock execution always gathered a good crowd and the fly and bottle boy always collected a few coins afterwards.

The trick began with Mary's confession. The conjurer let the crowd feel the razor-sharp blade of his axe; tonight he'd let a woman slice a loaf with it. Then 'Mary' laid her head on the block, and the conjurer – Will did think this was something of a cheat – laid another small block over her so her head stuck out of a hole. The tall, black-caped magician raised the axe, the blade glinting in the light from the flaming torches. Down it swung.

Will had worked out that it was the bang and puff of smoke that was the key. The bang was off to one side and lured your eyes away for one instant and the smoke was in front of the block and obscured the girl's head just long enough as the axe came down. If you ignored the bang and stared at the block, you could just see her whip her head back and throw out a fake severed one. It was dangerous though. She left it until the blade was inches above her. He guessed she took her cue from the bang so, if that was late, there would be a real head in the basket.

But again they had timed it perfectly. The conjurer held up the fake head dripping blood and the audience gasped and applauded. Will watched intently, as it was the next bit that baffled him. Surely today he would see how they did it. The conjurer placed the head down on top of the block, slung the axe down so it stuck in the ground, and then turned around in mock surprise as the head started to talk. Again he had missed the swap. How! He would have to come yet again and he didn't really want to be seen hanging around at such common entertainment.

'I would have killed your queen,' the girl was hissing. 'I am in league with the great Satan.'

She was good. God, she would have made a better Beatrice than any of those boys and the audience were enthralled. He wondered if he could use some of these tricks onstage. A dead woman coming back to life. Well, maybe one day.

There was a sharp crack and an officer on a white mare, swinging a whip above his head, rode into the tight-packed crowd, knocking people hither and thither. Soldiers from the militia ran in from all sides of the square, armour gleaming in the torchlight. One tried to grab the bottle boy who ducked under his metal gauntlet. The conjurer stood waiting for them onstage, cursing wildly in Welsh, until a soldier swung the pole of a halberd to take out his legs and they dragged him away still spluttering in rage. The officer dismounted and strode over to where the woman's head was trapped. He took hold of her hair and yanked her upright. He was left holding the dummy head. The crowd jeered and hooted and the officer angrily threw the head away.

Will knew him, the recently knighted Sir Crispin Proute,

one of King James's new favourites. You could see why. He was big and handsome, with a jaw that they could have used as a battering ram. His crimson uniform, gilded with silver and gold braid, looked as if it had been stolen from the costume store at the Globe. He surely must have invented it himself. There were more and more of these young gentlemen who wanted to play at soldiers strutting around London as 'officers' in the militia. A tiny old woman with no teeth followed behind him aping his swagger and the crowd cheered.

There was a distant bang that rattled the nearby windowpanes. An illicit gunpowder factory had caught fire around lunchtime and there had been explosions all through the day. London was always blowing up, falling down, catching fire or just sinking into its soggy clay – a great, ever-growing beast of a city, steaming in the rain, stinking in the heat, still clamouring beneath fog, smoke or darkness with the sound of haggling, hammering and breaking glass, its teeming citizens swarming like fleas in its fur.

A soldier shouted. He'd found the young woman from the show hiding behind a fried eel stall, but before he could grab her she was away, leaping light-footed over a low cart. There was something about the way she ran – Will was sure he knew her from somewhere.

ANN

The man raised the knife, lifted the bottom of his scarf for a moment and licked the flat of the blade as if blessing it. He stepped towards her with the nonchalance of someone about to snuff out a candle. The only weapon Ann could see nearby was the half-full bottle of rubbing alcohol and she reached out and picked it up. The man gave a snort of derision.

She hurled the bottle and it struck a beam above him and covered his hair in alcohol and small shards of glass. He shook his head disdainfully at her terrible aim. She picked up the flaming candle and hurled it at his alcohol-soaked head. He saw what she was trying to do just in time and swatted it away with the hand holding the knife.

'Oh, I remember you,' he said. 'You're a cunning bitch.' And he took two quick steps towards her, slashing ahead of himself with the knife.

She leapt backwards so the table where her dead father lay was between them. The candle that had missed him had fallen on the sheet, and some of the alcohol they'd washed him with must have soaked in, because it flared into flames. The man circled the table in pursuit, those pale eyes never leaving her. She backed away from him, but stumbled over something and fell. She'd forgotten the body lying on the floor.

She could only see the man's eyes but she was sure he was smiling as he raised his knife. She yanked the now flaming sheet off the table, swung it around and chucked it at his head and shoulders as he lunged. He leapt back but this time he was too late, and his scarf caught fire where the rubbing alcohol had soaked him. He ripped it away but now his face and hair were on fire. She scrambled to her feet and darted past this human candle and out the door.

A strange thought jumped into her brain. Was this the first time alcohol had saved a Marlowe? As she reached the alley she looked behind her and the man came running around the corner, still on fire, batting at his flaming hair. You couldn't fault his determination. She picked up her skirt and ran.

She looked behind her again as she turned the next corner, and saw him throw himself into an ice-covered horse trough outside the old stables with a crack and a splosh. Now she'd have a few seconds to get away, so she turned left into Tanner's Yard then doubled back up the steps towards the Nunnery gardens.

Why was this happening? Why had he killed the coffin maker? Was he a thief? He didn't seem like a thief and everyone in Canterbury knew that her father had drunk away anything worth stealing long ago. Anyhow, surely she must have lost him by now. She decided to wind her way through the backstreets to the Flying Horse, but then the killer's words came into her head.

'I remember you. You're a cunning bitch.'

If he knew her, he'd know she lived at the pub that she and John ran. She stepped into an alley that smelt of soap and horse piss and paused to have a think.

She smelt him before she saw him, a faint waft of something burnt. Had he managed to follow her or was he just combing the streets? She looked behind her. The alley was a dead end. A vagabond woman and a child she hadn't seen at first lay on some straw beneath a high stone wall. The woman was asleep but the child's eyes were wide and staring. She held her finger to her lips. Her only chance was to stay very still. She held her breath.

His dark shape glided past, walking almost silently, and she smelt the stench of charred flesh, the smell of hell itself.

He disappeared. She could hear her heart thumping so loud that surely he would hear it too and come back. But he didn't. She counted to a hundred, then pressed a silver penny into the child's hand and tiptoed out of the alley in the opposite direction to the man.

Who was he? Had he followed Dove to the cottage to kill him? Or was he already there looking for something when Hal had disturbed him? But then it hit her. The masked man had killed Hal, but then, rather than fleeing, had waited in the house. There was only one reason he'd do that. He'd come there to kill Ann.

FRIDAY

WILL

The strangling of Desdemona was very realistic tonight. Xander Cooke, the boy playing Desdemona, had been upstaging Othello again and Burbage was taking it out on him in the death scene. Richard Burbage, the world's greatest tragedian according to Richard Burbage, did not tolerate overacting in anyone but himself. The strangling went on and on. From backstage, Will could see Burbage's face turning red beneath his black make-up, either with rage or the effort of throttling him. Now Xander's legs were kicking.

Will started to run on from backstage to drag Burbage away but Xander's legs stopped moving and Burbage stepped away and started his final monologue, panting slightly. Xander was still and Will hoped he was just unconscious and not actually dead. Burbage fell to his knees and his voice broke into a sob as he said, 'Then you must speak of one who loved not wisely but too well.'

Will kept telling him it was too much, and to let the words do the work, but Burbage loved a bit of weeping.

Behind Othello, Desdemona stirred, croaked and gasped. Burbage's voice rose louder but Xander couldn't help groaning and spluttering as he sucked in air. Someone in the crowd laughed. Burbage stopped speaking. Someone had had the audacity to laugh in his final scene. Will braced himself.

Burbage strode over to Desdemona and went back to strangling her. Will went to run on but Hugh Berrycloth, playing Cassio, was quicker. He'd always liked Xander. He grabbed Burbage and tried to drag him away before he killed the boy. Othello turned around and punched him and Cassio punched him back. The crowd cheered. Othello ran at him and knocked him over and they both fell on the bed flailing at each other as Desdemona tried to crawl away. This made it look as if not only had Desdemona survived, but that Othello's suspicions of Cassio were justified.

The crowd on All Saints' Day had spent the day in the pub and were always more raucous than usual. They stomped and hooted and the pit and the gallery started rival chants for Othello and Cassio. Desdemona's robe got caught under Burbage's boot and her gown was torn off, leaving a bare-arsed boy clambering for the wings, which set the audience off again. Most of the cast had gathered behind Will and looked at him, not knowing what to do. He wanted to let the fight go on in the hope they did some proper damage to each other, but then Burbage and Berrycloth rolled into one of the torches that lit the stage and it fell over and set some drapes on fire. A couple of stagehands ran on with a bucket of water and poured it over the burning fabric. Will picked up another bucket of water, walked onstage and poured it over Burbage and Berrycloth, which got another cheer. He signalled for the cast to come on and take their bow.

The crowd clapped and roared, so at least no one would be asking for their money back, but for heaven's sake, it was a theatre and not a bear pit. Burbage was on all fours and Will stepped on his hand.

'Sorry,' he said as Burbage yelped satisfyingly.

A woman in the sixpenny seats onstage called out Will's name and he saw her standing on tiptoe, her mass of blue-black hair piled high. She put her fingers in her mouth and whistled.

He waved to her and when all the nobles, notables and luminaries gathered onstage, as they always did after a performance, she came and found him.

'They want me to marry the tsar of Muscovy,' she said to Will.

'How old is this one?' asked Will.

Her smile tightened. Frances Strange – eldest daughter of the late Lord Strange, earl of Derby, descended from the blood of two kings, rich as Croesus, famed for her wit and beauty – liked to make fun of herself but no one else could.

'This one is fully grown,' she said crisply, 'not like…' She waved her long hands with those pointed scarlet nails as if they would conjure up the answer.

'The Sicilian one?' Will offered.

'Yes, though he was very grown-up for eleven. He wrote me a love poem in Greek.'

Will could barely hear her with the noise around them. Tonight, the throng mingling on the stage with the actors was even louder than usual, perhaps excited by the fight they'd seen onstage.

'No, this one's a man,' said Frances, 'and very handsome.' She poked Will. 'Are you jealous?'

Was she flirting with him? It seemed highly unlikely. He'd risen in the world, but nowhere near the giddy heights where she sauntered; if anything she was flirting with the theatre – with that, she was besotted.

An unstrangled boy actor was hovering beside Will.

'Mr Shakespeare, sir. There's a woman at the back door waiting to see you.'

'Oh, lucky you,' said Frances.

Frances was dressed in a shimmer of silk and taffeta, sky blue and black. The gold thread and tiny jewels sewn into her bodice glittered, and a string of fat pearls glistened around her throat. Yet she was never quite contained by what she wore. Hats tilted crookedly, feathers fell off and fluttered to the ground, pins came out and her mass of black hair slipped loose so she had to sweep it away from those unexpectedly blue eyes. Straps and hoops that shouldn't have been seen somehow appeared, and buttons were done up wrong. It made Will think of her undoing them – or, when he'd had a few drinks, of him undoing them. He was never sure if this chaos of clothing was accidental or artful.

He asked, 'So have you met this tsar?'

'God no, I've told Mama that if I must marry a foreigner, I'm holding out for an emperor.'

'I hear Persia is nice this time of year,' he said.

'Doesn't the emperor of Persia have a thousand wives?'

'I'm sure you'd be in the top ten.'

She glowered and waggled an admonishing finger.

Burbage emerged, one eye bruised and half closed, and the crowd onstage applauded and cheered. He beamed and raised his arms above his head like a champion.

'He'll probably start a fight every night now,' Will muttered.

'Of course, it's James behind this marriage nonsense,' said Frances, speaking of the king of England as if he was a pal. She put on a Scottish accent. 'Ay, the wee lassie's got a claim to my throne so I'll see her married off to the king of somewhere far away and dangerous.'

She had an uncanny gift for mimicry and it made Will laugh. He was allowed to laugh at this and she laughed too, with a big unladylike guffaw.

Timothy, the boy actor, was at his sleeve again.

'Mr Shakespeare, sir, the woman is still waiting at the back door.'

'Thank you, I will come in a moment.'

He watched this gangly bundle of limbs walk away. His voice was breaking. It was a pity, the lad had a gift for comedy, but he'd have to move on.

'Did you know my father had a bastard?' Frances asked with one of her dizzying changes of direction. Will didn't, though he knew many things about her father, Lord Strange, that he was sure she didn't. He knew that he was behind the death of his best friend Kit Marlowe and had led a plot to kill Queen Elizabeth. He knew that Lord Cecil had hushed the whole thing up and that Lord Strange had been poisoned.

Almost no one knew that. 'Yes, he's turned up from abroad and he's running around London,' Frances went on. 'And all the women and half the men are in love with him. You should get him to play Othello. He has a touch of the Moor in him.'

Will realised that he had met her half-brother here at the Globe. He had complimented Will on *Timon of Athens* but told him that if Kit Marlowe had written it he would have livened it up with some explosions.

An owl brooch, with sapphire eyes that matched Frances's own, fell off and she waited for Will to stoop and pick it up.

'I want to meet him,' she said, 'but my family tell me I mustn't because he's beneath me. Nearly as beneath me as you are, Will.'

She liked to mock him and yet he was the only one at the Globe who she spoke to as an equal. He'd come a long way from the boy with one groat tucked in his hose who'd jumped on the back of the actors' cart as it left Stratford.

A small woman walked towards him, her wet black hair plastered across her face, her ragged gown splattered with mud.

'Will!' she yelled.

He saw she only had one shoe.

It was Ann Marlowe.

BELLA

If ever Bella needed a vicious dog to protect her it was now that a man with a knife had broken into her house.

Her old brute of a dog, Perro, had died at the improbable age of eighteen on the same day as Queen Elizabeth. Bella had somehow felt that the outpouring of grief for the old queen, the muffled drums and tolling bells and men sobbing in the street, was also for Perro, for she too had been fierce, indomitable and reassuring.

Bella needed a dangerous dog for her dangerous work because a weapon on a leash made men treat her as an equal. She had found a grandson of Perro in a litter of thirteen, born in Lambeth on that same day as her old dog had died. The dog grew as huge and ugly as Perro, but despite Bella's attempts to train him, Tamburlaine was incapable of violence.

So then she had to hope that the sight of him walking beside her on a chain, pink speckled jowls swaying slowly from side to side, slobber dripping from his great jaws, a piratical black marking around one eye, would, at least, inspire terror in anyone intending her harm. But then he would lollop over to a stranger, put his huge paws on their shoulders and enthusiastically lick their face. She bought him an iron spike collar that made him look more brutal – that was until he went and sat at the feet of a stallholder, fixed them with adoring eyes and offered them a paw. Who had taught him that? Certainly it was not her.

Soon all of London knew that the huge mastiff, who weighed more than a hundredweight and had jaws that could crack an ox bone, was a soppy giant who made a noise suspiciously close to a purr if you scratched his massive, knobbly skull. Mothers would smile as children barely big enough to walk tottered over to him and laughed as his rough tongue licked their faces. Babies pulled his tail, their big sisters draped him in daisy necklaces and their bigger brothers tried to ride him. She had named him after a merciless emperor but created a licker of toddlers. The one time he had seen her attacked he had sat watching it happen wagging his tail. Was he really a dog? She knew his mother was one but what was his father? Perhaps a sheep.

At first, she felt a kind of discontent as everyone admired Tamburlaine. Was it jealousy? There had been a time men stared at her as she passed. Now they stared at her dog. Slowly though, she realised it was changing her. Before she had been an unspeaking foreign woman who walked the streets with a terrifying dog but now everyone smiled to see her coming. Children asked her hundreds of questions. How old was he? Did he eat custard? Did dogs dream? Could he jump over a horse? And she found herself answering them.

Even her work was different. When she turned up to bring Lord Cecil intelligence, the thugs he gathered around him, the square men with tobacco-stained beards and faces of rotting leather, would grin like babies as they scratched Tamburlaine's mighty head with the hilts of their daggers. Once he licked the face of Lord Cecil himself, the tiny, twisted, sharp-tongued, single-minded, brilliant obsessive who ran England, and the face smiled.

Now though, she wished she had her old, vicious dog for she had come home, shut the door and a man with some sort of mask obscuring his face had stepped out of her orangery and cut off her escape. The part of his face she could see was freshly scarred from burning. Tamburlaine pranced in front of him proudly holding a stick he had found, his tail wagging furiously.

She pulled out her blade from the sheaf in her skirt and

wondered if she could get to the drawer where she kept a loaded pistol. The man stepped towards her holding a long knife, his feet making no noise.

'Go now,' she said, 'or the dog will tear you to pieces.'

He gave a brief snort as if he did not want to waste time on laughing. So he knew who she was and the dog's reputation. That was worth knowing. Tamburlaine squatted on his big rump, dropped the stick at the man's feet, and stared at him adoringly as he pulled a pistol from beneath his singed cape and wound back the wheel lock to cock it.

'Put the knife on the table,' he said in a surprisingly mellifluous rumble. 'I just want to talk.'

He did not want to use the gun because of the noise. He would disarm her and then kill her with the blade.

'I can talk holding a knife,' she said, edging towards the drawer.

'I took your gun,' he said.

Sadly the man was no idiot. She wondered for a moment if this would be it, this would be the time she did not escape.

He stepped carefully forward still holding the pistol. She hoped he would not fire it. It would scare the dog. Tamburlaine was terrified of fireworks and thunder but loved people. She knew he was wrong, that explosions in the sky were harmless and it was humans who were deadly.

There were muffled voices from outside and the man glanced over his shoulder.Tamburlaine gave an excited woof and loped towards the door. Someone was outside and he was eager for more visitors. A fist pounded on the door and an aristocratic voice shouted, 'The king's militia. Open the door now!'

She ducked beneath the edge of a table in case the man was going to shoot her but he backed away silently in his felt boots towards her orangery. The last thing to disappear around the corner was his gun. She heard the door to the yard click.

'Open the door now,' shouted the voice at her front door.

'I'm coming,' she said, but a hammer smashed through a wooden panel. And then another.

The militia loved nothing more than breaking down doors – except, perhaps theft and violence. She tucked her dagger away, reached the door, unlocked it, and a soldier swinging a hammer fell into the room. The dog licked his face.

'Thank you,' she said. 'Who told you he was here?'

'Aha, she admits the devil is in the house,' said a voice, and Sir Crispin Proute's large frame, in his child's uniform, stepped out of the darkness. He pointed a large pistol and roared to the soldier, 'Stand back, idiot, and I'll shoot the dog.'

'No, no, no, sir,' said the soldier, standing and blocking his shot. 'I know him, he's as gentle as a lamb.'

Reluctantly Proute put the gun down.

There was another voice behind him.

'Have you got the witch?'

Sir John 'Rich' Spencer, the wealthiest man in London, tottered towards the door, dressed in a tight red silk coat that made him look like a giant cushion. A servant carried a wide chair which he placed behind him.

Bella felt real fear for the first time that night. 'Rich' Spencer's new pastime was arresting and interrogating witches. Was the arrival of him and the lackeys a coincidence and nothing to do with the man in her room?

He toppled back like a slaughtered ox into the waiting chair.

'Bring her familiar too,' he wheezed.

The soldier tied a rope around Tamburlaine's iron collar.

WILL

After Ann had left on the cart for Canterbury twelve years ago, he'd tried to forget her, though the phrase made no sense, for to think of forgetting her he first had to think of her. But bit by bit she came into his mind less often and created less turmoil when she did. Yet now here she was – pale, fierce and bedraggled. He hurried over to her.

'A man tried to kill me,' she said.

He was shocked but not surprised. Not many Marlowes died of natural causes.

'I'm sorry,' he said, not knowing what else to say.

The hum of conversation had dropped. Everyone was looking at them without quite looking. Painted eyes glanced sideways, finely trimmed beards bristled with excitement, ostrich feathers in silk hats quivered expectantly.

Ann glowered back at them as drips from her soaked gown formed a small, dirty puddle on the floor.

There she stood amidst all those frills and fripperies, something real gusted onto the stage of the Globe – mud her make-up, woodsmoke her perfume, a small twig of bramble adorning her hair.

He could see her breathing hard, sense the desperation that had brought her here. He reached out a hand wanting to console her, realised he shouldn't touch her with everyone watching, then didn't know what to do with it. It was left flapping in the air. Finally he gestured with it to guide her backstage away from all the prying eyes. She stayed where she was.

Frances Strange was hurrying over. Now the play was finished, she wasn't going to miss this drama, but the last thing Will wanted was her breathless enquiries. He needed to get Ann somewhere else before all London was gossiping about the two of them.

'Let's get you some dry clothes,' he said, and to guide her he touched the small of her back. He felt her shiver and for a moment the world reeled around him like a room in which he lay drunk. Had twelve years changed nothing? He wasn't going to let all that start up again.

ANN

Will guided her backstage. She squelched into a curtained-off room which turned out to be the costume store. A couple of actors were sitting there smoking pipes.

'Can you go somewhere else, please?' Will asked. They bowed and walked out. He shouted after them. 'And ask one of the boys to fetch in some hot soup.'

'Yes, Mr Shakespeare,' said one of them.

'*Well*,' she thought, '*he's gone up in the world since the last time I was here. Not surprising he's ashamed of me*.' She dropped her soaked and ripped cloak and it slapped wetly onto the floor.

As he rummaged among the costumes looking for something for her to wear he asked her what had happened.

She told him about the man with the knife and what he'd said and how he'd hunted her, about how she'd gone to her sister's, tapped on the window and managed to tell Dot what had happened, all without waking the baby, told him how it wasn't safe for her to go back to the Flying Horse so she needed to flee. She didn't tell him how the thought of going back to her husband filled her with misery.

She skated over the journey – how she feared the killer would check the night carts leaving Grassmarket, so she had walked out on the Whitstable Road, cursing the biting wind that chilled her and the full moon that lit her up like a target.

She didn't tell him how crossing Rough Common she'd heard hoofbeats on the road behind her and leapt into a ditch skinned with ice to hide but needn't have bothered. It was just a mule train carrying lambskins to the port. She crawled out of the wet mulch of autumn leaves and a kind pair of brothers put her on the back of one of their animals – Bessie, who they swore had the sweetest nature of any mule they'd ever known. Bessie carried her to Whitstable as the grey dawn broke ahead of her.

She did say how she'd paid for passage on a two-masted Dutch Fluyt heading for London but not that she used some of the half-guinea that her husband had grudgingly given her for her father's funeral.

The hold was crammed with goats at one end and drunk Hessian mercenaries at the other so she stayed on deck wrapped in the sheepskin the brothers had given her, and tried to make herself small in the wind and sleet. The flask of gin she bought to keep herself warm was gone before they passed the smudged outline of Canvey, and when she was unable to feel her hands, she knew she must go below. She chose the end with the goats.

The rest he knew – how bruised, bloodied, soaked, shivering and stinking, she turned up at the Globe. She shouldn't have come. She felt like a small, mauled creature a cat had dropped on some satin sheets.

He handed her a cloak of purple and gold.

'Is there a gown?' she asked, unable to stop herself from trembling. She hoped he knew it was the cold and nothing to do with him.

All he could find was a garish red robe that he told her was Francescina's from *The Dutch Courtesan*. Well, that would have to do. Her fingers were still numb lumps as she fumbled at the loops to take off her kirtle. Will stepped outside, though heaven knows it wasn't as if he'd never seen her undress.

She peeled off her sodden petticoat and smock and stepped out of them. There was a sheet of shiny metal on the wall opposite that the actors used as a mirror, and she looked at herself. She stared back, small, wet and naked.

'*Well*,' she thought, '*that's all I am*.'

She put on the gown and cloak, told Will she was done and he came back in. Burbage's booming voice passed by outside and Will stuck his head out of the curtain.

'Dickie,' he said, 'have you got your flask?'

'Dickie' indeed! He really had gone up in the world, she thought, as Dickie handed Will a fine silver flask and Will gave it to her. She unscrewed the cap, smelt brandy and tipped it back. It was only a quarter full so she drained it and it lent her its moment of false warmth. The only shoes that fitted her were from Will's new play and she put on Desdemona's white and gold slippers.

Will asked her if she wanted to wait for the soup. He kept asking these questions. What she wanted to eat or wear, but never the question that hung between them – why had she come? Why had she? It was an unfortunate necessity. She hadn't wanted to come straight to Will, but Canterbury was too small to hide in and there was no one else she knew in London. Well, there was her cousin, both her cousins, but she'd quarrelled with one of them – well, both of them if she was being honest. Anyhow, that just left Will. She really had had no other choice.

She said no to the soup. A giggling couple tumbled through the curtain, saw them, apologised and hurried away.

'Let's get you back to my house,' Will said. 'I'll send word ahead for the maid to make a fire and have a hot meal ready.'

'Your undermaid or your overmaid?' she said, surprising herself that she had time to mock him on a day like this. 'Perhaps your coachman can convey us there.'

'It's his night off,' said Will.

She presumed he was joking but wasn't sure. There were flashes of the old Will but how much he had changed since she had last seen him. He had never dressed theatrically like Alleyn or her brother – those purple-lined capes and raffish hats. Yet now he looked more like a prosperous merchant than a playwright, expensive clothes as close to a gentleman's as the sumptuary laws allowed, his hair slightly balding and a neatly trimmed beard she suspected had been dyed. And there was something about his voice.

He reached out and pulled a piece of twig from her hair.

'So the killer,' he said. 'Why did he go to your father's house if he wanted to kill *you*?'

'It's quieter,' she said, 'I was meeting the coffin maker there.'

'The coffin maker?' Will was puzzled.

'My father died.'

She wondered if he was going to say how sorry he was, like everyone had in Canterbury.

'So,' he said, 'at least there's some good news.'

To be fair he hadn't changed entirely – she was grateful for his lack of hypocrisy.

There'd been a moment, after he'd died, when she'd looked back through her father's violence and drunken self-pity for a glimpse of a better, kinder man, but Dot had said to her, 'He's dead. Don't look a gift horse in the mouth.' Dot was right. He'd be in hell now and if there was anyone she felt sorry for it was Satan.

'I'm sorry about your mother though,' said Will. 'That must have been a blow.'

It had been. But at least now she didn't need to tell him how she'd found her mother curled up dead beneath the washing hanging out to dry in the garden. She wondered how he'd found out. As far as she knew, London high society didn't gossip about the mothers of pub landladies in Canterbury. Perhaps some Kent merchants visiting London had told Will, knowing how he knew her. Or perhaps he'd been asking around about her. Why would he do that? Not that it mattered one bit.

Anyway, if he knew about the death of her mother he'd surely know about the death of her babies, and that was something she really didn't want to talk about.

‘I was thinking,’ he said, ‘the killer must have known you were meeting the coffin maker at your father’s cottage.’

She realised what it was about his voice. He’d almost lost that West Midlands’ accent – it was still just there but nothing like the soggy warble she’d once made fun of. He’d retaliated with impressions of her Kentish burr.

‘What am ye a doing of?’ he’d ask her, grinning. She’d reply in his thick accent, ‘I’m just slummocking about.’ Back then they’d liked being different to everyone else.

He was looking at her, still waiting for an answer to his question.

‘I doubt he knew I was meeting anyone,’ she said. ‘I’ve been going there every evening since my father died.’

‘Then he knew that.’

She wondered for a moment if he thought she was making the whole thing up, that she was using it as an excuse to come to London and see him.

‘Half of Canterbury knew that,’ she said. ‘Knowing everyone else’s business is their only pleasure.’

He nodded.

‘So,’ he said, ‘have you any idea who wants to kill you?’

She didn’t. She only knew of two people in this world who often wished she was dead.

Her husband and herself.

WILL

Ann was unsteady on her feet, whether from the shock or the brandy he wasn't sure. At first she'd seemed just the same as he remembered her, but as she'd wiped away the rain and scraped off the mud, he saw how she'd changed. Time seemed to have scoured her, deepened the hollows under her eyes, worn away any spare flesh, so she was even more herself – fiercer, more determined and more sorrowful. He wanted to scoop her up, to take her in his arms and lay her down in a different world where everyone she knew didn't die around her. But he also wanted her gone from the theatre.

Everyone who knew about their past relationship was whispering eagerly and those who didn't would be asking how he knew this strange, bedraggled woman. He guided her towards the back entrance. There was an excited yelp and Frances Strange hurried alongside them, her make-up smudged and more of her black hair adrift.

'Will, there's still a girl waiting to see you.'

He was confused. He thought the message earlier had been about Ann.

'She says she knows you from long ago,' said Frances. 'She's exceedingly pretty if you like milkmaidy sort of girls.'

'You better see her,' said Ann.

'No, no,' he said. 'We need to get you somewhere safe and warm.'

'Let the girl in,' Frances shouted to no one in particular as she linked arms with Ann. 'Now, Will, you must introduce me to your unfortunate friend.'

'Frances Strange,' he said, 'this is Kit Marlowe's sister.'

He regretted it as he said it, but it was too late.

'Ann Marlowe,' he said quickly.

'Who's that?' she said. 'No, I'm not Ann. I'm just Kit Marlowe's sister.'

She shook herself free of Frances's arm and faces started to appear around corners.

He knew with Ann how grief or fear came out as anger – well, most things did – but he'd never worked out how to deal with it. Frances was watching, her blue eyes sparkling with glee.

'Mr Shakespeare,' said a voice beside him.

He turned to see a tall young woman in a plain blue-grey gown who held herself like a dancer.

'I'm in some trouble and I didn't know who else to come to.'

'All these damsels in distress, Will,' said Frances. 'You better ask them to form a queue.'

The young woman stepped closer and into the lantern light.

'You probably don't know who I am.'

But he did.

'Mary, Queen of Scots!' he exclaimed.

It was the girl from the magic show whom he'd last seen fleeing from the soldiers.

'Don't you see?' cried Ann. 'It's Lizzie.'

And then he saw it. It was the small Dutch refugee girl who had found Christopher Marlowe's body all those years ago and became entangled in the search for his murderer. That wa's why the girl in the magic show had seemed so familiar. He felt himself beaming and his astonishment made him want to laugh.

'Lizzie, it's really you,' he said, as Ann ran forward and hugged her.

'You'll help her, won't you?' said Ann.

'Of course I will.'

It was strange, he thought, Ann and Lizzie, both in trouble on the same night.

BELLA

They took her through the streets tied to the tail of a mule which neither she nor the mule much enjoyed. Tamburlaine was led behind her on a rope by one of the militia and the dog kept stopping to sniff out new smells. The soldier holding the rope tried to drag him away, but each time he braced all four legs and the man could not move him until he was ready. The late-night drunks and prostitutes, who would usually have thrown mud or stones at a captured witch, recognised the dog and instead stepped over to pat him or give him treats.

Bella tried to talk to Sir Crispin Proute, who pranced ahead of the mule in a strange parody of a military march.

'Sir Crispin,' she started.

'Sergeant-Major Colonel Proute,' he corrected her prissily. 'His Majesty promoted me this morning.'

Promoted him from what? Idiot? As far as she knew he had never been in the army.

And 'sergeant-major colonel'? She was sure the rank did not exist. Probably no one dared to tell that to the king. Proute was his favourite favourite this month. He had been made Keeper of the Royal Clock, a job with pay but no job. It was rumoured he would be appointed Yeoman of the Removing Wardrobe. What dizzy heights could he reach? Perhaps even Keeper of the Swans.

A young woman leading a female donkey was selling asses' milk and she stepped over to Bella and gave her a cup for free.

They got to the end of Coopers Street, which would have led them to Bridewell where they usually took witches, but they passed it and continued east.

Proute had a small fluffy goatee on his massive chin that strangely made her think of a spaniel mating with a Great Dane. 'Sergeant-Major Colonel Proute,' she said meekly, resisting a crazy impulse to laugh as she said his rank. 'Do you know who is responsible for my arrest?'

'I do,' he said. 'I will tell you who is responsible. Satan.'

So he too was one of those men who used the hysteria that England was being taken over by witches as an excuse to torture women. She was surprised they hadn't made Satan a woman. Women were usually held responsible for all evil. But then, of course, Satan had power so, yes, he was a man.

She looked behind them. Sir 'Rich' Spencer was being carried by four men in a sedan chair led by a herald. Spencer claimed that his interest in witches was strictly scientific, just as some priests' interest in boys was strictly educational.

Her mule turned a corner and ahead of them loomed the great grey stone walls of the Tower of London and her heart shivered as she realised that was her destination.

They went across the moat and struggled to unfasten her from the mule. These men could identify witches – if only they knew how to untie knots. She was taken through the gate and up a flight of green-slimed stone steps to a corridor of cells. There they waited.

A tall, stooped man she recognised as the half-mad conjurer who performed in Amen Court was led down the corridor, shouting in a language that sounded a little like Breton. She wondered if her arrest as a witch was a pretext and she had been brought here for some secret reason, but it was all probably just blind chance. Everyone looked for patterns when there were none – shapes in the stars, as if joining a million dots of light would explain darkness.

She heard a wheezing noise on the stairs and realised they'd been waiting for 'Rich' Spencer, who finally appeared and filled the narrow corridor. There was a long silence as he gathered his breath.

'Put her in a cell and search her for teats upon which the devil has sucked.'

Something shrivelled inside her. She would try and leave her body behind. She had borne such humiliations before and she supposed she could do so one more time.

SATURDAY

WILL

Will knew why night after night he couldn't sleep. It wasn't his circumstances. He was respected, renowned and passably rich. Even the boastful Ben Jonson acknowledged him as the best playwright in England. Lords and ladies flattered him, actors begged him to write parts for them, fishmongers and prostitutes would quote his words as he walked by, costermongers, constables and coalmen would ask him, 'What's your next play about?' He had no idea.

In the worst of the plague in 1603 he had shut the doors of his new house and written. As a fifth of London died, he wrote *Timon of Athens*, *Measure for Measure* and *Othello*. When the theatres reopened, he held two of them back so his work appeared regularly through 1604 and 1605, but as for new plays, he couldn't finish them – he couldn't even start them.

He had tried to plunder the stories of Holinshed, who had been the source of *Richard III*, his greatest success, but nothing stuck. *The History of Queen Voadicea* wouldn't work with a boy playing the lead. His *Tragedy of Gumundus*, King of the Africans, hadn't gone well. There were the bloody histories of the Scottish kings and the story of the Welsh King Llyr, but when he sat down to write, nothing happened. He missed writing, missed those moments when he could take refuge from existence in a world of his own making.

He tried drinking and he tried stopping drinking but neither helped. He tried writing by day and by night, at his desk and in a tavern, even in a mad moment he'd tried writing backwards.

He feared he'd never finish another play. He knew if he didn't how quickly the lords and ladies would shun him and the actors cross the street to avoid him. That was why he couldn't sleep, why he roamed his house at night, wrapped in a fur bed cover, exhausted but awake, listening to the dogs barking and the drunks yelling, despairing each time the church clocks struck another hour.

He paced up and down the corridor silently as Ann and Lizzie were asleep. Two unchaperoned women staying in his house. The babble of gossip was the last thing he needed now his application had gone in to the royal chamberlain.

Outside, Holy Sally on her night-time walk was muttering the only words she ever spoke, 'I have seen his face.' It must be twenty past three – Holy Sally might be mad, but she was punctual.

A light was flickering beneath Lizzie's door but he could hear her steady breathing. She must have fallen asleep and left her candle lit. He walked as quietly as he could – the new beeswax-polished elm floorboards creaked when they shouldn't have. There was a glimmer of light under the door of his study where it had been hung with too much of a gap. He must get that carpenter back.

He opened the door and found Ann sitting at his desk. He caught the end of a sudden movement as if she was hiding something, the candle flame flickering from the rush of air. Had she been drinking from the bottle of sack he kept there? After what she'd been through she probably needed it.

'Can't sleep?' he asked her.

Of course she couldn't sleep. She was up in the middle of the night. He knew her better than anyone in the world, but often she was the hardest of all to talk to. There were so many things they couldn't say and so many they'd said too often.

'It's not just tonight,' said Ann, 'I always have trouble sleeping.'

She seemed at pains to point this out, as if being kept awake by thoughts of her attempted murder made her look a weakling.

He told her how he too couldn't sleep, and pictured the two of them, fifty miles apart, each wandering around in the middle of the night listening to the owls hooting, and the dogs howling. Ann looked out at the sleet spattering against the window. The anger he'd sparked at the theatre seemed to have gone. It did this, rose suddenly and vanished just as fast, and he could never keep up. It was like the English weather, he was always dressed for what had just passed.

'What do you do when you can't sleep?' she asked him.

He thought of all those hours alone in his darkened house.

'I think,' he said.

She shook her head at this stupidity.

'Not surprising you don't sleep.'

'So what do you do?' he asked her, sitting down on the Portuguese credenza in which he kept his paper and notebooks.

She shrugged.

'Knit, darn, sometimes I pray.'

The surprise must have showed in his face. It wasn't that he thought Ann was an atheist, just that she and God didn't have much in common.

'Why not? At least it's someone to talk to. God's a better listener than John.'

She'd broken one of their unspoken rules and mentioned her husband.

'And at least God doesn't judge me,' she said.

'I thought that was the point of God.'

She smiled. 'Not mine.'

'And does he talk to you?' he asked.

'Don't be stupid. He's God.'

He liked it when Ann was Ann.

She stood up, stretched, and Francescina's costume shimmered red and gold in the candlelight.

'Are you hungry? Shall I get us some bread?' he asked.

She shook her head and sat down next to him on the credenza. There was the rumble of a handcart in the street below and the man pushing it was murmuring a song, the twenty-third psalm, 'The Lord is My Shepherd'.' Ann shuddered and then quickly turned to the window to disguise her distress.

'What?' he asked.

She hesitated, went to speak, then didn't.

'Tell me,' he said.

She shook her head. 'It's nothing.' But he could see she was trembling and it took a lot to make Ann tremble.

He reached out to take her hand, hesitated, drew back and instead just touched her wrist with two fingers, then feared that gesture was more intimate than the one he'd avoided.

In here they played these games. Outside murderers roamed the streets and it was so cold that birds dropped dead from the sky.

'I've been going over and over it and I can't work out who would send someone to kill me,' she said.

'Send someone?'

'I think he was a hired killer.'

He looked sideways at her and saw her mouth crimped and her brow wrinkled as she thought.

'Everyone's always killing each other in Canterbury but they just batter each other over the head with a log or something. He was different. It was like he was doing a job. He looked almost bored – well, until I set fire to him.'

Will struggled not to smile.

'Didn't you say he knew you though?' said Will. 'Called you—'

'A cunning bitch,' she said. 'Yes, it doesn't make sense, does it?'

A dog started to howl. Holy Sally was coming back and he could hear the shiver in her voice. Only drunks, criminals and the mad were awake at this hour. He wasn't sure which of these he and Ann were.

Will wondered whether to say what was in his head. Why not? She'd mentioned her husband first.

'Could it be anything to do with John?'

'Why would it be anything to do with John?'

He wasn't going to tell her about the Canterbury wine merchant he'd met at his dancing lessons and how Will had invited him to an inn afterwards, bought him drinks and asked him about the landlady of the Flying Horse.

He wasn't going to tell her how the wine merchant told him that, late at night, people passing the pub heard John Cranford shouting drunken threats at his wife. He wasn't going to tell her of the dread and helplessness he'd felt and how when she'd first turned up at the theatre he'd thought it was her husband she was fleeing.

'I just wondered,' he said.

She was staring hard at him.

'John never hits me,' she said. 'He'd like to, but he's too lazy to get round to it.'

Had she guessed what he was thinking?

'How's your Anne?' she asked.

He supposed he'd asked her about John first.

'Nothing's changed,' he said.

His Anne knew that he only ever visited her to see his children and she spent the time he was there abusing him. He supposed he deserved it. He tried not to think of her because then he thought of his dead son. To wipe Hamnet from his mind seemed like a betrayal but thinking of him just made it worse.

After he had died people who'd known his boy told Will how he'd been so handsome, so clever, so happy, how he'd climbed to the top of their tallest tree or helped them push their cart all the way up Onion Hill as if that would make him feel better now his son was none of those things, could do none of those things ever again.

St Paul's chimed the half-hour and the old sea captain in the attic across the street shouted at the bells to leave him alone.

'His parrot used to join in,' said Will, 'but it hasn't for a while. I think it might be dead.'

Ann looked baffled. He went to explain then didn't. He wished they hadn't broken their unspoken rule and talked about their spouses. They might as well be fifty miles apart again. He stood up.

'I might have another go at sleeping,' he said.

ANN

After Will left she went back to reading the pile of poems on his desk. They were all sonnets, all dated, the most recent ones at the bottom of the pile. She read them in disbelief. They were outpourings of tortured love to an aristocratic, exotic, dark beauty who could only be Frances Strange.

How had such beauty been inspired by that hollow coquette? She wondered how an intelligent man could have such terrible judgement in women – then remembered he had once chosen her.

Obviously, any affair between Will and Frances was impossible given her rank – and her youth – and her beauty. Perhaps that was what he wanted, just something in his head – he spent far too much time rattling around in there.

She finally managed a couple hours of sleep before Lizzie knocked on her door and told her breakfast was ready.

Will's parlour smelt of linseed oil and beeswax which must have been from all the newly bought furniture. She, Will and Lizzie sat at a fine Flanders table with intricate linenfold panels. Carved in the middle were Will's initials. She traced out the *W. S.* with her finger as Will's maid, Judith, brought them ham soup with warm baked bread and a choice of bramble or plum jam.

'You know you can stay as long as you need,' said Will.

'*Need, not want*,' she thought. Need ended a lot sooner.

She had no desire to go back to Canterbury and her murderer – to her father's charred body which must smell by now and her husband who smelt all the time. Still, she wasn't going to stay here in this fancy house where she was so out of place – carpets from Persia on the floor, silver cutlery on the table and, hanging in the hall, a portrait of Will, in a fine ruff that she bet he'd rented for the occasion. You could see that these days he cared about what people thought – not people like her who spent their days working, but people like Frances Strange who spent their days deciding how many feathers they should have in their hats.

He even had a strange contraption, with candles set above what looked like the workings of a large clock, attached to a spring-loaded steel pan and flint.

'What's that?' she asked.

'It lights candles half an hour before you get up, so you come downstairs and find them burning.'

'So why aren't the candles lit?' she asked.

'Because when I tried it, it nearly set my house on fire.'

She wanted to laugh, and then she did and Lizzie joined in. Lizzie was slim and quick-limbed, her face both boyish and beautiful, flushes of pink suddenly appearing on her cheeks like in a child's drawing. She had eaten all the soup and bread and scraped the jam off her plate. Will saw she was still hungry and asked Judith to bring her more. He turned to Ann.

'Are you alright to stay here while Lizzie and I go to Finsbury?'

'I'm not going to stay,' she told him.

The worry on his face looked real.

'But where will you go?'

'You could come with me,' said Lizzie. 'I'm sure Mr Kemp wouldn't mind.'

Will was taking Lizzie to Finsbury to stay with Will Kemp, the comedian. Kemp and Lizzie had had a special bond since Lizzie was a little girl.

'I'll do that,' Ann said. 'Too many people know I'm at Will's. I'll be safer out of London.'

Ann wasn't sure how pleased Kemp would be to see her,

but better there than here. She watched Will to see if he was relieved she was leaving but he still looked worried.

'I've decided,' she said before he could say anything else.

'Are you sure?' he asked.

There it was. It wasn't as if she was going to say, *No, I'm not sure*. He wanted her to go.

'I'm sure,' she said.

A boy arrived with some felt boots for her to wear and Will offered her one of his fur-lined cloaks to go over the gaudy stage costume. She told him she didn't need it, but he put it over her shoulders anyway.

Judith actually curtseyed to her and Lizzie as they left and Lizzie had to stifle a giggle.

'Where's Mr William off to now?' Judith asked.

She was pink and anxious, her hand always hovering in front of her cleft lip.

'He never tells me anything,' she complained.

Lizzie told her they were going to see Kemp in Finsbury.

'Finsbury,' she said, shaking her head as if it was a barbarian land. 'It'll be bitter out there.'

It was bitter enough right here. The cold came looking for Ann as soon as she stepped outside and she was grateful for the cloak. There had been some icy winters since the turn of the century but she couldn't remember a November this bad. It seemed to get colder every year.

They passed a flock of geese being herded along the road by a pair of busy black and brown dogs and a boy dressed in an animal-hide coat that looked as if it was made from their forebears. The flocks of geese and turkeys left Norfolk in August so they reached London in plenty of time for Christmas. London sometimes seemed like a great mouth eating the rest of England.

She kept going back to the masked man with the knife. There were two things she couldn't get out of her head – the smell of his burnt face and the words he'd spoken to her.

I remember you, you're a cunning bitch, he'd said – given

away that he knew her because he'd never thought that she'd live to repeat it. He remembered her but did she remember him? That voice churned up a sense of dread – that deep, familiar voice. Was she imagining it? No, she was sure she'd heard it before. But where?

WILL

A single snowflake floated down and landed on Ann's chin. She swatted it away as if it were a wasp.

It was better that she wasn't going to stay with him and set the gossips prattling. Respectability meant nothing to him – it was just a high wall built around greed and debauchery so no one could see in, but what a lot of people didn't understand was that he had a duty to appear respectable. Everyone who worked at the Globe depended on him and unless he maintained his reputation the licences and permissions wouldn't be granted.

So, yes, it was better Ann was going with Lizzie. He'd hire a couple of toughs to keep watch on Kemp's house just to make sure that nothing happened to them.

Outside the dye factory in Clerkenwell, the waste water had frozen and their boots crunched through icy puddles of red, blue and yellow. Lizzie flipped forward and walked on her hands for a dozen yards, picking her way upside down over the brightly coloured ice. She stood up and cartwheeled around the corner, scattering a flock of sparrows. It was as if she got bored being the right way up.

He couldn't resist asking her how they swapped the heads for the second time in the Mary, Queen of Scots trick. She seemed pleased he couldn't work it out. She told him that when Glendower the Great picked up the fake clay head, he stuck it on a nail that protruded from the upper wooden block. The nail was on a small plank on a pivot so she could swing it and make it disappear in a flash.

‘Then, as I do that,’ she said, leaping up to touch an ironmonger’s sign hanging high above them, ‘I put my head up through a hole behind it.’

‘But I’d have seen that,’ said Will.

‘No, your eye goes to the axe which he plants in the ground.’

‘No,’ said Will. ‘I stayed looking at the block.’

‘You think you do but you don’t,’ said Lizzie. ‘And Glendower twirls his cape so the corner flicks in front of the block and obscures it for an instant and that’s enough.’

He’d been sure he’d stayed watching the head, but she must be right because he’d missed it.

Small children were playing football with a frozen fox’s head as they walked through Highbury village and the windmills on top of the hill creaked as their sails turned slowly in the breeze. The washed clothes laid out on the bushes to dry were speckled white with the frost. Two small boys had each picked up a stiff, frozen stocking and were using them for a sword fight. They ran off laughing when their big sister chased after them.

Ahead of them a noisy crowd blocked the lane. It was a holiday – a time to pray for the dead, but this lot were shouting and jeering. As they got closer he could see they were heaving on ropes slung over the branches of two oaks that stood on either side of the road. They were raising a large wooden cage with an old woman inside it.

‘Here too,’ muttered Ann.

The mad witch-hunting frenzy had come south with King James, who had written his own book on witchcraft, *Daemonologie*. Where once England had seemed to be emerging from superstition, now the darkness was creeping back in, seeping through the cracks of this broken land.

Drunks saw flights of witches sailing through the night sky surrounded by thousands of bats. Women who gave birth to deformed children were shut in their huts to die. Whispered rumours grew wilder as they were hissed from ear to ear, absurd surmise became fact, and the sickly and feeble, too weak to do harm on their own, gathered in mobs. Most humans had some pity but mobs had none. Immigrants were beaten, Jews and Gypsies butchered, old scores were settled, cranky old women trussed, bridled and chucked in rivers, young women stripped and their bodies scoured for the devil's bite marks. It was Christmas every day for the angry, vengeful and perverted. If Satan truly existed, he must be having a nice lie-down while men did his work for him.

Bacon had said that if only the country were a democracy and, like the ancient Greeks, held elections, they'd no longer be ruled by these vain, narcissistic tyrants. Like fish, kingdoms rotted from the head down, and the king's infatuation with the dark arts was at the heart of it. Will had heard all the whispered stories about him. The king was convinced of his supreme intelligence, but was bored by matters of state and spent his days hunting. The courtiers lied and told him it was his crossbow which had killed every wild boar or stag, while huntsmen pulled out their iron bolts and stuck his silver ones into the dead beast for him to find.

This mob was chanting something about Old Nick and the old woman joined in and conducted them with her scrawny arms.

Mothers watched blankly as their children threw mud and stones at their elderly neighbour in the cage. The old woman picked up a piece of mud that had made it through the bars and ate it. Like so many 'witches', she was probably just suffering from the insanity of old age. Two constables stood watching, drinking from a bottle and doing nothing. Will turned to the other two but Lizzie had vanished.

'Where is she?' he asked Ann, but she hadn't seen her go either. 'Do you think she's scared of the constables?' he asked. 'Perhaps she thinks they're still looking for her.'

The mob started to run back away from the road and he saw why. The thatch on one of the small cottages was on fire.

'Get water,' someone shouted, but the pails of water were

frozen solid. A boy jumped on the roof to try and beat it out before it spread to the other buildings. Anne was staring at the fire, a flicker of flame reflected in her dark eyes, but he saw something else. She was terrified.

'I've worked out who it was who tried to kill me,' she said.

'Who?'

'It was the voice that did it,' she said. 'Remember that evil thug who came after us when Christopher was murdered, the big one who sang in the street beneath your room when they barricaded us in there. The one who worked for Lord Strange and tried to kill us both.'

'Could it be a coincidence?' he asked. 'Could someone have hired him to come after your family? You may not have enemies, but the Marlowes certainly do. I mean, did your father die of natural causes?'

'Is gin a natural cause?'

'But the man you think it was,' he said. 'Do you think he's just a thug for hire?'

'The man "I think it was",' said Ann. 'You don't believe me, do you?'

Could she really remember a voice and a half-seen face from twelve years ago? And yet he found he too could picture him, the man who had supervised the killing of Lizzie's family. Even now, he felt that sense of evil and saw those dead, colourless eyes.

'No,' he said, 'I believe you.'

LIZZIE

Lizzie ran back to join them, looking over her shoulder at the mob trying to put out the fire. At least they weren't tormenting the poor woman any more. She was glad she'd set fire to the cottage. It was easy. There'd been some embers smouldering in the grate and she'd scooped them up in a pan and thrown them on the thatch. The villagers deserved it for what they'd done to that old woman, and, let's be honest, she liked the excitement. 'You have no fear,' Glendower had told her, but she knew the truth – she liked fear too much.

It had been the mania for witchcraft that had stopped the magic show touring. In 1604, the plague had kept them in London but when, at the start of 1605, it dwindled and they had hitched the mule to the wagon and set out for the small towns where the show thrived, everything had changed. There were mutterings and mumblings from the crowd and they had heard voices saying Satan had taught them their tricks.

Glendower had made it worse. He always spoke as if his magic came from secret powers and not the routines they had worked at so hard. He talked of his forefathers, the mysterious Cunning Folk – or *Dynion Hysbys* in Welsh – who could dive into rivers and vanish like eels, or pass through secret doors and speak to the dead. Glendower mostly passed through the doors of pubs and spoke to barmaids, but he brought trouble to their wagon. In Basingstoke, a crowd set fire to it and chased her, shouting that she was a child of the devil. She'd had to hide under some planks that bridged a ditch and it had ruined her one good robe. Once they had hated her because she came from Holland. Now, they hated her because she came from hell.

Most of the cobbles in the road had been stolen and the mud had frozen into ruts and ridges as Lizzie, Ann and Will turned the corner into the main street of Finsbury Village where Kemp now lived. She really wanted to see him but she feared he'd be angry that she'd squandered his generosity and run away from the school he'd paid for, to go on the road.

His room was in a crooked house – rotten wood beneath broken eaves, the cobwebbed windows half full of cracked panes and half of waxed brown paper. His landlady said he was up on the first floor and let them in. They climbed the stairs, stepping over the missing floorboards, and knocked on his door. There was no reply.

Will made a face. He must think Kemp was sleeping off a hard night drinking so he knocked again louder. There was silence. The smells of the landlady's cooking wafted up the stairs, but with them was another smell, fainter yet sweet and rotten. She looked over and saw Ann had smelt it too.

WILL

Kemp had found a landlady much like himself – short, square and hostile. She grumbled answers to their questions through the crack in the door and said he'd just be asleep. They went back upstairs and rattled at the bolted door.

Ann went to say something but didn't. He knew that it would have been about the smell – that she was worried there was a corpse in there. But he was sure it would turn out alright. After all it was Kemp in there and even alive Kemp was no rose.

'When did you last see him?' Lizzie asked.

It had been a while. Kemp no longer acted. He'd started getting drunk before performances as well as after. He'd slurred his lines and missed his cues. The crowd had stopped laughing and that's what had really hurt him. He raged at the idiocy of audiences and the mediocrity of Tarleton who started playing the parts he'd once have played.

He moved to cheaper lodgings outside London and came to the theatre less and less. The other actors shunned him, for they saw in him their future – out of favour, out of fashion, out of work.

Will had promised to visit him but, now he was a partner at the Globe, there was always something else to attend to – meetings, rehearsals. When was the last time he had seen Kemp? Was it as long as a year ago? Surely not.

'Not for a bit,' he said to Lizzie, and banged on the door again.

He swallowed back a rising panic. Yes, there was that sickly odour but Kemp couldn't be dead – it just wasn't like Kemp. He'd joked about death when he caught the sweating sickness on tour. 'Rather hell than Norwich,'

'We could call the constables to break down the door,' Will said. 'Or I could get a carpenter from the theatre.'

Lizzie looked out of a small window.

'Or I could break in,' she said.

Will looked out of the window and saw there was a sheer drop into a small yard at the back of the house and no way of reaching Kemp's lodgings. His room had windows but they were shut and the jettied wall stuck out over the yard so climbing in was doubly impossible. Ann was banging on the door now but there was no answer. He peered through the small gap between the door and the frame but could see nothing, only a fat iron bolt holding it shut. He turned to speak to Lizzie but Lizzie wasn't there. There were just her shoes on the floor. He looked out the window again and spotted her in the small courtyard down below. He wondered how she had got out there so silently.

He went to speak but Lizzie put her finger to her lips and with one leap she was on top of the back wall of the yard. She was so lithe and fast and fearless. Ann squeezed in beside him to see. The wall was only one brick wide, but Lizzie tiptoed along, her bare feet seeming to grip the brickwork. She reached the end, pirouetted around and tied up her robe in a knot around her middle. He saw what she was going to do, but before he could shout, 'No!', she swayed backwards, sprinted forwards and launched herself sideways and up at Kemp's window. One arm stretched out and her fingers grasped a ledge. He heard Ann gasp at the same time as him. Surely she must fall. But her other arm reached up and clawed at the roof and got a grip. She grinned in triumph.

They watched Lizzie push at the window with one hand but it wouldn't budge. It was one that was still filled with glass and not waxed paper. She put both hands back on the ledge to rest for a moment, then reached swiftly with her other hand and punched one of the small panes of glass out of its lead surround. She reached through it, unlatched the window and heaved it open. She reached through and pulled herself in. They turned back to the door and almost at once heard the bolt drawn back. It opened. Lizzie's face was shocking, for only seconds ago it had been grinning. Now it was pale and stiff with horror. Will felt the world around him buckle and sway.

ANN

'He's dead,' said Lizzie, but they both knew already. Will stepped forward but Lizzie still blocked the door. 'You might not want to see. He's hanged himself.'

'Thank you,' said Will. 'But I do.'

He was strangely polite at times of crisis. She followed him into the room.

Kemp hung from a rope cast over a beam, a stool on its side on the floor beneath him. A mouse scampered out of the folds of his doublet, across his face, up the rope and ran off across the beam.

'His spirit,' whispered Lizzie.

If Kemp had a soul it wouldn't have been a mouse, thought Ann, it would be something much noisier.

The smell wasn't that strong but it clung inside her nose and throat. She shoved open another window and perhaps it was the draught, but Kemp's corpse started to twist slowly on its rope. Poor Kemp. Poor, poor Kemp. Ann couldn't really make out his features in the gloom and was glad. She had seen enough dead faces for a lifetime.

Will hurried to the body. 'We mustn't leave him here. We must get him down,' he said urgently, as if they could still save him.

Ann searched under the pile of dirty plates and found a knife. Will grasped the short square body around the waist so it wouldn't fall and she stood on the stool and hacked away until she cut through the rope. Will staggered under the weight of the body. She thought he would lay it down, but instead he stayed there holding it in a one-sided embrace. A tear rolled down his cheek. Finally, he lowered Kemp gently to the floor as if putting a sleeping child to bed.

'I wanted to come and see him,' he said. 'I was about to set out once, but there was a problem at rehearsal.'

'It's not your fault,' she said, thinking that perhaps it was, that this is what happened when you put new respectability ahead of old friendship.

Will looked down at Kemp, whose face had fallen to one side, a stubbly ball of nothing.

'It's not as if I could have saved him,' he said. 'He couldn't live without the laughter. It's not as if a couple of visits would have made any difference.'

She wanted to offer him some comfort, reach out a hand and touch him, but such things were difficult with hands that had once touched each other so much and so often.

'Do you think he could have been murdered?' asked Will and, before she could say 'no', he was off. He said how it could be the same man who had killed the coffin maker and tried to kill Ann, how he could have tried to make it look like suicide. His enthusiasm for murder was indecent. He wanted it to be a murderer that had killed Kemp and not despair, so none of it was his fault. 'It's possible though, isn't it?' he said.

Lizzie said it for her.

'The door and the window were bolted from the inside.'

'Yes, but…' Will started, his eyes flickering around the room eagerly looking for some way to explain it, but he found nothing and his shoulders slumped. He looked miserably down at Kemp again.

To hell with their history. Ann put her arms around him.

'I'm sorry,' she said.

He smelt the same as she remembered and different, of ink and lamp oil, but also a new expensive cologne. His cheek was damp.

This is how I deal with my own sorrow, she thought, *I comfort others*. She could have told him that she knew the pattern of grief, how it gripped you and clung to your every thought and moment, but how, after a time, after a long, long time, it grew weary of you and the grip loosened, and though it never let go entirely, you had room to breathe again. She could have told him, but she was sure he knew it already.

'I'm going to wash the body,' he said.

She went to tell him that an undertaker could do that, but there was no point. He had to do his penance. Will walked over to Kemp and knelt to undress him.

She and Lizzie walked down the stairs. They told the landlady what had happened and asked her for water, soap and rags. Ann realised she looked disturbingly like Kemp and, like him, she was kinder than she first appeared.

'Oh dearie me,' the woman said. Her gown was so mended that there were more patches than garment. 'He was famous once but no one came to see him any more.'

It sounded as if Kemp had been complaining to her.

'The man who came to see him a couple days ago was the only one for months.'

Ann couldn't help asking.

'What did he look like?'

'He was young with a black eye. It was the day that the factory blew up and I'd gone out into the street to see what was happening.'

The mystery visitor sent thoughts flying through Ann's head for a moment, but the bolted door – it wasn't possible.

The landlady went off to get some water.

'He owed me five weeks' rent,' she said as she limped away. God knows what she was cooking but Ann reckoned she preferred the smell upstairs.

Lizzie whispered to Ann. 'Could he have said something to Kemp, this man who visited him?'

She hadn't thought of that. Could he really have brought news that made Kemp kill himself?

She heard the door to Kemp's room open and Will shouted down the stairs.

'He didn't kill himself. The stool's too short.'

BELLA

A face was looking into the barred window of Bella's cell, which was odd for it was on the second floor. The face had huge, soft brown eyes, a nose like a donkey, pointy ears and two small furry horns. Perhaps she was a witch after all and had summoned up a demonic familiar? If it was, Satan must have been in a good mood for it looked so gentle. It blinked those big eyes, wrinkled its nose and swung its head away. Pressing her face to the bars of the window, she glimpsed a long yellow and brown neck. It was a beast she had never seen on any of her voyages, but she had heard that King James had demanded a long-necked animal called a giraffe to add to the menagerie he kept at the Tower. The king of France had one and James wanted one taller. Many exotic animals had been brought at huge expense from Africa, India and Cathay, shipped in crates or made to walk, prodded north through Europe. Few survived the journey and those that did reach London shrivelled and died.

A voice outside her cell said, 'I'm going to open the door.'

It was Lord Cecil himself. She heard the key turn and the door creaked open and pushed against the body of the soldier, who lay at her feet on the floor.

She had killed the man sent to strip and search her. Clearly her patience was not what it used to be. They really should have taken her knife. She had thought the others would have killed her then and there, but they just locked the door and fled. Perhaps they really did think she was a witch. Oh well.

She rolled the body away from the door so Lord Cecil

could get in. He stepped in alone and placed a lantern on the floor.

'May I have your knife?' he asked.

'Don't you trust me?'

'I don't trust anyone, as you well know.'

She took the knife out and held it carefully by the blade so he could take the hilt.

He gestured at the body.

'What came over you, Bella?'

She wondered the same thing, why she had lost her usual calculated self-control. She feared that she had let in too much humanity, that she could not suppress her outrage and disgust and had recklessly rebelled against the brutal rules of her world.

'I had a headache,' she said.

'Ah yes, a headache,' he said. 'I believe that's why Genghis Khan slaughtered the entire population of Samarkand.'

A wooden stool was handed around the half-open door and he took it and sat on it, his small, twisted body propped against the door, his dark eyes flickering in the lamplight, his feet resting on the body of the man. She sat on the stone shelf opposite.

'Sir John Spencer was most upset,' he said. 'He wanted to chain you to the wall and put you in a witch's bridle.'

She thanked him for saving her, but wondered whether he had arranged her arrest as part of a strategy? That would explain why they had spared her when she stabbed the soldier – because they knew Cecil required her. His nose wrinkled and he looked down at the corpse on which he rested his feet.

'He's starting to smell.'

'He smelled before I killed him,' said Bella.

Cecil smiled. 'A confession. Now, there's a choice of charges. Murder or witchcraft. Do you wish to be burnt or hung? I can put in a word for you if you have a preference.'

He liked to tease her. Sitting across from her, he looked like a portrait by an inferior artist, stiff, posed and not quite real, perhaps because he held himself so rigidly to reduce the pain in his back.

'There was a lord in Scotland found guilty of murder and witchcraft,' he said. 'King James had him both burnt and hung, though I don't know in what order.'

'So you believe in witches then?' she said to Cecil.

'Only since I met you, Bella.'

He was surely too busy hunting real conspirators to care about witches.

Cecil called around the door for wine and asked, 'Will you join me in a bottle of claret?'

'I only drink virgin's blood,' she said.

She thought it was wise to engage in this repartee for it made her seem unruffled and calm and therefore useful to him and therefore worth saving. She was relieved that her mind had returned to making these fine calculations.

The bottle and two glasses were passed around the door, and he filled one and handed it to her. She took it but saw her hand was unsteady and she worried that it betrayed her fear. Perhaps that was what he had been waiting for because he got down to business.

'I have a proposal for you.'

'Does it involve me staying alive?'

'You never know.'

She forced a smile.

'There is a gentleman who wishes to interrogate you,' he said.

'"Rich" Spencer?'

'I said a gentleman, not some jumped-up member of the hoi polloi.'

'Like you,' she said.

Had she gone too far? But he smiled.

'Yes, like me. And like you.'

'I haven't jumped very far.'

He got back to business.

'When you meet him I want you to admit that you're a witch.'

'Things don't go well for women who admit to witchcraft.'

'Things go worse for women who don't do what I ask,' said Cecil.

He had done with teasing her. His face grimaced and he shifted position on the stool. His back must be hurting.

'So this gentleman you're bringing to interrogate me…' She hesitated to finish her question.

He was dangerous when he was in pain.

'He is one of the Scots who came south with His Majesty.'

He gave no hint of his opinions though she knew he despised this foppish cluster of spongers. A Scottish mercenary she knew had joked that the men who had come south had raised the average intelligence of both nations.

'He is a favourite of His Majesty who shares his interest in witches and wishes to converse with one.'

A shadow passed across the cell and she looked up and saw the giraffe peering curiously through the window again. Cecil saw it too and shook his head sadly.

'These sad beasts,' he muttered, and waited for it to disappear as if it might overhear their conversation.

'Is this why I was arrested,' she asked, 'to provide a subject for this gentleman?'

This time he snapped angrily.

'I don't get men like "Rich" Spencer to do my work for me.'

She was not sure she believed him. If Cecil needed her to be a witch it would, at least, explain her arrest, though not the man who had come to kill her. Who'd sent him? There were so many possibilities. Her memory palace had a whole floor devoted to men who wanted her dead.

'I have one request,' she said.

He grimaced again. 'Don't haggle with me, Bella.'

'Whatever your answer I will, of course, do what you ask, my lord. This is purely a request, not a condition.'

He reached into his Italian goatskin bag, took out her pipe and a small silk bag containing her hashish and passed them to her.

'You want this, I imagine.'

'I am grateful for that, but what I was going to request was that I may have my dog in here with me.'

He shrugged.

'You're growing sentimental, but I suppose we might as well swap a dog for a dead body.'

He rose and spoke through the half-open cell door.

'Bring her familiar.' There the smallest crinkle of a smile on his face. 'I wish to interrogate that too.'

'Thank you, my lord,' she said. There was one more question she had to ask. 'This gentleman. Will he torture me?'

Cecil was silent for a moment.

'I shall avoid that if I can.'

ANN

As soon as they stepped through the door, Will asked Ann to stand on the stool.

'You're the same height as him,' he said.

She did as he asked. Lizzie helped him get the noose off Kemp.

'He always made me laugh when I was sad,' Lizzie said as she yanked the rope free.

She was walking this way and that with a nervous, jumpy energy that Ann had thought must be her way of showing grief. When Lizzie was little she had brought out a side to Kemp that no one had seen before. The morose drunk became almost a jolly uncle.

Will held up the noose so its frayed ends, where she had cut through it, joined up with the frayed ends of the rope hanging from the beam. There was a big gap between her neck and the noose.

'See?' he said. 'It's not long enough.'

'It will have tightened when he stepped off the stool,' Ann said. She was trying to keep the weariness out of her voice but not doing a very good job of it.

'Not that much,' said Will.

He so wanted to believe Kemp had been murdered.

Lizzie reached under the bed and pulled out a rectangular oak box stained with Kemp's stage make-up. She handed it to Will. Ann stepped off the stool and Will, silently, reluctantly, placed it on the stool. Now the ropes would have fitted perfectly.

'He wouldn't have kicked it all the way under the bed,' said Will, but his shoulders were slumped. He didn't even believe himself any more.

'I'll fetch the soap and water,' Lizzie said. She turned towards the door, but then stopped. She fingered a nail – a single nail, about two inches long, hammered into the door frame.

'What?' asked Will.

'There's a trick with a locked coffin that Glendower taught me,' she said, running out the door.

When they had shut Kemp's door, Lizzie tied a loop around the bar of the bolt and positioned it so it was as close as it could be to closing. Will crowded close watching her and Ann had to pull him back to let Lizzie work. She greased the bar with some lard she found in the bottom of a pan in the grate, then tied a loop of string around the nail in the door frame and out through the crack between the door and the frame. She tied a second length of string around the loop she had attached to the bolt, ran that across the room around the bed leg and back under the crack beneath the door.

'Stay in here,' she said, went out and shut the door.

They watched as the first length of string yanked taut around the nail. It pulled the bolt closed. Now Lizzie tugged the other piece of string that looped around the bed leg. The first yank did nothing but then she jerked it harder and the loop around the bolt came free and they watched as she reeled it in. Both pieces of string disappeared beneath the door. The door was bolted and they were left inside with no sign of what had been done. They let Lizzie back in.

Ann touched the nail. Was that really enough evidence? Lizzie saw her doubts.

'Three inches up or down and it wouldn't work,' she said.

'He was murdered, there's no doubt,' said Will. He'd got what he wanted. It wasn't despair that had killed Kemp. He might have abandoned his friend because Kemp didn't fit in with his new fancy ways, but he wasn't responsible for his death.

'Someone tried to kill Ann and someone did kill Kemp,' said Lizzie. 'Is there something going on?'

Was there? She'd had a rough couple of days and her brain wasn't at its best. She looked across at Will as they walked back down the stairs to talk to the landlady but he was slumped in silent grief.

'You, me and Kemp all know why my brother Christopher was killed,' she said, 'and someone's tried to kill or arrest all three of us.'

'And Bella,' said Lizzie. 'They've arrested her as a witch.'

'What?' said Ann. 'Why didn't you say sooner?'

Maybe she said it too harshly because Lizzie took a step back. Ann knew how she reached for anger the way her father had reached for a drink.

'They were talking about it at the theatre door last night,' said Lizzie, 'I'm sorry, I meant to tell you,'

'I didn't mean to be sharp,' said Ann. 'But you're right, Bella did know too.'

Bella did, indeed, know too, because she'd helped kill him.

'So something's happened to just about everyone who knew,' said Lizzie.

'Apart from Will,' said Ann, but he didn't seem to hear her. Ann rapped on the landlady's door.

She opened it at once and Ann wondered if she had been standing at the door listening to them talking as they came down the stairs.

'The man who came to see Mr Kemp with the black eye,' Ann said. 'Is there anything else you can tell us about him?'

'He said he was an actor.' Her baggy face looked like it was coming apart at the seams.

'And did you believe him?'

'Oh yes, he was one of us.'

Ann didn't understand.

'I used to be a tumbler in a travelling show.'

She must have thought Ann didn't believe her, because she took a step back, threw herself forward and balanced upside down on her hands with her feet against the wall.

'See,' she said through clenched teeth. She continued to stand there on her hands. 'You'll have to help me,' she continued. 'I can get up but these days I can't get down.'

Lizzie grabbed her ankles and lowered her gently. Ann was going to ask more questions but suddenly Will spoke.

'What about the Widow?'

So he was listening after all. And he was right. Agnes – the Widow, as everyone called her – had been with them, along with Kemp and Lizzie, when they had discovered that Christopher had been murdered to keep Lord Strange's conspiracy to overthrow Queen Elizabeth a secret. If they were in danger then so was she.

'We need to warn her,' said Ann.

ACT TWO

THE WIDOW

She had lost count of the gentlemen who had turned up at her shop or 'bumped into her' in the street, moustaches combed, hair shimmering, faces pink and shiny, their cocky charm all they'd taken away from their schooling. It was the worn footwear which gave them away, for while they could stretch to a fancy doublet, what they couldn't afford were new boots. They kept coming, the impoverished second and third sons of foolish country gentlemen who had bought shares in diamond mines in Yorkshire or schemes to turn lead into gold, sons with expensive habits and no money, unfit for work, skilled only in swordsmanship and flattery, who needed a rich wife to pay for their hawking, hunting and whoring and were prepared to marry a well-off widow in trade. Gentleman so desperate they'd stoop to marrying her.

At first she felt sorry for their puppy-eyed befuddlement – their shock at how their raffish looks and documented ancestry got them nowhere with a mere shopkeeper. But many of them got angry when she sent them packing back to their cold, mouldering manor houses in Something-or-other-shire. They didn't know she was set up very nicely thank you with the other widow on the sign above the door, Louise, whom she loved. She loved her laughter and her smell and seeing her small shoes neatly lined up as she came through the door. She loved Marie and Henri, the children she'd brought with her when she'd fled France. She loved how she did the books, checked and double-checked in tiny, neat columns, and she loved the profits that totalled up at the bottom of them.

Widows were the only women that the law permitted to run a business and theirs was flourishing.

Let's face it, that was mostly down to her. She could down vodka toe to toe with the beaver-coated Russian merchants who sold her gum and pitch, and argue with the Essex builders about brickwash and the right ratio for red ochre, alum and small beer. With the gold-toothed Genoese captains, she could joke about their tall stories of pirates and sea monsters before she haggled them down on the price of turpentine. Who'd have known it, but she put these men at their ease and they liked doing business with her.

She and Louise joked about who would come in next and, when they were both in the shop, they couldn't resist teasing their would-be husbands and telling them that they were already engaged to earls and dukes. The day identical twins walked in wanting to marry them both, they burst into laughter.

So Agnes, the Widow, wasn't one bit surprised at the handsome young man who walked into her shop and greeted her with a smile that would melt a brick. Very well, this one really was good-looking, with his dark skin and surprising pale blue eyes, and unlike the others he hid any hint of desperation beneath his swagger. There really was a lot of swagger though.

'I believe I'm talking to "the Widow",' he said.

That's when she saw his boots – fine white calfskin with fashionable loose cuffs that fell nearly to his ankles. Perhaps this one was different.

'How may I help?' she asked.

He smiled. 'I am charged with equipping this winter's expedition to Virginia.'

There were indeed three ships moored at Wapping, ready to sail for America, the *Susan Constant*, the *Godspeed*, and a small one, whose name she couldn't remember. She thought that it was Sir 'Rich' Spencer supplying them. He provided rotten beef and biscuits, charged twice the going rate and he and one of his mates who gave him the contract split the profit.

‘We can certainly do that,’ she said, ‘and I’m sure at a better rate than you’re getting now and with discounts for bulk.’

‘I was told I’d be glad I came here. My associate Mr Johnson had some dealings with you.’

A Mr Johnson had bought tools and tarpaulins. She hadn’t realised it was for the Jamestown expedition. It hadn’t seemed in sufficient bulk, but Mr Calfskin Boots must have guessed what was in her head.

‘The private gentlemen travelling to Virginia must provide for themselves,’ he explained. ‘There may be further orders but, for now, they require four hundredweight of salt as a preservative and to trade with the natives.’

She told him a price expecting him to haggle but he agreed at once.

‘May I see it?’ he asked.

‘You want to look at the salt?’

‘At that price I surely deserve a look.’

‘Very well,’ she said. Louise was in Rochester buying Kentish malt so she called up to Marie who loved to stand on a box so she could see over the counter and mind the shop. She came running down.

‘How old are you?’ asked her customer.

‘I’m six,’ said Marie.

‘How old do you think I am?’ he asked.

Marie wrinkled her forehead in thought. ‘Fourteen.’ That was as high as she could count.

‘Close,’ he said. ‘I’m a hundred and forty seven.’

The little girl laughed.

Agnes lit a candle and led the way to the cellar.

‘Are you going on this expedition?’ she asked.

‘I wish I could.’ His voice lost that smooth confidence for a moment. ‘What an opportunity to rip up the rules and create a new world of our own.’

‘A new world in the New World,’ she said.

'Yes,' he said sadly. 'But I'm stuck here having to do things according to the old rules.'

Agnes led him through the cellar door and lit a lantern from the candle. He closed the door behind them.

LIZZIE

Lizzie reckoned she could run to the Widow's chandlers shop in Bishopsgate in twenty-five minutes. She liked to run places when she was sad. She felt as if each pace wore away a tiny piece of misery and when she got there, if it hadn't gone, she was at least lighter. Today though it wasn't working and tears for Kemp came into her eyes. She ran faster.

She took a shortcut through St Paul's Cathedral, in the North Door, dodging through the black-robed moneylenders with their click-clacking abacuses, past the man from Cathay selling dead baby dragons and live snakes tied by their tails and draped over the pews, nearly slipping where the boys had pissed on the smooth marble floor to make a slide. She went out the Chain Door and, in the few seconds she had been inside, a hailstorm had started. She ran on through a flurry of icy pellets rattling around her ears and bouncing at her feet.

She spotted Bob Grizzle the chestnut seller, hailstones bouncing off the bald dome of his head. He stood in front of his fire stripped to the waist in all weather, his big belly gleaming a rosy pink. Bob meant she was in Blowbladder Street, so only a short run away from Amen Court where their magic show had been performed.

To go there would only delay her for a couple of minutes. There was a chance that Evan, the fly and bottle boy, would be there. If anyone from the magic show got separated they always went back to the last place they'd been together.

It was the job of the fly and bottle boy to collect money at the end of the show. He had to keep one thumb over the end of the bottle with a fly in it so he had only one hand to hold the hat and couldn't steal the money. Glendower called him a simpleton but he wasn't that simple for he had a magic trick all of his own. He had made a tiny slit in the lining of the hat, and learnt how to shake it so a couple of the coins stuck beneath it. These he kept when Glendower the Great emptied the hat.

As she and Evan had grown older, he'd fallen helplessly in love with her, and bought her copper rings for her fingers, gypsy bows for her hair and, for her fifteenth birthday, a duckling.

Lizzie had spent seven years on the road with the magic show. She had started when she was eleven, soon after her father had died in an explosion in an illegal gunpowder factory like the one that had rocked London a couple of days ago. They had handed her the copper medal that he kept around his neck which was all they could find of him. It showed David fighting Goliath and had been minted to mark the resistance of the tiny Netherlands against the mighty Spanish. Now it was on a lace around her neck.

Alone in London, she had gone to find grumpy, kind Kemp who had always helped her when he could. He was more generous than she could have imagined, paid an elderly lady to house and feed her and found a school run by Ursuline nuns who believed girls should be educated. The nuns were kind enough but the lessons were dull. She only liked theology, for the Bible was as full of blood and murder as her life had been.

One morning she reached the school gate but found herself walking on by. She wandered the streets and ended up sneaking into a theatre and crawled between the legs of the crowd to the front of the pit. The story of murder, madness and betrayal thrilled her. She kept returning and started to creep backstage, where they seemed to think that she, with her short-cut hair, was one of the boy actors. Why couldn't she perform like those boys did? She learnt her favourite speeches and, when the streets were dark and she was alone in the blackness, she spoke them as she walked to give her courage.

'*Come, night, come, Romeo, come thou day in night;*
For thou wilt lie upon the wings of night
Whiter than new snow on a raven's back.
Come, gentle night, come, loving, black-brow'd night
Give me my Romeo; and, when he shall die,
Take him and cut him out in little stars,
And he will make the face of heaven so fine
That all the world will be in love with night
And pay no worship to the garish sun.'

That's what she was doing when she met Glendower the Great, crouched in a doorway sobbing silently.

'I've lost my girl,' he said in an accent made more sing-song by the booze. 'Are you bendy?'

She kept her distance as she always did with men who spoke to her in the street, but she told him, 'I can do five cartwheels in a row.'

He rubbed his chin and she heard the rustle of fingers on stubble.

'You've got the job,' he said.

Later, at the theatre, she asked a boy actor if the conjurer was safe.

'He won't touch you,' the boy said, so she accepted his offer. It was only afterwards that she found out that Glendower the Great had lost his previous girl because he performed a trick more drunk than usual and nearly sawed off one of her ears. He was very tall with big eyes, a big mouth and a huge nose. Fortunately, he had a massive head and they all just about fitted on there.

He was pleased she was a Dutch refugee for he hated the English. 'Thieves, murderers to a man, and they think they own the world,' he said. 'And a language ugly as sin.' She took him in hand and stopped him drinking before shows as she valued her ears, but sober or drunk Glendower had much to teach her. She learnt the magic tricks and, outside plague years, they made enough money to buy the odd new costume and eat lamb on Sundays.

Now Lizzie looked around Amen Court but in the hailstorm there was hardly anyone there and definitely no Evan. She waved at the Hungarian gypsy band sheltering miserably under an oilcloth they all held over their heads. Then she saw it under a cart, beneath a blanket so rotten and full of holes that not even a beggar had taken it. She walked over, checked to see no one was watching her, picked it up and put it in the burlap bag she carried.

WILL

Kemp's body lay on the floor at his feet. Kemp, brilliant, grumpy Kemp, with a head like a plucked turkey and a face that could have sunk the Armada. Kemp, who forgot Will's lines and wrote them all over the set – who read them off wooden trees, swords, once from the face of a Roman soldier, but still made audiences roar with laughter.

Kemp who loved dogs, pies, farting, words starting with K and Lizzie. Kemp who hated people, wasps, foreigners, royalty, hills and soup. 'If it's liquid why isn't it beer?' Kemp who gave money to beggars but only if he was alone, who secretly loved men but never told anyone, not even Will. Kemp who claimed to have the blood of comedy royalty in his veins – to be the son of the famous jesters Will Sommers and Jane Foole. Kemp who in a bad mood could have put a damper on the Second Coming and in a good mood could have cheered up Armageddon. Kemp, whose pantaloons usually held a bottle of sack and a veal pie, and once a baby hedgehog. Kemp, who he'd abandoned and who was now a cold carcass at their feet. Will was going to find out who had killed him and make them pay. Only he had no idea who it was. All he knew was that it had something to do with Kit Marlowe's murder.

Twelve years before, when Will and Ann, along with Kemp, Lizzie and the Widow, had exposed Lord Strange's plot to supplant Queen Elizabeth, Ann's would-be assassin was one of the few plotters to survive. Could he be seeking revenge? But if he was, why had he waited until now?

Then there was the man with the black eye who Kemp's landlady thought was an actor. They couldn't be sure he was the killer but he seemed to be the only one who had visited Kemp. He remembered the fight onstage at the end of *Othello* and told Ann about it.

'I remember wondering where Burbage got his black eye,' she said.

'I don't think it could be him,' said Will. 'The landlady would surely have recognised him. But Berrycloth had a black eye too.'

They agreed they should start by going to the Globe and questioning him.

'Of course, you could just lie low,' he said to Ann.

She shook her head.

'I'm tired of hiding away and waiting for things to happen to me,' she said. 'Let's go meet trouble.'

It was a flicker of her old recklessness and it made him realise how she'd changed – how she seemed more daunted by a world she'd once defied. He didn't want to leave Kemp but knew he must. He gave the landlady money for a coffin and he and Ann hurried away.

He'd forgotten what being in danger was like, the exhausting fear and suspicion, every dark alley a danger, every stranger a threat. They cut through small passages, glancing behind them to see if they were being followed. The sleet turned to a thin snow that seemed to gust into their faces in whichever direction they walked. He saw the large, dark shape of a man come round a corner behind them and he grabbed Ann's hand and they ducked into a crowded fish market, slipping on the slithery fish scales and stumbling over the cats that ran under their feet. They doubled back the way they came and saw no more dark shapes following them.

He feared for Ann. There seemed even less of her than there had been before, her small frame slighter, her face tight over its bones, her throat so slim. He knew better than to underestimate Ann Marlowe but it would take so little to hurt her.

They took a private wherry across the Thames, because London Bridge was a bottleneck that could easily be watched. They sat in the stern, an oilskin spread over their knees. Flakes of snow settled for a moment on the dark, swirling water before they melted. At least the Thames smelt less when it was this cold. The stiller water at the edge of the river had frozen and the prow of the boat had to break through the ice as they edged up to Southwark Wharf.

'What's your next play about?' the boatman asked as he helped them onto the landing.

'A shipwreck on a magic island,' he said. He always said that now. He had no intention of writing it, but it usually stopped the questions.

'Is it true you wrote *Hamlet* in a day?' the man asked.

'No,' said Will. 'It was more like a day and a half.' Rubbish, obviously, but these stories were good for business.

They walked up the green-stained stone steps crisp with frost.

'When was the explosion in London?' Ann asked suddenly. He thought back.

'It was the day before you arrived,' he said. 'Thursday. There were explosions all afternoon. Why do you ask?'

'Because the landlady said that's when the man turned up at Kemp's. But that was the same day as that big bastard killed the coffin maker in Canterbury.'

'Which means he couldn't have been involved in Kemp's murder,' he said.

She nodded.

'So,' he said, 'either the murders weren't connected after all.'

She finished his sentence. 'Or there's more murderers out there than we thought.'

LIZZIE

There was a jumble of overhanging shop signs in Bishopsgate fighting for attention – cut-outs of scissors, anvils, boots and barrels, bright painted beer jugs jangling on chains, buckets and hammers and giant keys – but the widows had gone for something different: cut-out silhouettes of their faces, nose to nose, swung in the wind.

She went into the Widow's shop and the little girl peering over the counter told her that Auntie Agnes had gone off with a very old man, giggled and pointed to the cellar door. Lizzie went through it into the darkness and felt her way down the stone steps; the only light came from the shop behind her.

'Hello!' she called.

A man's voice echoed from what sounded far away.

'We're here.'

Lizzie gave her eyes a moment to adjust to the dark but she still hated its clammy grasp. She stooped beneath the low beam and made her way down a narrow aisle, between stacked barrels, boxes and sacks, identified with bright splashes of different coloured paint.

The further she went from the door, the darker it got, until she had to feel with her hands against either side of the passage, the goods now only identified by their smells – piney resin, stinking sulphur, the tang of glue. Her heartbeat battered against her ribcage like it was trying to get out. She usually liked that feeling but not in this darkness.

'Hello,' she called again.

'Around the corner,' the man's voice shouted.

The giggling little girl had set her at ease, but now, in this clotted gloom, she felt alarm. She could just make out a brick wall ahead of her and to the left a faint glow of light. She wanted to run through this darkness to make it go quickly, but the passageway was too narrow and treacherous.

One day, in a small town near Ludlow, Glendower had watched her step out of the wagon and seemed surprised. 'You're a looker,' he'd said. 'Men are going to be a problem.'

He'd gone and found her an ivory knitting needle sharpened to a fierce point and given it to her. Now she took it from her hose and clenched it in her hand as she inched around the corner.

'Who are you?' the man's voice asked.

'Who are you?' she asked back.

'Edgar,' he said.

The light was getting stronger and she could make out a man holding a lantern. She stopped walking.

'Where's the Widow?' she asked.

'Getting me some salt from the back arches.'

She must have been standing next to some barrels of molasses – his voice had the same sweetness as that smell. Now she could see his face and what a face it was, lit by the lantern, like the Dutch portraits she'd seen in the great house where they'd once been asked to perform. He was smiling and he stepped forward cautiously like a hunter trying not to scare a deer. A rich breath of perfume mingled with the molasses.

'Agnes,' she called out past him. 'Are you there?'

There was no reply.

ANN

Just outside the stage door to the Globe an exceedingly tall, gaunt young man, walking with the excessive care of a drunk, came up to Will. His strikingly white face stuck out of his black ruff as if it had just escaped from a dungeon.

'Tell me,' he said, putting both hands on Will's shoulders. 'How do you take any pleasure from life when you know it's going to end in death?'

'You stop being so miserable,' said Will.

'Really? Really?' said white-face. 'Would you enjoy a delicious meal if you knew that someone was going to poke you in the eye with a dagger at the end of it?'

Yes, he'd definitely been drinking. She wondered where he'd got the alcohol from, because she could do with some right now. Will went to speak but death's-head-on-a-mop didn't give him a chance.

'You look at a beautiful woman…' he started.

She hoped the thought had been prompted by looking at her but she doubted it.

'…what do you see but a skeleton briefly lent some flesh?' He gripped Will's doublet with both hands. 'Tell me, how do we live when we die?'

'I like sleep,' said Ann. 'So I think I'll like death.'

He seemed put out that she'd spoken and those spindly legs carried him carefully away.

'He must be a playwright,' she said to Will.

He nodded. 'John Webster. He had his first play on last winter.'

'And what was that called?'

'*Christmas Comes but Once a Year*.' He must have seen her surprise. 'I think he wanted to start with a crowd-pleaser,' said Will.

'Was there a scene,' she asked, 'where some carol singers were battered to death with a yule log?'

'Sadly, no.'

'Or drowned in their own blood in a wassail bowl.'

He laughed. She liked to make him laugh.

'If only there had been,' he said.

'So was this play not a success?'

He shook his head.

'It was the last play Kemp performed in. He promised Webster that if he brought him back, he'd remain sober but…' He spread his hands. 'He killed every laugh. In one performance he vomited over Captain Christmas.' Will thought back. 'Though, in fact, that did get a laugh.' Will was smiling fondly at the memory. 'But poor Kemp, there was no way back for him after that. Webster threw a stage weight at him.'

Looking at the knife-thin Webster she was surprised he could lift it. He walked away, his pointy shoes picking their way through the muddy puddles.

'So you'll question Berrycloth?' she asked Will.

'Yes,' he said.

Will stopped walking.

'No, I'm being stupid,' he said.

'About what?'

'The man with the black eye turned up at Kemp's place on Thursday afternoon. Berrycloth only got his black eye in the fight on Thursday evening.'

'Could it be a different actor?' she asked him.

Behind him Webster walked into a shop sign and fell over.

'I'll talk to the man who runs the Globe,' said Will.

WILL

In 1602, when half the actors were down with the sweating sickness, Will had got Sam Bull the doorman to play Thersites in *Troilus and Cressida*. He might as well have cast the door. Sam was a terrible actor, which was odd for such a talented liar.

His desk in the entrance was a stall where he sold this, that and the other, mostly stolen. Burbage nicknamed him Autolycus after a shapeshifting thief in Greek mythology. Everyone else called him Bollock. Still, if anyone knew what was going on at the Globe it was Bollock.

Will asked him if any of the actors apart from Burbage and Berrycloth had black eyes. He thought and shook his head.

'Whyburn has the pox. And Hancock, but he always has.'

'What about the stagehands?'

'Oh, they've all got the pox, but no black eyes. But I'll keep an eye out, Mr S.'

Sam reached beneath his desk, pulled out some gloves and handed them to Ann.

'Very cheap,' he said, 'rare kidskin imported from France.'

She held them up to the light.

'Made by Jeff Nutt down in Slough?' she asked.

Bollock started to be outraged then gave up and nodded grudgingly.

'Pigskin soaked in milk?' Will asked Ann.

'Yes,' she said as they walked towards the stage. 'Your father would be proud of you for once.'

He and Ann might not have a clue why everyone was getting murdered but they knew their leather.

'The actor with the black eye,' said Ann. 'He could be from any of the theatres.'

'We can go to the Swan later and ask there.'

The black eye wasn't much of a clue but it was all they had.

A couple of the boys were mixing buckets of calves' blood, oatmeal and vinegar to make the stage blood for *Alarum For London*, and God knows it needed a lot of blood. The plot about the sack of Protestant Antwerp by Catholic Spanish troops was just an excuse for endless slaughter, torture and rape. Will and Burbage had quarrelled about it.

'We might just as well put public executions onstage,' Will had said.

'I tried that,' said Burbage, 'but they wouldn't let us sell tickets for it.'

Sam Bull coughed from behind Will.

'Tell you what, Mr S, just remembered, Berrycloth had a black eye before Mr Burbage hit him. He covered it up with make-up for the performance.'

'Is he in?' Will asked as he slipped him a coin.

'Not seen him.'

'Tell me if you do.'

LIZZIE

The smiling man came closer, one hand holding the lantern, something glinting in the other. She didn't know her heart could beat that fast and her feet no longer seemed to be touching the floor, but she didn't want to step backwards and show fear. She gripped the needle tightly. She tried one more time. 'Agnes.' He was within three paces of her… two…

'Hello, who's that?' came Agnes's voice from behind the man.

'It's Lizzie,' she called.

'Dutch Lizzie?'

'Yes.'

The man was in front of her, his scent stronger. It was a magnifying glass he held in his other hand.

'Hello, Dutch Lizzie,' he said. 'I'm English Edgar.'

He tucked the magnifying glass in his doublet and held out his hand. She went to shake it but then realised she was still holding the knitting needle. He saw it and laughed.

'I see you're a dangerous woman.'

'It's a dangerous world,' she said, then swapped the needle to her other hand and shook his hand.

It was how people greeted each other back in Holland, but it was rarely done in England and certainly not between men and women.

'As you're Dutch,' he explained, 'I fought in the Netherlands.'

'For which side?' she asked. As well as the English troops

who'd fought alongside the Dutch there were the English mercenaries among the Spanish who'd slaughtered their way through her town.

'The right one,' he said.

She realised she was still holding his hand and let go. He had the face of a gentleman but the rough palm of a workman. Her bag slipped from her shoulder but she caught it before it fell to the floor.

'What have you got in there?' he asked.

'My head,' said Lizzie.

He smiled and it was a bit like an animal baring its teeth.

'I like the one you've got on your shoulders.'

She didn't know if she should explain how she had found the clay head that Glendower had fashioned for the execution scene, which she threw on the floor when the axe came down and was executed. Instead she opened the bag and held it up.

'I like to carry a spare.'

'If only King Henry's wives had done that,' he said.

A voice came out of the darkness.

'You two stop flirting.'

The Widow appeared, handed Edgar a small bowl and turned to give Lizzie a hug. With her turned-up nose and her small face splattered with freckles, the Widow barely looked grown-up, though she must be in her mid-twenties now.

'Look at you,' she said to Lizzie, and shook her head as if she couldn't believe it. 'Dutch Lizzie, eh?'

'I'm more English Lizzie, now.'

There was still a lot of hatred for the refugees from the war. She'd seen a handbill nailed to a church door only the day before accusing the Dutch of *washing as often as once a week, even in winter*.

'Oh, it's you who gets executed, isn't it?' said the Widow. She must have seen the show. 'I had no idea.'

'Executed?' asked Edgar.

'She's in that magic show that performs in Amen Court.'

'Is that so?' said Edgar, but something made Lizzie think that he already knew.

The bowl the Widow had given him contained a spoonful of white crystals and he tested one with his tongue.

'This salt is better,' he said. 'Thank you, I'll take three hundredweight if you drop the price to a pound.'

'The best discount I can do is a halfpenny on a pound but take four hundredweight and we'll call it five guineas and two shillings.'

Edgar was taking a while to catch up.

'That's about a three farthings discount in a pound,' said Lizzie. She'd always had a head for sums.

Edgar grinned. 'How can I say no?'

They walked back towards the bottom of the stairs.

'May I carry your head for you?' asked Edgar.

The Widow sighed. 'You two. You only just met.'

A small voice came out of the darkness.

'There's a man upstairs, Auntie Agnes. Do we sell coal tar?'

'Indeed we do, love. Run back upstairs and tell him I'm just coming.'

'What's the man like?' Lizzie asked the little girl.

'He smells of horse wee,' she said and they heard her footsteps running up the stairs.

'Marie, wait,' shouted the Widow, and turned to Lizzie. 'Is there something wrong?'

Agnes had always been able to read people, probably why she had done so well in business. That and the freckles which made men underestimate her. Lizzie hesitated to answer in front of Edgar.

'Tell me, Lizzie,' she said.

'We think you might be in danger.'

'We?'

'Will and Ann and me. Everyone who got involved back when Christopher was murdered.'

'Marie, come back,' the Widow shouted.

The little girl came running into the light and put her hands on her hips.

'Make your mind up,' she said.

'Don't be rude, Marie,' said the Widow gently.

A voice with a thick foreign accent came down the stairs.

'Is that you Agnes?'

The Widow breathed out. 'It's fine. It's Horsepiss Pete.' She took Marie's hand, shouted, 'Coming,' and headed for the stairs.

Edgar turned to Lizzie. 'I haven't introduced myself,' he said. 'I'm the son of Lord Ferdinando Strange – Edgar Strange, the well-known bastard.'

WILL

Will heard a woman shout his name and turned to see Frances Strange bounding across the stage towards him, a blaze of orange taffeta.

'Will,' she called again. 'Burbage has agreed I should write a play. It's going to be a tragedy.'

'Bloody right it is,' he heard Ann mutter beside him.

'I'll be coming to you for advice, Will.' She looked past Ann as if she wasn't there, and remembering what had happened the night before, Will hurried to reintroduce her.

'You know—'

'Kit Marlowe's sister,' Ann got in quickly.

'Of course,' said Frances Strange. 'She was nearly murdered.'

'That's me,' said Ann. 'I'm Kit Marlowe's sister who was nearly murdered.'

Frances Strange must have registered something because she turned to Ann.

'I'm sorry about what happened.'

Ann gave a low harrumph. Will had a feeling this would end badly. It was a bit like in his performing days when he'd been trapped onstage in the first act of a terrible play knowing there were four more acts to go. There was a short pause so obviously Frances Strange turned the conversation back to herself.

'I've decided I'm going to seek out Othello.'

Will was puzzled.

'That illegitimate half-caste half-brother of mine, that's

what they call him now,' she said, a little peeved that he hadn't been paying enough attention to her life. 'Have you met him?'

'I have,' said Will.

He was a charmer and a chancer, a taker of liberties and a stealer of hearts.

'Do you know who his mother is?' he asked Frances.

Lord Strange had been obsessed with Bella and Will wondered if it was her.

'No idea,' Frances said, toying with the cluster of pearls which glistened around her neck.

'But I'm going to meet him. I don't care that people say he's beneath me.'

'Surely he's not as far beneath you as Will,' said Ann.

Frances Strange laughed, her real big honk of a laugh, not her society ripple.

'Surely you don't mean Sir William here?'

Will interrupted. 'So what's your tragedy going to be about?'

'"Sir William?"' asked Ann.

'Oh yes. "Sir William",' said Frances Strange.

'Is your play contemporary or set in the past?' Will asked. 'Is it going to be set in England or abroad?'

'They're going to knight you?' Ann asked incredulously.

It was too late to stop it.

'No, he's going to buy a knighthood,' said Frances Strange. 'Though I think they should give him one for free.'

Will tried not to look at Ann, but in the end he couldn't help it. He wished he hadn't.

'Sir William Shakespeare,' she said very slowly to get maximum contempt into each word.

'I was considering it, yes, but only as a business decision. It would be useful on playbills.' It was pointless defending himself, it was too late, yet on he went. 'There's so many new writers now you need to stand out,' he said. 'It's a competitive situation.'

He ran into the brick wall of Anne's face and finally

stopped. Should she be relishing this so much when a murderer was hunting her down?

'So you're going to pay the king – what is it, thirty-five pounds to become a knight?' she said.

'Seventy,' said Frances Strange.

'Seventy?' asked Ann.

'Yes, he charges double if you come from, you know, trade.'

Some words from Kit Marlowe's *Doctor Faustus* came into his head. *Mountains and hills, come, come, and fall on me*. But they weren't going to and Ann would never stop mentioning this until the day he died – probably long after. He must make sure she never found out he was having fencing lessons.

'I understand now,' said Ann. 'You think they haven't come for you because you're too respectable to kill.'

Frances looked intrigued. 'Kill?'

'You think you're one of them now,' said Ann. 'But you're not. People like you are the ones they really despise – the tradesmen's sons trying to crawl up the back stairs into the gentry.' She turned to Frances. 'That's right, isn't it?'

'I'm not sure I'd call a knight "gentry",' said Frances. 'Now what's all this about people being killed?'

A woman bustled over to them followed by Charlie, the youngest of the boy actors.

'I'm sorry, Mr Shakespeare, but she insisted on—'

'It's fine,' he said quickly. It would have been fine if Satan himself had come to interrupt but it turned out to be Kemp's landlady.

'You said you'd pay me if I had any new information,' she said.

Will took a shilling from his purse and saw it was one of the new ones with King James in profile looking handsome and raffish. The landlady didn't look impressed.

'I've come all the way from Finsbury through snow, sleet, hail and all sorts.'

He gave her another sixpence. She looked at it gloomily, and finally handed him a round stone about the size of a plum.

'It was in Mr Kemp's mouth,' she said. 'The undertaker found it.'

He didn't want it in his hand any more but he didn't know what to do with it.

'In his mouth?' he asked.

'Just left there,' she said.

'But why would anyone do that?' he said.

'As a knight,' said Ann. 'You probably know the answer to that.'

BELLA

In a dog, you watched your own life speed by. The gangly, bounding, impulsive puppy made you think of your youth. You watched the dog grow – become strong and bold and work out how to make the most of its place in the world. But then as the years crawled by for you, it grew older, grew lame or deaf or blind, grew weary and grouchy and only wanted to lie in front of the fire. You still loved it, still scratched its bony old head and dropped morsels into its toothless mouth, but you asked yourself, 'Who will do this for me when I'm old and weak? Who will adore and protect me?'

Bella might not be that old, but she knew she was vulnerable; her novelty had faded, her contacts were not what they used to be and her value to Lord Cecil as an agent had fallen. Yet locked in this stone cell he was the only one who could offer her protection, the only one who could stop this favourite of the king from torturing her. She did not know how hard he would try.

The cell door creaked open, and Cecil appeared.

'This is Sir Stuart Henry,' he said. 'He has recently arrived from Edinburgh and brings with him a deep knowledge of witchcraft and a renowned intelligence, so if you lie, he will know at once.'

Should she cackle demonically, convulse, screech? She decided to do nothing. Cecil had warned her against overacting. There was only one small lamp in the cell and she could barely make out the man who came in. He pointed to the mask that covered his lower face, and spoke to Cecil in a broad Scottish accent.

'You should cover your nose and mouth, so the creature cannot send satanic vapours to infiltrate your being.'

'I had not thought of that,' said Cecil. 'Wise words.'

He pulled out a scented handkerchief and held it to his nose. Cecil treated the man with deference so he must indeed be close to the king, though he certainly was not one of the beautiful young men with whom James surrounded himself. She now could see he was wearing a long sword that almost dragged along the ground. His face was white – the white of a frog's belly – and his pale blue eyes blinked continuously. She had the illusion that if he took off the mask there would be no mouth or nose there, just that stretched white skin.

'Surely she should be kept in a witches' bridle?' he said.

Bella had seen women forced to wear these brutal spiked mouthpieces that men would not stoop to use on the most savage of dogs.

'We've taken it off,' said Cecil, 'so she can answer your questions.'

Sir Stuart considered this and finally, grudgingly, seemed to accept the logic.

'I had a blacksmith in Edinburgh make one of my own designs which also has iron prongs which stop up the nose so no evil vapours can pass in and out of the creature's nostrils. I will have you sent one.'

'I would be most grateful,' said Cecil.

'So this fearful brute is her familiar,' said Sir Stuart.

Tamburlaine yawned amiably and rolled over, exposing his pink belly in the hope of a tummy rub.

'I'll wager she has a tail and it has none.'

'In this case not,' said Cecil. 'We did check that.'

She wondered where the king had found these men who came south with him, for the Scots she had met in London during the Old Queen's reign were tough, sinewy men with dry wits and sharp minds. Everyone knew that Cecil found it near impossible to get the king to turn his mind to statecraft. Though Parliament convened in a couple of days, His Majesty was reluctant to break off from his hunting. That, probably, was why Cecil was pandering to Sir Stuart, so he could use him as a route to the king.

Sir Stuart stepped closer and prodded her.

'Fully corporeal,' he murmured excitedly.

He seemed both contemptuous and aroused. She could see now that he wore a thick stuffed canvas waistcoat beneath his coat, the kind worn by men who feared being stabbed – with good reason in his case.

'So what have they discovered so far?' he asked Cecil.

'Very little, but they are simple men who lack your intelligence and subtlety.'

Cecil had once advised her, 'You will hear yourself being ridiculous, but it is impossible to flatter a vain man too much.'

'She did however once speak of the future ruin of this kingdom,' Cecil whispered to Sir Stuart, 'so I thought it was wise that you, our foremost expert, should interview her.'

Sir Stuart finally spoke to Bella herself. 'Tell me your witch's name.' He was stuttering with excitement. 'What has Satan christened you?'

'I'm just Bella,' she said.

'Oh, it speaks,' he said, his voice mired in disgust. He was both repelled and fascinated by her, just like Sir 'Rich' Spencer. What compulsion possessed these men? They were always going on about how witches shrivelled men's penises. She suspected most of them had shrunken penises a long time before witches got there. 'You'll witness, Cecil,' said Sir Stuart, 'that they can't hide their satanic name. If you speak it they scream.'

'I didn't know that,' said Cecil, his face expressionless. 'That's fascinating.'

'Are you called Hecate?' Sir Stuart asked her. 'Circe? Jezebel?'

It would be suspicious if he guessed straight away, but this could go on all day.

'Juniper?' he asked. 'Melania?' He sputtered as he spoke and his face was sheened in sweaty excitement.

Her rage rose inside her and she had to look away. She felt a sharp pain in her thigh and yelped. He had jabbed her with the point of his sword.

'Hah! Now I've got your attention, you vile, leaky troll.'

Now she was really scared. She had met sick-minded men like this before. Brutal ship's captains who ruled their little floating shack like it was the world and they were God; the bored sons of the rich, damned by their wealth and lack of talent; bishops who cloaked warped desires in purple robes; men with no limit on their power who slipped further and further into the cracks of darkness. Yes, she had met many men like this before. Though none this stupid. That made him the most dangerous of all.

Blood was running down her leg. She looked to Cecil with a plea for help.

'I don't know if this assists,' he said, 'but when she was first interrogated, blood came from her ear and formed the letter Z on her cheek.'

'Yes, yes, yes, why didn't you say before?' said Sir Stuart.

Cecil was clever. There were not many names beginning with Z. Sir Stuart fixed her with those flickering eyes.

'Is your name Zena?' he asked. 'Zuzanka?'

She screamed and, though it was an act, it was a scream of rage and horror and dread.

Sir Stuart leapt back as if she had bitten him.

'Sweet Jesus, the voice of Beelzebub is indeed a hellish thing. Now, sloven, tell me the truth or I shall say your name again and again until you convulse in agony.'

She put on a small, scared croak. 'Please do not, kind sir. I shall not lie any more. You have bested me.'

'Tell me all you know about the future of this land,' he said.

She must not look at Cecil as she said what he had told her.

'Satan will have England for his own,' she said.

But Sir Stuart was staring over her shoulder.

'Sweet God, the devil, the devil is here,' he gasped.

'It's a giraffe, Sir Stuart,' said Cecil.

The creature was peering in the window behind her again. Its long lashes blinked up and down over its big, gentle eyes.

'I can see Satan in its face,' said Sir Stuart. 'I shall tell the king to have it destroyed. Now I don't have much time.' Sir Stuart was now playing with a small pistol, a beautiful thing, its walnut handle decorated with pearl inlay. It had five revolving barrels; he must be a very rich man.

'Now what were you saying?' he said.

She was terrified, but she still had to take the contempt out of her voice as she repeated. 'Satan will have England for his own.'

'Yes, yes, and how will he do this?' His pale eyes were blinking furiously as if his brain was sending a message asking for help.

Cecil had positioned himself so Sir Stuart could not see his face and she could. He gave her an almost imperceptible shake of the head. She must not give it away too quickly or it would be suspicious.

'The blossom will smell of sulphur and the cows' udders will flow with blood,' she said. She felt a warm tongue on her ankle. Tamburlaine was licking the blood that had dripped down her leg and soaked through her hose.

'Look, look,' said Sir Stuart, 'her familiar revives itself, with the blood of Satan's bitch.' His voice was quivering and stuttering again. 'You're lucky to see that, Cecil, it's very rare.' He fumbled in his doublet, pulled out a notebook, ink and a quill and wrote eagerly, muttering, 'Fascinating, fascinating.'

She struggled not to exchange a glance with Cecil.

Finally Sir Stuart looked up.

'So where were we?'

'The cows' udders were flowing with blood,' said Cecil, his face a blank.

'Don't delay me with your riddles,' Sir Stuart said to her. He started to lift his sword. Cecil be damned. She was not going to be pricked again.

'Satan sits on Saint Peter's throne,' she cried. 'On his throne in Rome.'

Sir Stuart wrinkled his brow.

'What is she talking about?'

Cecil shook his head. 'I cannot divine it.'

Sir Stuart was truly an idiot. She was going to have to spell it out.

'Satan has infiltrated the Vatican.'

Sir Stuart's mouth was slightly agape.

'In Rome,' she added. 'The Vatican, the seat of the Catholic religion.'

Sir Stuart slapped his head like a bad actor. He finally had it.

'She means the papacy.'

'By God, I think you're right,' said Cecil.

'He will fly north in a vapour,' she said, for Sir Stuart seemed to like vapours. 'He will slither into the minds of Englishmen who love their king and turn them into beasts who will rid themselves of God's anointed majesty.'

Sir Stuart looked truly alarmed.

'Surely not.'

She had delivered Cecil's message. Now she convulsed, clutched her hands to her throat, closed her eyes and slipped to the floor.

'Perhaps Satan is punishing her for telling the truth?' suggested Cecil.

The warm stink of Tamburlaine's breath huffed in her face. He was worried for her.

'Vile infamy!' she heard Sir Stuart cry, and she half opened one eye and saw him stagger towards the door. Cecil went to follow him but Sir Stuart waved him away. 'No, no. I need a moment alone to think straight.'

However long it would not be enough.

He had gone, and she opened both eyes, gave Tamburlaine a reassuring pat and heaved herself wearily to her feet. Cecil gave her a brief nod which signified his approval. She wondered, should she let on that she knew? He would guess that she had guessed, she thought, so it was probably better to demonstrate that she hid nothing from him.

'So it's true,' she said, 'the king is a fool.'

She was disappointed that it had taken her so long to realise that Sir Stuart Henry was indeed King James. Not only did he share the king's love of interrogating witches, but he had taken the first two names of his father, Henry Stuart Darnley, and reversed them.

Cecil was staring at her. Had she made a mistake? Was he going to deny it? Finally he spoke.

'You see what I have to deal with.'

ANN

Sir William Shakespeare, indeed! Whatever next? She didn't know Will any more. When he'd first come to London, yes, he'd learnt to act like them, eat and dress like them, but he'd seen through them, seen them more clearly than they saw themselves.

But now he wanted to be one of them, cared about what they thought of him – cared about what they thought of him and her. His affection for Ann was a youthful whim crushed by the real world, that great mass of stone and brick, of money, reputation and responsibility that rose up around us, a prison disguised as a house and a home.

There was a yell and she turned to see Lizzie bounding towards them, dodging between a short man carrying a tall stack of pies and a pale-faced meandering drunk she realised was John Webster.

'The Widow sent you these,' she said, and handed Will a paper bag containing half a dozen nuts, about the size of Kentish cobs but flatter and longer.

'They're earth nuts,' she said. 'A Portuguese sailor brought them back from Terra de Santo something-or-other.'

Will offered Ann the bag but she shook her head. Lizzie told them that the other Widow had now come back from Kent and was minding the shop while Agnes hid at a friend's house.

Webster's white face appeared suddenly over Lizzie's shoulder and made Ann jump.

'William,' he asked, 'what happened about my advance?'

'We gave it to you and you bought a pelican.'

Webster looked puzzled, touched the top of his head as if he might find the bird up there and wove off through the crowd.

'He has more money than me,' muttered Will. 'His father is the richest coachmaker in London.'

The trumpet that blew one hour before a performance sounded and they opened the gates, and through a gap in the wings she saw the keenest groundlings running for the best spots at the lip of the stage.

Around them actors buckled on their silver-painted armour, and the boy playing Desdemona was asking where his shoes were. You could see how much Lizzie loved the theatre. She grinned as she watched the hubbub around them. Iago snorted snuff to 'clear his airways', Burbage sat in a purple armchair with his eyes closed while a woman in a silver gown massaged his head, and a nervous actor paced back and forth muttering Cassio's lines.

'Why are you learning Cassio?' Will asked him.

'Well... um...' He was reluctant to answer.

'Because I fired Berrycloth,' said Burbage, his eyes still closed. 'He assaulted me, for God's sake. I knew you'd approve.'

Will didn't look like a man who approved.

'Where's Berrycloth now?' Ann asked Burbage.

He opened his eyes and swung his handsome head around to her with a slow disdain she'd once seen him turn on an actor who'd trodden on his lines. Here was another man who didn't like being asked questions by women.

'She asked you where Berrycloth is now,' said Will.

'Oh, he flounced off and said he was joining the Admiral's Men.'

Will went to ask him more but he held up his hand.

'Not now. Can't you see I'm replenishing?'

They let him replenish and Will took a key from his purse and handed it to Lizzie.

'The theatre owns a secret house,' he said. 'It's where Ben

Jonson hid when the king wanted him arrested. You'll be safe there.'

'How safe?' asked Ann. 'Jonson's in the Tower.'

'He kept leaving to go to brothels,' said Will, crunching on the nuts. 'Lizzie'll be safe there. You could go too if you wanted.'

Here he was trying to get rid of her again. She told him that she didn't want to. Perhaps she should just go back to Canterbury. Yes, it was dangerous, but her life seemed a small, useless thing. Either the murderer would kill her, or her husband would bore her to death.

At least the murderer wouldn't run his fingers over the dusty table and say, *I don't ask for much, I really don't.* At least he wouldn't lecture her about her failings. Though, come to think of it, he had. *I remember you, you're a cunning bitch*, he'd said. Yes, even the men who came to kill you couldn't help but give a bit of criticism first.

She must have let out a little laugh because Will looked at her and said, 'Well, at least you amuse yourself.'

'Someone has to,' she said.

Will called over a sturdy young actor to show Lizzie the way to the house. You could see she didn't want to leave the bustle of the theatre, but she followed him out.

Ann started to tell Will that she was going to go back to Canterbury, but she stopped herself. That would sound pathetic – as if she just wanted him to beg her to stay. Instead she reached down and took one of the nuts. They were sprinkled with salt and instantly made you want to eat another.

Burbage came striding towards them.

'There's a whole company of militia at the door,' he said to Will, 'and they say they've come to arrest you.'

WILL

Will's first thought was that Ann would say, *I told you so. I told you they'd come for you*. She only seemed happy when she was mocking or scolding him. He was sick of it. But when he turned to look at her she seemed to be choking. Perhaps it was a reaction to what had happened in Canterbury. He'd seen similar things in people days after a terrible shock.

'I can put them off for a moment,' said Burbage, 'but you need to get out the side door as soon as you can. And take her with you. They want to arrest both of you.'

He reached out to take Ann's hand, but she was clutching her throat and her face was swelling. Her breath came in desperate gasps. This was more than panic.

'Go now,' said Burbage.

Will took Ann's arm, but as he did so her knees buckled and she fell to the floor. Her throat looked hugely swollen and her face was so red and distorted it didn't even look like her. She tried to speak but only made strange noises. Will had felt fear when he'd heard about the soldiers but now he felt utter terror.

'Go on your own,' said Burbage to Will, his voice filling the theatre as it always did in crises, but Will wasn't going to leave Ann. He knelt beside her. What was going on? She was sweating, her face was pale and her throat made horrible gurgling sounds as she tried to breathe. She looked as if she'd been poisoned but all she'd eaten were three or four of the earth nuts. He'd eaten more and was fine.

A grandiose voice boomed from the stage. 'We've got orders to arrest them, where are they?'

Will looked up. It was Proute, the king's favourite, the one with the ridiculous goatee who had led the arrest of the magician. He wore a new toy soldier uniform, bright pink with his head sticking out of a high wired ruff, that made him look like a boiled tortoise.

'They're not here,' said Burbage, striding onto the stage to confront him. The early theatregoers applauded as if the play had started.

Will tried pulling Ann's hand so the two of them could crawl away before they were seen, but she couldn't move. Bubbles were frothing on her lips and her throat choked with an inhuman rattle. Will fought back panic but each breath he took filled him with more cold terror.

'Oh, there you are,' boomed Proute's contemptuous voice. 'Come with me straight away.'

'Can't you see she's ill?' said Will.

'My men will carry her.'

Will didn't care about being arrested. He feared he was watching Ann die. Had she survived murderers and the plague to be killed by a tiny nut? She was making sounds which should never come out of a human. Proute and Burbage were shouting at each other in their booming baritones then another voice cut through.

'Leave this theatre, now.' It was Frances Strange.

'Who the hell are you?' asked Proute and drew his sword. He couldn't have properly seen her.

'Who am I? Who am I? I am the woman who will send you to be racked in the Tower. I am the woman who will watch while they pluck out your eyes with hot irons. I am Frances Strange, daughter of the earl of Derby, descendant of Henry the Seventh and Henry the Eighth. Who the hell are you?'

'I am Sergeant-Major Colonel Proute,' he said, but the voice had shrunk.

'Well, Sergeant-Major Colonel Proute,' she said, all seven

syllables laden with contempt. 'Go now, and don't return until you have a warrant signed by the king.'

He hesitated, then spoke very loudly to try and get some authority back. 'The theatre is surrounded. Do not on any account leave.' And he went.

Ann's lips were blue, her eyes popping from her head, the rasping creak of her breathing growing weaker. Will held her head in his hands and yelled her name, and thought he saw a twitch of recognition.

'Her throat is too swollen to breathe. We need to cut a hole in her windpipe,' said Frances, who was suddenly kneeling next to him. 'I need a thin-bladed dagger.'

'What?' he said.

'Arabian doctors do it. You just have to take care to miss the main artery.'

A hand reached over and gave Frances a narrow dagger.

'No,' he said.

'Do you want her to die?' she asked Will.

Ann's feet began to twitch and tap. Her whole face was going blue. Will's own breath was coming in short gasps. He had to think how best to save her but black panic flooded his mind.

'Alexander the Great saved one of his soldiers this way,' Frances said as if that was conclusive. She positioned the tip of the knife just below Ann's Adam's apple. 'Shall I do it?' she asked Will.

Will didn't know. He stared at Ann's face and saw her life draining away.

'Will,' Frances shouted. 'I have to do it quickly or she'll die.'

'Very well.'

He'd said it.

She took a deep breath and lifted the blade ready to plunge, but at that moment Ann gasped. Was she saying 'no'?

'Stop!' shouted Will.

She threw back her head and out of her mouth came a

creaky hiss but it was a breath of a sort. The feet stopped twitching and she sucked in air.

'I think she's breathing again,' he said. He stared at her eyes and there was something there as if she was seeing him at last.

'Put the dagger away,' said Will.

Frances Strange stuck it hard into the wooden floor with a sulky flounce.

ANN

The first thing she heard was Frances Strange's voice. Perhaps she was in hell. But then she could make out Will's face staring down at her.

'Ann,' he said again and again. 'Ann.'

His face was pale and terrified. She wanted to speak but she couldn't. She heard her breath coming in desperate rasps. Still, at least she was breathing, sucking in sweet, sweet air.

'Are you back?' he asked, and something wet fell on her face. Was it a tear?

She tried to move but her limbs had no strength and her body felt like it had melted onto the floor. She could recall some of what had happened, the shuddering panic, the swirl of dizziness as her body stopped working, and then the blackness. Not really black, but a terrifying nothingness full of shouting and screaming. Will lifted her head in his arms.

'Do you know where you are?'

Back on earth, she thought, and she was grateful to be there. She'd considered throwing her life away carelessly. She'd said to the whey-faced playwright that she liked sleep so she'd like death, but she'd glimpsed it now, been to the edge of oblivion and wanted so much to return to life.

'Ann,' Will was saying. 'Can you hear me?'

She managed a nod.

Frances Strange's face loomed over her.

'I scared off Corporal-Major-Sergeant What's-his-name but he'll go running to the palace, get told to stop being a fool and come back. You need to get up and go now.'

'She's too weak,' said Will.

Ann managed to lift an arm and Will reached out and held her hand; it felt as if his strength was flowing into her, and she moved some more.

'Ann,' he said again. How many times had he said 'Ann'?

She smiled. There, that was something else she could do.

'Can you move?' he asked her.

She wasn't sure about that.

He raised her so she was sitting up. Life was trickling back into her nerves and muscles.

'Stand her up,' said Frances.

'Not yet,' said Will.

If they gave her a moment she might be able to. Her legs were part of her again. Now someone else was there. It was Burbage.

'Proute's at the door again,' he said. 'He hasn't had time to go for a warrant so there's someone outside telling him what to do. He says that if you don't come out, he's going to send the soldiers in.'

'Tell him we're coming out,' said Will. 'It will give us a couple of minutes.'

Ann wasn't sure what was happening. Frances must have seen her confusion.

'They've sent a company of soldiers to arrest Will,' she said.

Ann looked up at Will.

'I told you so,' she said.

LIZZIE

Edgar Strange had pressed the note into her hands as they parted. In it were two pennies and it read, *This is the entrance fee for St Paul's tower. I will be there at four fifteen.*

She didn't like how he presumed she didn't have the entrance fee. She didn't, it was true, but all the same it irked her. Anyhow, she knew better than to meet a man she'd only just met after dark. Of course, it wasn't quite after dark. He had timed it for sunset, so she could leave before darkness set in, but even so.

He had a bit of flair, she'd give him that. He couldn't be much older than her but he was running around in a pale green Hungarian horseman's coat lined with mauve silk, that had cost him over two guineas. She knew because he'd told her. Of course he had.

'Two guineas, you were robbed,' she said to him and he'd laughed.

She liked his laugh, his laugh made her want to laugh too, but his smile unnerved her, those almost girlish lips curled back, that flash of white teeth… It made her think of an animal about to bite, it unsettled her and on the road she'd learnt to listen to her fears.

She did want to see the tower though. Glendower had gleefully told her how, in a great storm, the steeple above it had been set on fire by lightning, and how in the inferno, the great bells that could be heard from Wallington to Walthamstow, from Gunnersbury to Gravesend, had come crashing down through the cathedral roof and shattered on the Purbeck marble floor below. Glendower loved stories where nature humbled man, particularly when the men were English. Still, that was no excuse to go and meet Edgar.

There had been boys before on the road. The sweet-natured blonde cooper in a village near Lincoln, healthy as a spring morning, who'd flushed pink every time he saw her and had driven poor Evan the bottle boy mad with jealousy. The slim gypsy with the scarred back in Banbury who'd sold hawks to courtiers. When she had gone back to his room, a dozen goshawks had stood on a rail, all hooded as if for modesty.

Then there had been the young priest in the great house where a Catholic lord who knew Glendower had invited them in to perform. The lord had been jovial.

'The Protestants hate magic,' he'd said. 'They want to take away the magic of the mass where bread and wine turn to flesh and blood.'

The priest had crawled from a hidden door in an oak panel and it was he who held the Bible on which they swore to remain silent about what they'd seen. Her fingertips had touched his. That was all, but she saw what he felt about her in those fierce, scared eyes. It was him she thought of the most; perhaps she liked the impossibility of it. She imagined his life, hiding alone in darkness, emerging to perform Mass for those hungry for their God, and she feared the terrible death waiting for him if he was caught.

Now, though, Edgar Strange, the bastard son of Lord Strange, kept her thoughts busy, the man who summoned women with notes and spent stupid amounts of money on silk-lined coats. Well, she wasn't daft.

Outside, the militia and at least one hired killer were looking for her. Inside she was sat in front of a fire in a hidden house with a stout bolt on the door and the large and amiable young actor Will had sent to guard her sitting behind it. Yes, she liked risk. When the axe missed by inches, when she got away with theft, that was when she felt most alive. Yes, she liked risk, but she liked risk when the odds were on her side.

EDGAR

Edgar had no idea whether Lizzie would come. He didn't even know if she could read. She was so unlike most of the women he knew, unlike anyone he knew – except perhaps himself. Well, she'd come or she wouldn't, he liked it up here anyway. He walked all the way around the open terrace that surrounded the top of the tower.

A pair of red kites wheeled in narrow circles at the same height as him, and as they came close he could see the ruffled red glow of their feathers and the tiny black dots of their eyes looking down for carrion in the streets. He imagined leaping onto the rail, spreading his arms and joining them, soaring above all the grimy entanglements down in the streets below. The sun had come out from behind the grey skies just in time to set. He would fly away above the glint of the river snaking its way down to the estuary, he would fly above the empty sea as darkness fell, and tell the stars his secrets.

Two portly merchants speaking what he thought was Swedish huffed and wheezed their way to the top of the stairs, their breath puffs of vapour in the cold. One passed the other a silver flask – good workmanship, you'd get seven or eight shillings for it in one of the pawn shops in Cheapside. They offered him a swig. It smelled of cherries and alcohol but he said no. He didn't like to drink when he worked.

The wind had dropped and smoke from the chimneys rose in plumes towards him and he could smell countless dinners cooking – all those ordinary lives. Night was crawling in, the shadows below inking out the people in the streets and leaving only darkness. One of the merchants leant out to see better, and rested on the wooden rail.

'I wouldn't,' said Edgar, and poked a finger an inch deep into the rotten timber.

The man stepped back and thanked him.

'There'd be time to say your prayers on the way down,' his friend said and they laughed.

There was a voice behind them.

'Hello.'

Edgar turned and there stood Lizzie, not one bit out of breath from climbing 150 steps. She threw him his two pennies and he caught one but dropped the other. He was shocked at how glad he was to see her and more shocked at how sorry he was that she'd come. He'd have to wait until the Swedish merchants left to kill her.

WILL

Two elderly men left the Globe Theatre through the hidden gate the actors used to avoid the admirers who waited for them outside. One of the grey-bearded old gentlemen held the arm of the other, who walked with a stick, and was unsteady on his feet.

There weren't going to be many costumes left in the store at this rate. Will and Ann had stuck on grey beards and donned the pumpkin hose, codpieces and cloaks that the Merry Wassailers had worn in Webster's *Christmas Comes but Once a Year*. He worried that Ann wouldn't be able to walk, but her strength had returned surprisingly quickly. They struggled against the shove of over 3,000 people squeezing through the narrow streets towards the theatre, bundled in coats, cloaks and hats, their breath white in the icy air. It would be a full house on the coldest day of the year. It often was – standing squashed together in the pit was one way to warm up.

A squad of Proute's militia came stomping towards them. He and Ann shrank away against a wall, but the soldiers pushed past them to join a fight between some of their mates and a bunch of Irishmen who ran an eel soup stall. The militia had halberds but the stallholders had boiling water and it looked like it would be a close thing.

'So we have the militia after us as well,' said Ann.

That's what worried him. Someone in the government wanted them dead as well. The large moustache that he'd stuck on his top lip was coming loose and Ann pressed it back on.

'What do we do now?' she asked.

It was a good question.

'We visit the Admiral's Men and find Berrycloth, he's our best hope,' he said, and heard his own lack of conviction.

'Where do we find them?'

'At the Fortune in Clerkenwell.'

What they couldn't do was ask at the Rose Theatre. He could hear the thuds and clunks of Henslowe's men still at work dismantling it.

Here in the cramped streets of the 'Liberty of the Clink', beyond the grasp of the City of London and 'Rich' Spencer, were the bear pits, brothels and theatres. Here men pulled the teeth from bears and murdered them with dogs, here men paid women for sex, and here men stood onstage pretending to be emperors, kings and heroes.

All this was under the jurisdiction of the bishop of Winchester, and his Right Reverence was raking it in. Kit Marlowe had joked, 'It's fine to sleep with a prostitute here, twenty per cent of your money goes to God.' Will told Ann how, last spring, the bishop had tripled the rent of the Rose and Henslowe, who owned it, had refused to pay and chosen instead to take it down and move it.

The Rose was where he and Ann had fallen in love, sneaking into the theatre at night through a secret back door. Before they started knocking it down he had taken the key as a keepsake. A key that unlocked nothing – that was an apt memento for him and Ann.

He wanted to tell her he was glad she was alive but he didn't know how to start. Here he was, better with words than anyone in London, but when it came to Ann, they were useless. In the end, he asked her if she was hungry.

'Still not hungry,' she said.

'Have I asked you that often?'

'Oh yes,' she said, but she was smiling. At least nearly dying had made her forget her anger at him.

As the light faded, an elderly woman running a stall lit an

oil lantern and hung it on a pole. Will took Ann's hand and guided her into the pool of light.

'Let's take a look at you,' he said.

The swelling had gone down and, though her eyes were still puffy and red, she looked like herself again – at least like herself with a grey beard glued to her chin. She idly fingered a ring on the stall.

'That's a powerful one,' said the woman. 'Protects you from plague, poison and getting struck by lightning.'

It was a stall dedicated to Saint Guinefort, the dog saint. Guinefort was a greyhound who'd been wrongfully accused of savaging a baby. The baby's father had killed her, but her image had reappeared in the village well and started curing the sick. She'd been made a saint but then the church had second thoughts about beatifying a greyhound and they destroyed her shrine and suppressed her worship. People, though, still loved her and, though illegal, her merchandise was popular. This stall sold Guinefort crucifixes, rings and sacred relics of the bones she'd eaten.

'Try it on, sir,' the woman said to Ann.

Will wasn't sure whether she really thought Ann was an elderly man or if she was just encouraging a customer.

'Go on,' said Will. 'You could do with some protection.'

Ann rolled her eyes at him, but put the ring on her middle finger next to her wedding band. It was poor quality – brass, with the outline of a greyhound etched on its head.

'That's a good fit,' said the woman. 'Meant for you, sir.'

It did fit perfectly and Will was surprised at how much he wanted to buy it for her. Was he trying to get a glimpse of what a normal life together could have been?

'We'll take it,' he said, and before Ann could protest, handed the woman a silver sixpence.

'Dog bless you,' she whispered as they left, quiet enough to deny it if challenged.

Ann took his arm for support and looked up at him.

'You knights know how to treat a lady.'

'I'd hoped that nearly dying would have made you forget that.'

'Oh no, it's all crystal clear.'

She scrunched her face in thought for a moment.

'Kemp's landlady,' she said. 'When she came to the theatre, did you see what she was wearing?'

ANN

Nearly everything that had happened at the theatre had come back to her, not in the right order, but piece by piece, so she had to fit it together. The landlady's visit had flashed into her head, bright and vivid, more like she was there watching than remembering it. She could see her telling them about the stone in Kemp's mouth. At the time, the strangeness of her words was all she had taken in but now she saw more.

'That silver chain,' she said.

A purple jewel sparkled for a moment in her mind.

'With an amethyst on it. She didn't have that when we saw her at Kemp's.'

'She might not have worn it at home.'

'And she had brand new shoes, shiny leather with brass buckles. Someone's given her money.'

Her thoughts were racing. Her mind seemed sharp and bright, as if nearly dying had given it a nice spring clean.

'She certainly can't be trusted,' said Will. 'She lied to us about Kemp being behind with his rent.'

'How do you know?' she asked him.

'Because I paid it.'

'But then she'd know you knew it wasn't behind.'

He turned away so he wasn't looking at her as if he was embarrassed.

'I did it secretly,' he said. 'Kemp didn't know who paid it.'

Was that kindness or guilt, she wondered. Probably both.

‘So she was rewarded for something to do with Kemp’s murder,’ said Will. ‘Is that what you think?’

‘Yes,’ she said, ‘but what for? Helping or keeping quiet?’

Her sharp, new mind didn’t have the answer for that.

BELLA

There were times that Tamburlaine slept so still that Bella put a hand on his side to feel his breath and make sure he was still alive, just as she had once done when her baby boy had lain in his cot. The dog, feeling her touch, rolled lazily onto his back, all four paws in the air. Tamburlaine was a proper dog, a big, ugly, filthy brute, not like one of those quivering lapdogs. The countess of Malmsey had mated a spaniel and a miniature poodle and created something that looked like one of the fluffballs Tamburlaine coughed up after breakfast. At least dogs like that would never catch on. She rubbed Tamburlaine's stomach – his upside-down jowls wobbled and he made a rumbling noise close to a purr.

The door scraped open and Cecil returned. He reached down to scratch the dog's nose. His glasses were hooked over his ears but facing backwards. It was a habit he had so he did not lose them when he was not using them, but when he turned his back on you, there were the spectacles, the glass shimmering as if he had eyes in the back of his head, as if he could still see you, look into your soul and know what you were thinking.

He sniffed the air.

'I hope your hashish has calmed you,' he said.

It had, but not enough. She feared Cecil, but at least with him there was a logic. The king she feared more. She knew what had happened back in Scotland to a woman called Barbara Napier. She had been tried for witchcraft and found innocent. James had arrested the jury and had her burned anyway. She risked asking Cecil a question.

'Is His Majesty still here?'

'He is being comforted by one of his young gentlemen,' he said.

He tried to sit but seemed stuck. She reached to help but he refused her arm, gritted his teeth and forced himself down.

'Most kings need a fool,' he said. 'James needs a king.'

There was a long shivery howl from the courtyard – she couldn't tell from what animal but it sounded like a cry for help.

'It's madness,' muttered Cecil. 'He surrounds himself with men who laugh at his jokes and now is convinced he's the wittiest man in England.'

This candour was unlike him.

'First courtiers flatter him, then they say the same things in private for fear that if they don't their friends will betray them, and finally, having said these things so often, they come to believe them.'

He seemed to have to say all this to someone.

'He's just spent the price of five naval vessels on an elaborate crib for Prince Harry, which will be too small for him in a year's time.'

But why was he saying such dangerous things to her? Did it mean he was going to have her killed? Tamburlaine licked his chin and he smiled. At least, if he did, he would find her dog a good home.

'I swear I will say nothing about the king coming here,' she said.

'No,' he said, 'and from now on you will never mention him by name even if it is just myself present.'

So there was a future. That was promising.

Perhaps he had come to release her now she had sent his message to the king. She wondered if he really thought England's much persecuted Catholics were a threat or if he just required them as scapegoats, but there was enough to worry about without concerning herself with that. As ever, Cecil seemed to read her mind.

'We shall tell the Personage that you and your dog turned yourselves into vapours and flew out between the bars.'

He grimaced and flexed his back against the wall.

'We shall also tell him that the evil vapours flew out of the enchanted giraffe and it is no longer enchanted, so he doesn't have to kill it. To get it to England cost the price of a small palace.'

She was pleased that both she and the giraffe would live.

'I will move you to a more comfortable cell,' he said.

What had he just said? She must not show any anger, yet it was getting harder and harder to submit to the whims of these men. She wanted to bang his oversized head against the stone wall. One day she would explode.

'My lord, I had thought you were going to release me,' she said.

'The Personage does not trust what you have told him. He has decided that witches in captivity always lie. He has decided that to hear the truth, he must go and visit them in the wild.'

'But, my lord.' She could hear the strain as she fought to keep her voice meek. 'If a witch lies in captivity, why wouldn't she lie when she was free?'

Cecil huffed in frustration. 'You use logic, sense and reason. Have you not heard they are dead? Let superstition, delusion and mad surmise govern you like everyone else.' He shrugged helplessly. 'You will return to your coven and the Personage will come there to speak to you again.'

She was not sure what he meant by this.

'Bella,' he said, 'we are going to put on a play.' And he left.

Bella despaired. Sailing once with a Portuguese captain searching for the fabled southern continent, she had shared her cabin with two frigate birds called Malta and Jerusalem. Frigate birds were unable to land on the sea, so if released would return to the ship if there was no land within fifty miles.

If it was closer, however, they somehow knew it and would fly off and the ship could follow the direction they took.

South-west of Ilhas das Papuas, the ship had struck a mighty whale, and despite two desperate days on the pumps they had been forced to abandon it in three tiny boats. The captain had taken one of the birds with them, and given it food and water even when there was none for the men. It was Jerusalem who had saved them.

After forty-six days, with the other boats lost, with half the crew dead and half the rest raving from drinking saltwater, the bird had been released for perhaps the fiftieth time. They watched as it circled above them, but this time it flew off trailing the long double ribbons of its tail. They followed it north-west and after two days found an island with fruit and fresh water streams where the bird was waiting for them.

Bella wanted a frigate bird now, something that would save her from this ocean of despair and lead her, as Jerusalem had, towards salvation.

WILL

They had been heading for the pier at St Mary Overie, so they could cross the river and head for the Fortune, but a house had collapsed and blocked the street so he led Ann towards Bear Garden Steps There should be plenty of boats heading north with the theatre crowd having crossed south. He'd get the waterman to take them to Puddle Dock and from there it was a thirty-minute walk to the Fortune Theatre, where hopefully they'd find Berrycloth. Smoke rolled down the lane from where they were burning the rubbish at Southwark Market and Ann started to cough and stopped for a moment to gather her breath.

Snow was falling again – big, fat flakes floating down through the black smoke. Will asked if she was alright but she ignored him.

'Were you going to let Frances Strange stab me in the throat?' she asked.

He mustn't pause. That would be suspicious.

'Do what? No,' he said, laughing at the absurdity of it. 'Stab you in the throat? Why would I do that? God, no.'

Now he was talking too much.

'Are you sure?' she asked. 'It's the last thing that's come back to me. I can see her holding a dagger above my throat.'

He was committed to the lie. It was too late to go back.

'I hear that lack of air does strange things to the brain. It can give you hallucinations.'

He tried to start walking again and slipped on an icy puddle and nearly fell over.

'She asked you if she should and you said "Yes",' said Ann.

'There was a thief whose pardon arrived when he'd been hanging for three minutes,' said Will, 'and when they cut him down, he told them that he'd seen the face of Jesus, and Jesus was a mouse. Which was a mistake because then they hung him for blasphemy.'

Ann still looked dubious.

'Do you think Kemp's landlady could have lied about the stone?' he asked.

She seemed reluctant to change the subject.

'It's possible.'

'Or the man with the black eye, for that matter.'

A distant trumpet sounded for the start of his play and they started walking again. The crowds were gone and the moon glimmered on the icy puddles. Even the yellow patches where people had urinated were frozen.

'She could have said about the black eye to confuse us,' he said. 'Perhaps she was involved with Kemp's murder? Perhaps they told her to let them know if anyone asked questions, and when she did they rewarded her.'

Ann made a face. She didn't seem convinced, but at least she was no longer asking about Frances Strange and the dagger.

Bear Garden Steps were deserted, which was odd this early in the evening. The stone stairs led down to a wooden platform that rose and fell with the tides, usually busy with watermen and customers, but there was no one. Then he saw why. The river had frozen.

The moon had come out and an expanse of white stretched in front of them all the way to the fires flickering by Three Cranes Wharf on the Queenhithe Shore. The river had frozen in 1604, the ice so thick that they had held a Frost Fair on it, but he'd never known it happen in November. Somewhere a man sang a song in a sweet, deep voice and a dozen geese flew in formation low across the ice, their slow flapping wings carrying them downriver and into darkness. They walked onto the dock past a stack of upturned wherries where the watermen had dragged their boats out of the river so they weren't crushed by the ice.

Gruff voices joined in as the singer reached the chorus. Will could just make out the words, an old soldiers' song, 'Let the Canakin Clink'.

'We'll have to risk London Bridge,' he said.

Ann jabbed him hard and when he looked put her finger to her lips. Her face behind her hand was taut with fear, her eyes wide in the moonlight.

'It's him,' she whispered.

He turned but couldn't see anyone, but then he knew – the soldiers' song. The man who had hunted them before, the man who had come to kill Ann, he had sung it all those years ago, that mellow voice, those empty eyes.

They were exposed, standing in the open on the platform. They must move but silently. At least if he was singing he hadn't seen them. The singing stopped suddenly.

A large shape appeared, framed at the mouth of one of the alleys that led to the river. Two more shapes joined him, the smaller one carrying a lantern, and they walked forward to the top of the steps. Will and Ann were trapped. He could see the face of the small one in the lantern he held, a wide grin, his teeth filed to points. The big man started a new song. It took a moment before he could work out the words.

'Two more pigeons for my pie,' he sang as he walked towards them.

ACT THREE

EDGAR

'What made you join a magic show?' he asked Lizzie.

She considered.

'It was that or be normal.'

It was snowing again and the flakes were landing on her hair. He watched them melt. He didn't like killing anyone who wasn't in the same game. Spies, criminals, soldiers, anyone who would kill you, that was fair enough, but not people who just knew something that they shouldn't. It wasn't as if it would keep him awake at night. The only thing that kept him awake at night was a woman in his bed, but this did offend his sense of fair play. He was glad when they'd gone along with his suggestion to use the Widow to get the salt they needed and deal with her later. But with Lizzie they'd been very clear and he knew what would happen if he didn't do as he was told.

The Swedish merchants were taking their time to go. They were on to a second flask – not as valuable as the first. They offered him a drink again and this time he took it. He needed it and the sooner they finished it the sooner they'd leave.

'Have you seen the show?' she asked him.

He nodded. The magic had delighted him. He tried telling himself she deserved to die for calling the martyred Mary, Queen of Scots 'satanic', but he didn't have much luck with that.

'Did you know that Mary turned up for her execution dressed all in black?' he asked her.

He wished he hadn't started talking about death, but now he had to go on.

'As she stepped towards the block, she slipped the black cape from her shoulders and everyone gasped because she was dressed beneath in crimson, the colour of blood, from head to toe.'

'So overdramatic,' said Lizzie, unimpressed.

He'd have thought she liked drama. He asked her what she meant.

'When Anne and Jane and Jane and Mary went to the block, everyone says how dignified they were, but why did they kneel and put their heads on the block at all? I'd have snatched the headsman's axe, leaped into the crowd, and wrought havoc.'

Of course she would have.

'You should try that in your show,' he said.

'I'm not sure it's a good idea to murder the paying public.'

The Swedes were still there. They were really getting their tuppence worth. Lizzie told him about the performance.

'They all gasp,' she said. 'When they think I'm a severed head, and I open my eyes.'

She smiled. Her smile was slow coming but worth waiting for. The snow was heavier and she stuck out her tongue to catch a flake.

'At first, I just went and said the words, "I can only speak the truth," but then I realised it's better if I wait. The further from London, the bigger the gasp was and the bigger the gasp the longer I waited and then I wouldn't just say it, I'd ask them, "Do you want to hear the truth?" And they'd murmur, "Yes," and I'd keep asking them and asking them until they roared it.'

'Isn't magic just about tricking people?' he asked.

She hesitated. Her cheeks were flushed pink from the cold and the melting snow in her hair shimmered. Even in this weather, she was bare-armed, wearing only a thin blue wool cape. If he was a gentleman, he'd offer her his black Astrakhan cloak. But then he'd lose it when he pushed her off the tower. She was biting her lower lip again as she thought, and somehow that gesture sent him into turmoil and he hoped she would keep thinking for a long time. Finally, though, she spoke.

'It's about showing them that the impossible is possible.'

He wanted to ask her why that was a good thing but he must stop asking her questions because the more she answered the more he knew about her, and the more he knew the less he wanted to kill her.

The two Swedish merchants finally said goodbye, doffed their hats to Lizzie and turned and walked down the stairs. Melted snow was dripping down her face and she licked it away with her tongue. She reached under her cloak and bought out two marchpane ducks with cloves for eyes, popped one in her mouth and offered him the other.

'Aren't they expensive?' he asked, surprised she could afford them.

'Don't worry,' she said, 'I stole them.'

He was slow taking the little duck so she ate the second one too, crunching it between her teeth.

'So you steal?' he said.

'Yes,' she said, and whipped out an arm, snatched his felt hat, put it on her head and stood there grinning, tiny shards of sugar stuck around her mouth. He told himself that it was better to wait until it was fully dark to do it. 'Do you have a knife?' she asked.

'Yes,' he said.

'May I have it?'

This was not the time to hand her a knife but he did anyway. She pointed down. Some of the lead that formed the gutter at their feet had been stolen, but in the sections that were left, initials, names and love hearts were carved into the soft metal.

She carved a *C* into the lead.

'I thought you were Lizzie,' he said.

'My stage name. Glendower gave it to me.'

'What is it?'

'You'll have to find out.'

He didn't suppose he would.

'May I have my knife back?' he asked.

She held it out to him, but with her hand clasped around the hilt so he had to take the blade.

'Careful,' she said. 'It's sharp.'

It was. He took it carefully with thumb and forefinger and she let go. He squatted down and started to carve his initials next to hers.

'I thought you were Edgar Strange,' she said.

He had started to carve his old name. He quickly changed the letter to an *E*.

'I am,' he said.

It didn't matter that she'd seen. She wasn't going to be telling anyone. For a moment, he was going to carve a heart around their two sets of initials, but it wouldn't be playing fair to do that, then push her through the rotten rail.

He stood up and they were facing each other. Her eyes seemed amused. He grabbed to get his hat but she leapt a step back. She was quick. He could imagine kissing her pale lips and wondered whether she would kiss him back.

More and more lights were showing – the glow of ovens in kitchens, of lanterns in shops, the distant fires of the charcoal burners and the brick kilns. Drunken voices came from beneath them, but now they could see nothing. Humanity was hidden, its presence only discernible in fire and noise. It was time. If he pushed her now her body would smack into the cobblestones below in darkness and it would take a while for a crowd to gather and work out where it had come from and by then he would have slipped away. Even if he was stopped, they'd believe him if he told them she'd leant on one of the rails and fallen. Everyone knew how rotten they were.

He moved to go around her as if he wanted to look out over the other side. Now she was at the rail and he was on the inside. She turned to face him and kissed him on the lips. For a moment he froze with surprise but then he kissed her too. She leant back and he heard the creak of the rotten rail behind her giving way and felt her falling back. He pulled her towards him before she lost her balance and fell. He tried to kiss her some more but she slipped sideways out of his arms and in a couple of steps was at the top of the stairs. She waved goodbye and sped down them so fast he couldn't have caught her if he'd tried.

'Where do you live?' he shouted after her.

'Nowhere.'

Her voice echoed up the stairs.

'Where can I find you?' she asked.

'I'm lodging above the Cock Tavern,' he shouted down.

That had not gone the way he'd intended. He'd saved her from falling and told her where he lived. He laughed to himself. He'd have to tell them that she hadn't turned up and hope none of them saw her wearing his hat. He peered over the creaky rail, making sure not to put any weight on it. There was just enough light close to the cathedral to see her come running out of the Chain Door and across the square. A dark figure came out of a doorway and followed her.

ANN

The big man persuaded his mouth to smile. It looked like a scythe.

'I've only orders to take you prisoner,' he said.

The scar tissues where she'd burnt him had wept and then frozen so it looked as if wax had dripped down one side of his face. That smile too was frozen.

'Come up here quietly and we'll make it easy, won't we?' he said.

The other two nodded obediently. Still he smiled. If he did nothing else that smile was enough to kill her.

'No ropes, no gags, we'll just walk you half a mile down the road to where someone wants to talk to you.'

He just wanted them to go somewhere quieter and darker to kill them, but she worried that this was just the kind of thing Will would fall for.

'Sod off. You must be joking,' said Will.

He'd changed more than she'd realised. The big man sighed.

'Yes, I'm joking. I'm going to kill you.'

Thank God, at least he stopped smiling. He pulled a knife out of his waistband and licked the flat of the blade just as he'd done before.

In amongst the terror Ann felt something else – sadness that she and Will would never have a chance to put things right between them, the thought compressed into a bare second.

The little one was talking now in a high, scratchy voice wavering with rage.

'Yes, Mr Words, I'm going to kill you, make her watch, then kill her. That'll teach you for being so clever.'

The podgy one leant over. His chins had chins. He whispered in the little one's ear.

'Right, no, small correction,' the little one hissed through his filed teeth. 'I'm going to kill her so you have to watch, then kill you.'

The big man shook his head at them like an indulgent father and turned to pointy-teeth.

'Don't touch the woman, Dogface, she's mine.' He led the three of them forward.

'The river,' Ann whispered to Will, 'we might as well try it.'

Her wobbly legs ran towards the end of the jetty. She wanted to step carefully onto the frozen river, but the men were close and she just leapt. She landed heavily, expecting the ice to crack beneath her, but it held. Will jumped with her and they scrambled out towards the middle of the river.

The three killers lowered themselves onto the ice and spread out to cut off any escape, Dogface with the lantern on the London Bridge side and the fat one towards Westminster. The moon slipped behind the clouds and it was all darkness save for a few flickers of flame on the far bank ahead of them. Ann's legs felt like they didn't belong to her, that they belonged to someone older and feebler, but she forced them to take one step and then the next.

'There's usually a channel where the river still runs,' gasped Will.

What could she say? They'd find out if they got that far.

When the moon came back out, the three men had gained on them and were close behind. She slipped and fell again and, this time, as she hit the ice, there was a creak and she could see a spider's web of small cracks beneath her and hear the rush of the river flowing beneath the ice. Will came back for her. She should tell him to go on, but she knew he wouldn't. She could hear the harsh rasping breath of the big man closing on them. She turned and saw he held a knife in one hand. There was a crack and a flash and she realised it wasn't a knife. He'd fired a pistol. She wondered how he'd missed. He was so close she could smell the acrid whiff of gunpowder.

There were bangs and flashes from both sides of them now. All three pursuers were firing. Will stumbled, grunted and fell onto the ice. He'd been hit.

There was another crack and a yell, but this wasn't a gunshot. The fat one must have fallen through the ice.

'Help me,' he bawled from the darkness.

Dogface was shouting something she couldn't hear but the big, burnt one yelled, 'Leave him!'

She crabbed her way across the ice to Will, who had got up on his knees. She couldn't see any blood but then you wouldn't in the darkness. She put her hands under his arms and he groaned as she heaved him up. They staggered forward, the two of them, but they were twice the weight on the ice and double the target.

Behind them the big man had stopped. She could see why: the ice around them was thinner, blue-black and coated in slush. Dogface with the lantern had joined him and they were arguing and she guessed the burnt one was trying to get pointy-teeth to follow them but he wasn't having it. The man who had fallen in was swearing and thrashing, and she could hear the sound of more ice cracking around him.

She dragged Will forward and felt the unfamiliar new ring scraping against her finger. It promised protection against plague and poison but there'd been no mention of gunfire and drowning. Will slipped from her grip, fell and lay beneath her, clutching his side.

'Come on,' she pleaded.

'You're lighter,' he muttered, as he rose to his knees. 'You go. Get help.'

The moon vanished again but tongues of light from fires

on the far shore flickered out across the ice towards them, and she could just make him out.

'Go on,' he said, and shoved her leg with one hand.

He was right. She was much more likely to make it across the thin ice. It made sense for her to go.

'Don't think you're getting rid of me,' she said.

The flickering lights weren't bright enough for her to see the surface of the ice ahead of her. She just had to step out into blackness, only a thin skin of frozen water between her and death. She took a step expecting to plummet, but it held firm. Another step and it creaked beneath her. Was it really better to be slow and careful? Wasn't fast and fleet just as good? God damn it, that's what she was going to do, run towards the answer. She sped forward into the darkness, holding her breath even though she was running, trying to step light-footed, as if that would help. She slipped, slid, teetered, slithered and fell. Her chin hit something hard and she reached out and felt a lump of frozen mud. She was on the bank. Her yell of triumph sounded demented.

She couldn't see Will or their pursuers. There was a weak cry from the man who had fallen through the ice, then silence, silence and darkness. She got to her feet and the moon half came out again, a glow behind the racing clouds. Now she saw Will.

He had lain down and spread himself out on the ice and was crawling slowly towards her. She remembered from somewhere, that was the way to cross thin ice, yet while she weighed about eighty-five pounds, he must be a hundred and twenty. He inched forward one limb at a time. Behind him was a thin black streak on the ice, blood from where he'd been shot. He moved towards her, one hand and then the other stretched out ahead of him as if he was reaching out for her. She wanted to reach out for him, took a step forward, realised it would only put more weight on the ice and stepped back again.

'Will,' she shouted. 'Stay where you are, I'll get help.'

She turned around and men had appeared on the bank, silhouetted against the lights.

'Run for a rope,' she yelled.

She felt something prickly in her mouth and tasted glue. The old man's beard had come unstuck and was caught between her teeth. She spat it out and brushed it away.

'A rope,' she called again to the men.

They didn't move.

'Please,' she called, and turned around to see Will still crawling. He was four yards away, three, she could see those dark brown eyes, his face clenched in concentration. It was the noise she heard first – a creak and a crack. Then he was gone.

There was a man-sized hole but no sign of him. She feared the current had swept him under the ice, but then his head appeared, spluttering. His arms flailed at the jagged rim but each time he tried to use it to pull himself up it cracked and broke away and just made the hole bigger. She could smell the rank stench of the river released through the opening. She saw him gather himself, subdue his panic and stop smashing at the ice.

'That's right,' she said. 'Stay there.'

As if he was going anywhere else.

For an instant she thought of asking God for help, but she hadn't done that for a long time and that wasn't really how she and God worked. She'd try mankind first. She turned to the men on the bank. Now she could see it was the King's Guard standing there – the same men who had come to the theatre.

'Please, help.'

'Seize the woman,' came that rotund voice, and Sergeant-Major Colonel Proute stepped out of the darkness.

'No,' she screamed. 'Help him!'

A soldier grabbed her around the waist and lifted her off her feet.

'No, no, help me help him.'

She was dragged up the bank pressed against the cold metal of his breastplate. Will, floundering in the freezing river, was being carried downstream. The current forced him against the lip of the ice and each time it cracked and broke. He clawed at the ice to the side trying to stop himself floating away, but that just broke away too, and the channel just kept getting wider and longer. He drifted further into the darkness.

Ann was deposited next to Proute and his big, pompous voice was in her ear.

'I thought I told you not to leave the theatre.'

'He's drowning,' she said.

'You brought it on yourselves.'

Will was disappearing, no longer struggling, just flapping weakly to stay afloat.

Humanity wasn't going to work with Proute, but she'd seen him give way faced with Frances Strange's threats. She wasn't descended from two kings, but she was descended from the Marlowes and they were worth a whole heap of kings.

'You had orders to bring both of us in for interrogation,' she said, making a bit of a guess. 'Your boss isn't going to be happy with you if you only bring me.'

'I'm not sending my men onto the ice,' he said, turning away and trying to light his pipe. 'I don't know if you noticed but they wear armour. They'd go straight through and armour is expensive.'

'I'll help him if you let me go,' she said.

'Light my pipe,' he said, and she realised he was speaking to the nearest soldier. Proute was struggling to light it in the wind, and the man came over with a tinderbox.

Now she couldn't see Will. She could only hear the cracking of the ice and the rippling of the water. She wanted to run to the river, but Proute would just tell his men to stop her.

She lowered her voice.

'If you don't bring us both in like you were told, someone's going to be very angry. Very well, you're one of the king's favourites now, but we all know that doesn't last for long. When he's lost interest in you, they're going to be coming for you.'

He spluttered, too indignant to form words. She thought he would hit her, but she went on quickly anyway.

'You've got to think ahead. Don't make enemies. Just let me go out there with a rope and get him, then you can deliver us and they'll be pleased.'

'What rope? I don't see a rope,' he said, but he was weakening. She could see her arguments were finally reaching his brain. The soldier had got his pipe alight for him.

'Then let me take a halberd.'

'Let you take a weapon? I'm not an idiot.'

She didn't have the time to put him right.

'I'm not going to defeat a regiment of the King's Guard.'

'It's not a "regiment", it's a "company",' he said prissily.

She could hear nothing from the river. Will could have drowned by now.

'Please, sergeant-major colonel,' she said.

'Oh, for God's sake,' he said, pointing at one of his soldiers. 'Go on, Pigface, give the silly wench a halberd.'

She went to the soldier he'd pointed at and put her hands out for his weapon. He handed it to her reluctantly. It was heavier than she thought and the end with the metal blade dropped to the ground and she nearly fell with it. Proute laughed. She took hold of the shaft close to the blade so it balanced and ran across the frozen mud to the river.

She heard Proute boom, 'If she escapes, you idiots will be in trouble.'

'Will,' Ann shouted, but there was no reply.

She followed the channel he'd cut through the ice as he'd struggled. It reached an end and there was no sign of him. She felt a black dread as if she was being pulled under the dark water herself. Then his head rose. There he was, his mouth gasping, ice clinging to his hair and beard, frozen, shot, exhausted, drowning but there.

'Will,' she shouted again.

She held the halberd by the blade end, stepped to the edge

of the beach of frozen mud and reached out the shaft towards him. It didn't reach and his head disappeared again. She edged out onto the ice and he came up again. She heard a gargling gasp for air. She stepped forward another pace. The ice held. She pushed the shaft towards him. She feared his hands would be too frozen to grasp it, but he clutched hold, and she pulled and he floated towards her and reached the lip of the ice nearest to the shore. He took one arm off the shaft and clawed at the ice, but it broke and he fell below the water once more.

'Help me!' she called over her shoulder to the King's Guard who stood watching the spectacle.

'Don't,' shouted Proute.

Will came up again, his arms moving too slowly to keep him afloat.

'Grab it again,' she shouted, and he did. 'And kick with your feet.' She remembered being told that once by her mother.

She leant back and heaved, but the blade of the halberd cut into her hands. She howled to fight away the pain and heaved some more, and though the ice in front of him broke, he was getting closer to the shore.

'Kick,' she shouted again, and she saw the water splashing behind him where he had been.

Now she could nearly reach him. She could feel her hands slipping on the blood where the blade cut into her but she pulled anyway. The ice she was standing on cracked and she plunged into the water.

LIZZIE

She only really feared darkness when she was still and it closed in around her. When she was running its black fingers reached out for her but before they could clutch her she was gone. She liked London when it was this cold, the streets deserted, the gutters no longer flowing with filth, the river crisp and glittering. Even the flag that flew above the Tower was stiff and still. It was as if the city had been frozen in time, a trick by a mighty magician, the whole of London bewitched, save for her flying through the empty streets. She was sure no one could follow her at this breakneck pace. She almost lost her grip, but managed to slither around a slick corner.

It was like ice skating on the frozen canals of Ghent when she was tiny, skimming past the boys who teased her, not tethered to the dullness of the everyday. It set her heart rat-tat-tatting against her ribs – almost as fast as when she had kissed Edgar Strange.

The guards at London Bridge were huddled under their cloaks around a brazier, their breath rising in white plumes mixing with the smoke. Above them, the severed heads of executed traitors were stuck on pikes, icicles hanging from their noses.

There seemed to be more and more of them each week and it made her fear for Glendower. She wondered where they were keeping him. If they questioned him about witchcraft, he'd make it worse with his talk of the ancient phantoms of the forests and the wraiths that floated like mist and stole your soul. And if they offered him a drink, he'd sign anything.

She was gasping for breath as she reached the small house at the end of an alleyway guarded by the young out-of-work actor who wouldn't stop talking. He was called Jake, or perhaps he'd played Jake, when someone was ill. That's right, he was called Nathaniel. He'd said he'd got so many laughs that Tarleton had pushed him up against a wall and told him that if he ever did that again, he'd get his face smashed in.

She knocked and she heard Nathaniel's voice.

'Lizzie, come in.'

But there was something wrong with it as if he'd forgotten to breathe. She heard the bolt being pulled back.

'Is that you, Nicholas?' she asked.

She could hear him swallow as he hesitated.

'That's right,' he said, 'it's me, Nicholas.'

He was warning her.

'Come on in,' he said.

She imagined a knife blade at his throat, or a pistol stuck in his back. Her heartbeat got faster again. If she turned and ran, would someone kill him?

The door crashed open, and a man burst out, his face hidden by a hooded cloak, a sword in his hand. She turned and fled, hoping she hadn't used up all her breath on the run there. Another man was blocking the end of the alley.

ANN

For a moment after she plunged into the river, Ann felt nothing, but then the cold hit her, clamped around her chest and squeezed. She flailed her arms to get her head above the water and came up. Will's face was in front of her, wild-eyed and speckled with ice. Both of them were still holding on to the halberd, but the heavy metal end pulled her under and she let go. The freezing water that she'd swallowed seemed to have filled her with a column of ice. Will's head sank beneath the surface. The hope that had given him strength had gone. He thrashed weakly and his face came up but barely above the surface, and he swallowed more water as he tried to breathe.

She could make out the shapes of the soldiers on the shore, watching them die. She tried to shout but the cold squeezed her chest so hard she couldn't speak. She reached for Will, but holding on to him they just seemed to sink faster. She heard Proute shouting furiously. One of the soldiers was walking towards them.

'Leave them. I'm warning you,' yelled Proute.

The man spat out a brown stream of tobacco and kept walking. Another soldier joined him, and then another. They were all walking down the beach now, armour glinting in the moonlight. They held out their halberds in a latticework of poles. Proute continued to rant.

Now the ice where she had been standing had broken, she and Will were closer to the shore and she could just reach the shafts. She put one arm over them and with the other grasped at Will's doublet. Her hand was so frozen it wouldn't grip but she hooked it inside his collar. She found a voice from somewhere.

'Grab hold. You're not drowning now.'

He clamped an arm over hers and the soldiers pulled and she felt them being dragged through the water and hooked up onto the Thames shore. Proute's ranting was an annoying noise echoing in her frozen ears.

The soldiers hauled her and Will to their feet but his legs just gave way and he slumped back to the ground.

'How bad is your wound?' she asked him through shivering teeth, but either her speech was incomprehensible or he was too weak to answer. A grizzled soldier with a grey beard spattered with brown tobacco stood next to her.

'Thank you,' she said, hoping at least those words were clear.

He grunted.

'You've lost a halberd, Shitbrain,' Proute was spluttering. 'I'm going to dock your wages.'

The soldier ignored this.

'Shall we do what you ordered, sir,' he asked, 'and take them to Lord Cecil at the Tower?'

Ann wondered if it would have been better to have drowned.

LIZZIE

Lizzie ran at the figure blocking the end of the alley. It was a narrow alleyway but if she feinted one way then went the other, she might get past him. She heard the rasping breath of the man chasing her, closer than she thought he'd be. The man blocking the alley had a half-brick raised in one hand.

'Run, Lizzie,' he shouted.

It was Evan, the bottle boy.

He hurled the half-brick past her shoulder, and she heard a pleasing crunch and grunt behind her. She half turned as she swung around the corner, and she saw her pursuer, one hand holding his bloody head, swaying, but still moving forward, sword in hand.

'Run,' cried Evan unnecessarily, and she ran, not for joy now, but for her life.

They pelted down a street she thought was Seething Lane, and into a maze of twisting alleys heading towards the river. He ran out of breath before her and stopped, hands on knees, wheezing in the cold air. She gestured at him to be quiet and listened. The streets were silent, no running footsteps, only dogs howling in the distance and someone snoring in a house next to them.

'I saved your life,' he said.

She wasn't too sure about that. If he hadn't been there, she'd just have run and not worried about a man blocking her escape. If anyone had saved her it was Nathaniel the actor. She feared for him. She'd thought it was risky meeting Edgar, but it turned out what would have been really dangerous was staying put behind the stone walls of the secret house. Well, there you were, take risks and you survived.

'I saved your life,' Evan said again. She couldn't see his face in the darkness, but he stood still facing her as if waiting for an acknowledgement.

'Thank you for helping,' she said. With Evan it was best to tell him what he wanted to hear.

He seemed satisfied and led her down towards the Thames. They came out of one of the cramped, dark alleys and there was the river, like a different world. The full moon lit a white expanse of ice that almost blinded her.

He went to move on, but she touched his arm and pointed. A single skater had come around the bend of the river, racing across the moonlit ice. She thought it was a woman, but she couldn't be sure, a slight figure, speeding in long, confident swishes along the river. Was she just using it to get somewhere? But, no, because she swept round in a circle, then more, one leading to another, tighter and tighter. She was just here for the joy of it. *This should be me*, Lizzie thought, *the first one out there, speeding across the thin ice*. She wondered where she could steal some ice skates from.

'Are you hurt?' asked Evan.

'Hurt? Why should I be hurt?'

'He slashed at you with his sword as you turned and ran. He must have come close.'

The moonlight shone pink through his sticky-out ears.

'I'm fine,' she said. 'How did you find me?'

'I followed you.'

She was disappointed. Could he have kept up with her when she ran from meeting Edgar?

'When I ran from St Paul's?'

He shook his head and started to walk along the path by the river.

'No, I lost you then, but I'd waited for you outside the theatre, and followed you and the man to the house, so I knew where it was. Then I followed you to the cathedral tower where you met the other man. Who are they?'

She'd seen *Othello* five times, so she knew how dangerous jealousy was. She decided it was safer to ignore his question.

'Why did you follow me? Why didn't you just come and talk to me?'

'I wanted to protect you. Glendower taught me how to be invisible.'

She doubted that, though had learnt something because she had never seen him behind her.

He was watching the skater. She was now sure it was a woman.

'That's your spirit,' he said.

That was a strange thing to say but then Evan was a strange boy.

'Whatever happens to you she will live forever.'

She'd never been fearful of Evan before but there was now something that worried her.

'Let's get you out of the cold,' he said. 'You can come and stay where I'm staying.'

'Where's that?'

'Here,' he said and pulled out a slat in a fence behind them.

Lizzie watched as her spirit, the skater, sped off upriver. She must have seen Lizzie watching because she waved as she went. Lizzie waved back just before she disappeared into darkness. She stared after her for a moment before she followed Evan through the gap in the fence.

It led into a yard. In it were a dozen or so sedan chairs crammed together so the carrying poles overlapped, their canopies frosted with ice. Evan opened the door of one of them and beckoned her to enter as if it was his mansion.

'This is where you sleep?' she said.

'They don't get a lot of business at this time of year.'

She stepped inside and it was so dark that she had to feel behind her for the bench. It didn't seem any warmer than it was outside. Evan got in after her and went to close the door.

'No,' she said, fearful of being shut in that darkness.

'Don't worry, I have a candle,' he said. 'I bought one in case you came.'

He lit a stub of candle from a tinderbox. Inside the sedan chair, he had a small canvas bag and a ragged blanket.

He picked something up – a brown half-eaten apple – and offered it to her. She shook her head, sure he was hungrier than her. He sat back on the bench opposite her and bit hungrily into the apple. It was then she saw his face clearly for the first time. He had one big black eye.

WILL

Will and Ann lay locked in a large stone room high up in the Tower of London, thawing out on the floor in front of a fire. Their sodden clothing made a puddle around them and they crawled out of it and got as close to the flames as they could without cooking.

Will had been too numb to walk so a couple of soldiers had taken an arm each and dragged him backwards through the streets, under Coldharbour Gate and up several flights of narrow stairs, but at least they'd been taken up and not down into the dungeons.

Getting the feeling back in his feet and hands was more painful than losing it, more painful than the wound in his side where he'd been shot. He tried to speak, but his teeth were grinding against each other as he shivered, and words wouldn't come out, not even a simple thank you to Ann.

'Your wound,' she said, and took off the bag he had around his shoulder that had stayed attached through everything. She lifted his shirt. There was a bloody hole just above his hip. 'I can see the ball you were shot with,' she said.

'How bad is it?' he tried to say, but just mumbled noise.

'It's only gone in an inch or so.'

She touched it and it hurt.

'You were shot from a few yards away. I don't know why it's so shallow.'

'Maybe it hit bone,' he tried to say.

She seemed to understand.

'No, it's just soft flesh. Maybe the pistol misfired. Shall I get the ball out?'

He tried to say they should wait for a doctor, but she couldn't have heard because she went ahead.

'No,' he said, and that did sound like 'no'.

She ignored it.

'What's seven times fourteen?' she asked, the Marlowe family's technique to distract from pain. He knew from before that it didn't work. There was a sharp stab of pain in his side, but that was all. She held out her hand and there it was, a bloody pistol ball flattened on one side.

'Ninety-eight,' he said, and she smiled.

The bolt on the outside of the door was pulled back, the door opened and someone threw in a bundle of clothes.

'We need bandages,' Ann shouted.

The door thumped shut and the bolt clanked across.

'You must stop saving my life,' he said, and those words were recognisable.

'What else was I going to do?' she said.

'Thank you.'

He'd finally said it. Ann grunted and shrugged. Gratitude always made her a bit crotchety. She poked at the heap of clothes on the floor with one damp toe.

'Can you undress yourself?' she asked.

He tried but his fingers were still blunt stubs. She knelt next to him, undid the buckle on his belt, pulled off his jerkin and yanked away his hose.

'Hands above head,' she said like he was a small child. He found it hard to raise his hands. She heaved off his sodden doublet and undershirt and it felt warmer with the fire's heat directly on his skin. She pointed to his underdrawers and looked at him questioningly, but he shook his head. He fumbled them off himself with the numb stumps that were his hands.

The clothes they'd been given were soldiers' uniforms, stained, but washed and smelling of wood-ash soap. She found some underclothes and threw them to him. As he did his best to dress, she took off her clothes. He looked away and she was amused at his modesty.

'After all this time,' she said.

When he turned back she was nearly out of her clothes. He'd forgotten the speed at which she dressed and undressed. She lifted her soaked shift over her head and dropped it on the stone floor with a splosh.

She stood there naked, the firelight flickering over her pale body, and shrugged as if to say, *so what?* The gesture somehow broke his heart. There she was, Ann, his Ann, Ann with no 'e', the woman he had loved more than anyone. She reached for one of the undershirts and dropped it over her head. It was so huge, the neck passed straight over her shoulders and it fell to the ground around her ankles. He laughed.

'At least I'm not so fat I fell through the ice,' she said.

He laughed again, and so did she.

The bolt clanked open and the same thing happened as before, only this time it was bandages they threw around the door.

Will helped Ann put some knots in the undershirt so it stayed on and felt strangely contented. It could just be a trick his battered body was playing on him but the pain had stopped and they were alive and laughing. Perhaps he should die then and there. Of course, he'd just been locked up in the Tower of London so he probably would.

Ann's hand was bloody from where the blade had cut it and he helped her bandage it. For the first time since she'd turned up at the theatre they were at ease with each other. Perhaps he should tell her what he felt about her and then he might find out what it was, but Ann must have sensed the danger because she got there first.

'We should cauterise your wound,' she said briskly, picking a stick out of the flames which was still red-hot at one end.

'No,' he said too loudly, and he found his numb legs could move faster than he'd thought.

He jumped away from her and saw the soaked shoulder bag he'd discarded with his wet clothes. There was a small hole in it – a pistol-ball-sized hole. He'd been shot through the bag. He reached inside and the pebble the undertaker had found in Kemp's mouth was split in two. He held up the halves.

'So that's why the ball didn't go through you,' said Ann. 'It hit the stone first.'

Kemp had protected him from beyond the grave. He knew it was nonsense, just blind chance, the sort of outlandish coincidence that these days led to old women being called witches and put in cages.

Ann took one half of the stone from him and rubbed at its smooth surface. It was not an ordinary pebble, but made of marble and smoothed perfectly round. Ann lowered her voice so he could barely hear her above the crackling of the fire. 'Do you think they really found this in his mouth?'

Whatever that moment had been it was over. They were back on nice safe ground talking about murder.

He thought about it, what the landlady had said.

'It's almost too strange to have made up.'

'Could you have made it up?'

'Well, yes,' he said.

'Of course, you're quite good at making things up.'

He didn't want it to be a lie because, coincidence though it was, he wanted it to be Kemp's pebble that had saved him. He felt a twinge of guilt that he'd had not time for his friend.

Ann told him how, in Canterbury, there had been a gang of moneylenders who killed men who couldn't pay them back and left a cut farthing in their mouths as a warning to others. Was the pebble also a warning?

'Could it be because he slept with men?' Will asked.

Kemp had always kept it a secret but there must be some who knew. They'd been cracking down on that too recently. The king took his favourites to bed with him and openly petted men like Proute, but he'd spoken out against homosexuality. He seemed to think it a sin in anyone except himself.

Mobs roamed the street and beat up men they called 'mollies', but then mobs beat up anyone, Catholics, Jews, foreigners, prostitutes, smaller mobs, and if they couldn't find any of the above, each other. He'd seen a mob batter a man unconscious for having one black shoe and one brown.

There was the rattle of the bolt being pulled back again and the door opened. What were they going to chuck into the room this time? It turned out to be a tall man in a spangled black cloak. Will took a moment to recognise him. It was the magician who'd been arrested, Glendower the Great.

Glendower was talking before they even closed the door. At first, Will thought it was Welsh as he couldn't understand a thing, but it was English, wild and whirling, at a frantic pace, breaking off every sentence before it was finished to start the next. 'A huge explosion,' he caught, 'double-hinged doors', 'bunch of English bastards', but that was it. Had Glendower been terrified into incoherence?

Will asked him to slow down and eventually he did, but then scolded Will for making fun of the Welsh in his plays and calling Owen Glendower boastful.

'I spoke well of his daughter,' said Will, 'and Henry the Fifth was proud to have been born in Wales and fond of Fluellen.'

Ann told them both to be quiet.

'Shall we not argue about what Will thinks of the Welsh and work out a way to stay alive instead?'

At that moment, the door rattled open and Lord Cecil walked in as if he had been listening all along. Perhaps he had.

ANN

'I thought I told you to stay out of politics,' he said to Will.

'I have, my lord.' Will bowed. He looked ridiculous in his baggy soldiers' clothes.

'Is that why you were chased across a frozen river by men firing guns?'

Will went to speak but Cecil stopped him with a raised hand and pointed at a chair in the corner of the room. Will picked up the chair and placed it close to the fire. Cecil thanked him, walked across and sat with a grunt.

'I wish I had your power,' he said to Will.

Will looked baffled.

'My power?'

'What is the capacity of the Globe?' Cecil asked.

'About three thousand four hundred, my lord.'

'So that's twenty thousand four hundred a week.'

'We don't always play to capacity.'

'No, but you usually do.' Cecil stretched and groaned. 'And you often play to more than capacity. I know how you pack them in.'

She saw Will go to speak but think better of it.

'So you have an audience of over one million a year. And you are just one of four theatres. Do you know how many people live in London?'

'Too many,' muttered Glendower.

Cecil ignored him.

'Two hundred thousand or so, which is about one hundred and forty thousand adults. One hundred and forty thousand people who could rebel. I can't reach them. Most of them can't read or write, but they can all listen and they go to the theatre again and again.'

'We are entertainers,' said Will cautiously.

'If only,' muttered Glendower.

'Entertainers?' said Cecil. 'Is that why Essex, on the night of his rebellion against Elizabeth, commissioned you to restage a play about the overthrow of a weak monarch?'

'Essex told me nothing of his intentions, my lord.'

'Is that so?' said Cecil. 'We could ask him if only his head was still attached to his shoulders. Now is there anything you need to tell me?'

Cecil could make civility terrifying and Ann could see why Will hesitated. She knew how these days it could just take the wrong phrase, the wrong word, and you were dangling on a rope by morning.

'I have asked many men that question,' said Cecil, 'and their failure to answer truthfully has led to a lot of heartache.'

So here Will was, damned by silence and damned by speaking. She knew she couldn't help, that a woman, a woman who ran a pub, must be silent.

'We have stumbled into trouble, my lord,' said Will, 'but we don't know its cause. Three men tried to kill us this evening, and Will Kemp, the comedian, was murdered two days ago.'

'Kemp,' Cecil said sharply.

Ann imagined that Cecil's face would never give anything away but perhaps he was less good at covering up anger, because that's what she saw.

'My lord, perhaps you have some idea who killed him,' she said.

She hadn't done a very good job of staying silent. Cecil turned slowly towards her and stared. His lips curled into what she thought was a smile, as if he was amused that she had spoken.

'Oh, it's you inside that uniform, is it? Have you noticed

how your visits to London always coincide with a lot of trouble?'

He knew who she was. That wasn't good.

'Yes, my lord,' she answered.

She heard herself keep on speaking. She seemed to be pressing the Lord Chancellor of England for an answer.

'I'm sorry to ask again, but I think perhaps you were angry that Kemp was dead, so—'

Will hissed a whispered, 'Ann,' and tugged at her sleeve as if that would pull her back from the brink, but she was going to finish the question whether he liked it or not.

'So I wondered if you knew that someone wanted to kill him.'

Cecil was no longer amused.

'You asked once which was presumptuous so I didn't answer. I think you understood that, yet you asked again. Do you wish to see what happens if you ask a third time?'

Strangely she did, though she knew she mustn't.

'She doesn't,' said Will quickly, still grasping her sleeve.

Cecil was still staring at her.

'No, my lord,' she said.

Yet he'd said he hadn't answered because she was presumptuous. Did that mean he knew the answer?

He exhaled wearily.

'Your presence here in the Tower is unconnected to your adventures. I instructed the militia to bring you here and I imagined they would do so with a firm request. Unfortunately it was Proute in charge and he does like to play at being a soldier. It seems we must indulge the idiot sons of the rich and influential. In Italy, they call it *nepotismo* – all those popes, succeeded by their sons.'

Pamphlets were flying around about the conclave to choose the second new pope of the year, which had ended up in a massive fist fight between cardinals.

'I'm magic,' said Glendower unexpectedly and he pointed at Will. 'You're words.'

Cecil sighed. 'Apparently he can make himself invisible. If only he would do so.'

Ann found herself smiling. Cecil turned to her.

'People are usually too scared to enjoy my jokes,' he said, 'but then, of course, you're a Marlowe.' He turned back to Will. 'But, yes, in this instance, our wizard is right. I've decided to harness your power. Together, you will create a masque.'

'Of course, my lord,' said Will. 'When do you need it?'

'Tomorrow night.'

WILL

Cecil was inflexible about the timing and guarded about the details. He would only say that it was for a highly important personage who loved spectacle.

'I'll need to talk to the set builders and choose the actors tonight, my lord,' said Will.

'No,' said Cecil. 'It will be a secret between us four and the actors.'

Will wondered how he would put on a spectacle without stagehands.

'The cast will be three witches,' Cecil continued.

'I will choose the three best and most discreet boy actors,' said Will.

'No,' said Cecil, 'the Personage would quickly see that they were boys and not women.'

Will was beginning to understand.

'So,' he said, 'this is an entertainment where the audience think it's real.'

'Isn't that what you aim at?' said Cecil.

'Temporarily.'

As plays ended, Will liked to watch the faces in the pit to see that moment when they remembered where they were and left the fiction he'd created for the world in which they lived – *God's inferior world*, Marlowe had called it.

Cecil seemed irritated at his answer. Despite his prodigious intelligence he never seemed to understand theatre.

'Well, this time do it permanently unless you want to shake hands with Mr Derrick.'

He could see Ann didn't understand. Thomas Derrick had been one of twenty-three men condemned to death for rape after Essex's raid on Cádiz. He'd been offered a pardon if he executed the other twenty-two. He'd swiftly hung them and from that found his vocation, rising to become the public executioner. He'd ended up executing his saviour, Essex, for treason. Unfortunately, he was a better ropesman than a headsman and had made a terrible hash of it – less decapitation and more whittling.

'Bella will be your chief witch,' said Cecil. 'Her life is a performance so I think she will serve you well.'

That was good. Will had seen her read once at rehearsals when the boys were all ill and it made him wish he could cast her and not them.

'You'll need two more. I want as few people as possible to know about this, so you might as well use Christopher Marlowe's sister here.'

'Ann, my Lord,' said Ann.

'I know your name, Ann,' he said. 'I know you run the Flying Horse with your useless husband John and that Shakespeare, here, is in love with you.'

Will noted that Cecil, who knew everything, didn't say that she was in love with him.

'My lord, I'm not an actress,' Ann said.

'Oh, really. You seem to have done some excellent acting over the years.'

Will didn't understand what he was talking about, but was that alarm he saw in Ann's face?

Cecil rose, grimaced and clenched his teeth as he stretched his back.

'The chief witch will magically disappear at the end of the masque and you will work with Glendower on this.'

'She will vanish into the void,' said Glendower. 'Even as we speak, there are workmen constructing a trap of my design out on the Isle of Dogs.'

'The Isle of Dogs?' said Will.

'Did I not mention that?' said Cecil. 'That is where it will be performed. One of my men will give you details of what the witches must predict. And keep it short or the king will fall asleep.

'The king?' said Will.

'Don't pretend you didn't guess.'

He hadn't.

LIZZIE

'How did you get that eye?' she asked Evan. She wasn't going to tell him how Kemp's landlady had told them that Kemp's last visitor was a man with a black eye. Well, not yet.

'One of the soldiers,' he said, 'when they attacked our show. He made a grab for me with his iron gauntlet, but me, I was too slippery for him. He did fetch me a blow on the eye though.'

'Have you ever been to Finsbury?' she asked.

He did that thing where he went still and balled his fists and his long, lopsided face looked as if it had got stuck. He used to have a trick where he would hold a piece of cloth over half his face, then change it to the other half, and he would look like two different boys. He'd stopped that when he'd become anxious about how he appeared to her.

'I don't like questions,' he said finally, and he sat back and closed his eyes as if he was going to sleep. So it was going to be like this.

'These are kind questions,' she said. 'Questions with smiles on their faces.'

He swallowed with a gulp and his knobbly Adam's apple bobbed up and down, but he kept his eyes closed and said nothing. The single candle Evan had placed on the bench beside her was getting low.

'Have you another candle?' she asked.

He shook his head. He knew how she couldn't sleep in

darkness and how it was getting money for candles which had first set her stealing.

Once, when the hawk seller wasn't looking at her, when he was staring at the sky waiting for a peregrine falcon to return to his glove, she had told him how her mother and brother had been murdered while they slept.

'So, that's why you need to sleep with a candle beside your bed,' he said.

She had never put the two things together.

The hawk had tucked in its wings and turned itself into an arrowhead that plummeted down towards them. He told her that when they dived, they sped faster than a bullet, but she didn't see how he could know. The bird pulled up and landed on his gloved hand with a lazy flop. He fed it a morsel of duck. That's when he'd asked her to marry him. She'd said no. She didn't want to be just another wild thing that he could tame with titbits.

The candle was nearly out, its light flickering this way and that. She would have to be quick because when it was dark, she wouldn't think straight.

'I need to know what happened,' she said gently. 'If you won't tell me, I'll ask the demons to show me.'

His eyes jolted open and he looked alarmed. Had he somehow been involved in Kemp's murder? It was hard to tell. Evan was odd that way. He acted as if he was guilty when he'd done nothing, yet when he wanted to he could tell lies like the best of them.

'You don't know how to speak to them,' he said.

The candle flickered and almost died and she had to keep the panic out of her voice.

'Glendower taught me.'

She looked upwards and blinked her eyes rapidly as if she was in a trance.

'Is that so?' she said. 'Tell me more.' She'd never pretended to talk to imaginary demons before and this wasn't her best performance. 'Really?' she said. 'I see.' She looked back down and Evan was staring stiffly at her, his wide eyes all she could really see in the last of the candlelight, so perhaps it had worked. 'They can see you walking into a small village near London,' she said. 'You're standing outside a house with a rotten wooden step beneath the door. You're knocking on the door.'

He was shocked that she knew and blurted out, 'Death was there.'

How did he know that?

'Tell me about Death,' she said.

He hesitated. She touched his hand.

'I'm your friend, Evan.'

'I wanted to look after you,' he said.

'You always do.' She smiled to encourage him. A big smile so he could make it out in the darkness.

'I knew Mr Kemp was your old guardian and that you wanted to go and see him, so I got his address off a carpenter at the Globe and I went to his house.'

'His landlady let you in, didn't she?'

Evan gave one tiny nod, as if he was fearful that someone was watching.

'And you climbed the stairs and knocked on his door.'

He sat very still and said nothing. She hoped he wouldn't clam up now.

'Tell me,' she said.

'Kemp didn't answer the door,' he said.

She waited.

'His spirit had left.'

It was all very well, all these spirits, but she wondered if Evan knew Kemp was dead by more earthly means.

The candle went out, and her panic rose, but then a tiny flame flickered back into life.

'Why did you think that?' she asked.

'Because Death was there,' he said.

'Tell me.'

The candle went out, this time for good, and the darkness

closed in on her like a liquid thing. Her chest didn't want to breathe, but she gritted her teeth, pushed herself back into the seat and grasped hard on to the handles on either side.

'Tell me what you saw,' she said.

He hesitated.

'Tell me now.' She had to keep the panic out of her voice.

'When I got there, there was a carriage waiting opposite, a fine carriage pulled by four black horses with black plumes. I heard the coach leave as I climbed the stairs.'

She pulled back the curtain of the sedan chair, but it was just as dark outside.

'Would Kemp's landlady have seen the coach?'

There was silence and she couldn't see Evan any more. She hoped he was thinking about her question.

'She must have,' he said finally, 'she was at the door.'

So she'd lied to them and only told them about Evan but not the other mysterious visitors.

'Did you see who was in the coach?' she asked.

'I saw the coachman jump up to his seat. He was tall and his cloak was black and his face was pale, pale white. Death is invisible but I saw Death's coachman.'

She wanted to ask him more but the darkness suffocated her into silence. She clenched her fists, closed her eyes and breathed slowly like she did in the trick where she squeezed herself into half of the box, while Glendower sawed her in two.

When she was a little girl Kemp had realised she was terrified of darkness. He had told her about Selene, Goddess of the Moon – how she wore a crescent crown and her flock of pearly-white owls flew around her head as winged horses pulled her chariot through the heavens, a silver streak across the night sky. And he told her that when clouds hid the moon, when the darkness was at its thickest and blackest, that Selene was still there above them and that he'd had a word with her, and because she 'fancied him something rotten' he'd got her to promise she would always keep an eye on Lizzie and protect her. He'd even got a carpenter at the theatre to carve her a little wooden figure of Selene with a crescent crown and an owl on her shoulder that Lizzie had kept by her bed.

She had lost it when the witch-hating mob had burnt down their wagon. That had been in darkness so Selene hadn't been doing her job that night. Still, as she sat hemmed in by the blackness, she thought of Kemp and his kindness and the Goddess of the Moon who was 'desperate to get into his pantaloons', and as she thought, the moon came out again and the faint wash of light flooded her with relief.

Now she could think properly again, she wondered if Evan had told the truth. Someone had made it look as if the door of Kemp's room was bolted from the inside. Not many people knew that trick, but he did. She could see Evan now and he looked asleep. She wondered for a moment if he was just pretending but he was snoring. He could fall asleep in seconds, especially after he'd been agitated. He fell asleep bolt upright in the wagon, between cues in the show, and once while crossing a busy street in Aylesbury.

She opened the door handle as silently as she could and stepped outside. He kept on snoring. She'd nowhere to go but she could face the night better if she kept moving.

She slipped back through the gap in the fence and headed down a narrow lane with a stripe of light against one wall where the moon reached in. She smelt the sharp stench of a farmyard, and through a window she saw the heads of a half-dozen cows looking out at her. She'd heard how, in London, they kept milk-cows in houses. She stared back for a moment, their slow chewing, the creak of the boards beneath them, that country smell calming her for a moment.

She thought of what Evan had told her about Death and his coachman but remembered instead the white-faced playwright, backstage at the Globe, who had once pinned her against a wall with his gin breath and told her how her life was meaningless: the playwright who hated Kemp for wrecking his plays; the playwright whose father was a coachmaker.

WILL

The room they were in was as comfortable as a room in the Tower could be. Fires crackled in hearths at either end, big baskets of seasoned oak and cedar beside them. There was food and drink, a desk, chairs, quills, ink and paper – paper that was still blank.

'Shouldn't you be writing our lines?' Ann asked him.

He told her he would in a moment.

'You should write as if your life depends on it,' Cecil had said as he left. Will thought this had sounded less like an expression and more like a fact, yet for months Will had written nothing.

That was not strictly true. He had written the titles of plays he was going to write at the top of valuable sheets of paper. He had crossed them out and written new ones, sometimes added subtitles, at least once a dedication, and he often wrote *Act One. Scene One* and *A forest in Bohemia* or some such thing. Beyond that – nothing. Now he hoped terror would work where alcohol and desperation had failed.

Cecil had been adamant that the 'Personage' must have three witches not two, as his study of the supernatural had revealed that witches only ever gathered in odd numbers. He and Ann had chosen Lizzie as their third witch. She loved theatre, they could trust her and she was used to working with Glendower. One of Cecil's messenger boys had been sent to the secret house with a message.

Glendower had left with a couple of the guards to check how the preparation work was going, though it must have been nearly eleven o'clock. He told them that he'd been taught by owls to see in the dark. Will sat at the desk and wished some owls would teach him how to start writing again. He picked up the quill and dipped it in the ink.

'I'll make a list of what we need,' he said.

'Just write the masque,' said Ann.

'We'll need a long box built,' he said, and explained how they used a long, narrow wooden box with a cannon ball inside, to rock up and down like a see-saw so the rolling cannon ball made the noise of thunder.

'Just write the words,' she said.

He rose, stretched and looked out the window. 'I'm thinking about that now.'

The ice on the windowpanes distorted the world outside and the flaming torches in the courtyard flickered and overlapped. He could just make out the huddled shapes of animals slowly dying in the English sleet. The king ordered that they should be wrapped in warm robes and given the finest care but stubbornly they refused to live and were fed to the survivors. Ann was breathing out in loud huffs to signal her impatience.

ANN

She couldn't understand why he kept putting off writing the script. In the past, he couldn't see a piece of paper without covering it with ink. He'd break off in the middle of conversations to scribble down some thought, and if he had no pen he'd tell her lines and ask her to help him by remembering half.

Resolve it into a dew. Some have greatness thrust upon them. They were still in her head. *Let slip the dogs of war. Like a pig entering heaven* – though maybe he hadn't used that one in the end. He was very drunk when he'd come up with that.

A scuffling noise from the end of the room made her look around and two crows came tumbling down the chimney in a big puff of soot, fighting each other. They fell into the flamesu, a ball of feathers, screeching and flapping wildly. One of them, then the other, escaped and flew into the room, one still on fire, the other smoking. The one on fire slammed panicking into a window and fell to the floor.

Will picked up a doublet from the pile of clothes and dropped it over the bird while it lay stunned. It started to struggle but he wrapped it tightly to put out the flames. A thin plume of smoke rose from the struggling bundle in his arms. There was an unpleasant smell that reminded her of something – it was the smell of burning after she had set the murderer on fire.

'What shall I do with it?' Will asked.

The bird had stopped struggling and he held it gently. Will

might have become obsessed with rank and privilege, but you had to give it to him, he was kind to crows.

'Shall I put it out the window or leave it inside to keep warm?'

'I think it got warm enough,' she said.

She pulled down on a stiff catch on the window, which came free with a jerk, and the cut on her hand started to bleed through the bandage. She opened the window and an icy gust swirled into the room. There were bars, probably to prevent anyone jumping while they were being interrogated, but Will opened the blanket so the bird could go through one of the gaps. It hopped onto the ledge and flew away into the night. Well, at least something had escaped from the Tower.

Ann gestured at the desk with the quills, ink and paper.

'You need to start writing.'

'You sound like Burbage,' he said.

She went to say it again but she saw his fear. His face was lit by the flickering fire and those dark eyes stirred as if there was ink swirling in his skull. She knew she could sound harsh so she tried to be gentle.

'What is it?'

He hesitated.

'You need to tell me,' she said.

He told her – how the words wouldn't come, how they seemed locked inside him, how he hadn't written for months.

'You said how you wanted to write about this mad obsession with witches,' she said, 'here's your chance. It doesn't even have to be good.'

'There's just nothing there,' he said.

She'd tried gentle and it hadn't worked.

'You writers and your "creativity",' she said. 'Do you think carpenters say, "Ooh, I can't put up those shelves today, I'm just not inspired. Maybe I'll have the spark on Monday"?'

He went to object but she didn't let him.

'It's not magic, it's just words. Write one down, then another and then just keep going. And if you need inspiration, imagine being stabbed to death and chucked in a gutter, because that's what'll happen to you if you don't.'

He shook his head and gave her a sad-eyed, superior look that took her back years. God, he could be irritating.

'I just need a moment to think,' he said. 'Let me be.'

She wasn't going to.

'We don't have a moment. If you won't write it, I will. I heard Cecil's man tell you exactly what needs to be said.'

She sat at the desk, picked up the quill and dipped it into ink.

'I know what you're doing,' he said.

'I know you know what I'm doing but I'm doing it anyway.'

She wrote *Witch One* on the paper.

'Wait, just give me a second,' he said, reaching for the quill.

She held it away from him.

'No,' she said, 'if it's going to be done it's best it's done quickly.'

'Alright, alright,' he said, 'I'll write it.'

She was amazed it had worked. Perhaps Burbage would pay her to browbeat other writers so he got his plays finished on time.

The remaining crow had perched on the ledge at the top of the carved wooden panelling that ran along the wall. It stood next to a wooden cherub and looked down with glossy black eyes as Will picked up the quill and started to write.

The door opened again and one of Cecil's lackeys came in – they all seemed the same, heavily bearded blocks of men criss-crossed by scars.

'The woman you sent the message to, Lizzie, she wasn't at the house,' he said, and left before they could ask him anything.

Will looked at Ann. Should they be fearful for Lizzie? There was nothing they could do for the moment.

'We'll need another witch,' said Will.

Ann had a thought. 'I know who it should be.'

WILL

Will was amazed when Ann suggested that the third performer should be Frances Strange.

'Would she even agree?' he asked.

'To act?' Ann laughed. 'She'd pluck out her granny's eyes to act.'

'I thought you despised her,' said Will.

Ann shrugged at this.

'She might save our lives. After we've done this, we'll know too much about how Cecil influenced the "Personage". He might kill us.'

Will gestured for Ann to speak more quietly. He knew there were rooms in the Tower where blocks in the walls had been carved away until only a sliver of stone remained so someone could listen from the room next door.

Ann was right though. Cecil wasn't a monster but he was extremely pragmatic. Two days in London and Ann seemed to have the political acumen of a courtier.

'Won't the Personage recognise Frances from court though?' asked Will. He'd meant to call her 'Frances Strange', as the familiarity of 'Frances' seemed to irritate Ann, but she let it pass.

'We'll use make-up and cover her face in warts and sores,' she said.

'Will that be enough?'

'We'll dress her in stinking rags and put filth in her hair. String rotting rats and owls around her neck.'

Will was beginning to get the idea.

'We'll throw toad blood in her face and stick lizard tails up her nose.' Ann was grinning. 'It's important so I'll do it myself.'

Will hadn't seen Ann this enthusiastic for some time. He went to ask her more questions but she picked up the quill he had laid down on the desk and put it back in his hand.

'Keep writing.'

Ann called for a messenger and sent a sealed scroll to Frances Strange with the invitation.

SUNDAY

EDGAR

Edgar woke up early with the cold. The fire in his room had long gone out and he went downstairs and followed the smell of smoke through the tavern to a room where one of the pot boys had started a good blaze.

He should never have told Lizzie he was staying at the Cock Inn. The others must never find that out. He wondered, though, if she would come. She'd come to St Paul's tower and kissed him, but he had no idea what it meant. She was so unlike most of the women he knew, the painted and primped daughters of the nobility, crammed into their silk and satin, who knew a surprising amount about how to avoid getting pregnant. They watched him across the banqueting halls as if he was a tasty canapé, a gentleman yet not a gentleman, intriguing but easily discarded, an escapade they could turn into one of their dreadful poems.

John Johnson ducked beneath the doorway and headed for the fire carrying a bowl of pottage in one hand, a pint of ale in the other and a slab of cheese between his teeth. He put it all down and crouched next to Edgar in that soldier's squat, getting as much heat from the fire as he could. The burns on his face were mostly scabbed over.

'Did the girl turn up?' he asked.

At the mention of Lizzie he got that liquid feeling in his stomach just like when the pikes of the advancing enemy first appeared over a hill. How should he answer? The man he'd seen follow her might have been one of theirs, which would mean they knew she had turned up.

‘She came,’ he said, ‘but there were a couple of Swedes up the tower so I couldn’t do anything.’

Cecil had taught him, always tell as much of the truth as you can. John stared at him, the flames from the fire flickering in those pale eyes, but before he could say anything, Nobbles and a couple of the other gentlemen came in and greeted them.

Nobbles shivered, and wrapped his hooded cape around him.

‘I think Dante was right. The heart of hell is freezing, not burning.’

‘No literary allusion before breakfast,’ said Edgar. ‘You know the rules.’

He heard the grunt of contempt from John at this fancy talk but Nobbles laughed, pulled a poker out of the fire and stuck it in his mug of porter to warm it up. It sizzled and steamed.

‘Have you noticed,’ he said, ‘that whatever drink you order here, it tastes slightly of urine.’

Edgar turned to John.

‘Get us a bottle of sack would you?’

John gave him a look which would freeze the sea. Edgar beamed back at him. Edgar had recruited him in the Spanish Netherlands. Unlike most of that pack of ruffians who brawled and whored their way from siege to siege, Johnson was a reliable subordinate – he was an expert on mining beneath enemy walls, he could sing like an angel and he loved killing. Around the campfires he and Dogface boasted of their murders as teenage boys might talk of girls.

Now, though, since the new turn of events, he was the one in charge. The fun of it was the others didn’t know that, and it was important that they believed John was just a soldier brought in for his brute strength, so he had to go along with it and do as Edgar asked.

‘Thanks, John,’ said Nobbles. ‘And while you’re out, get a couple of bottles of Madeira, the ones that come from Madeira, not that vile stuff they make in a cellar in Limehouse.’

He tossed John a couple of shillings.

‘Yes, sir,’ he said, still staring at Edgar, the scar tissue where he’d been burnt flaring red around his cheek and one eye.

Edgar’s father had been poisoned twelve years ago. He knew it should make him think life was dangerous, but it made him think life was short – if things went wrong, very short – so have a good time while you can. He knew it was unwise to rile John, but John wasn’t the kind of man who spared you just because you were nice to him. Also making him angry was enormous fun. John was almost out the door.

‘John, mate,’ he shouted, ‘while you’re at it, get us a mutton pie.’

ANN

Will put down the quill.

She went to ask him if he had finished.

'Have you—'

'Yes,' he said.

Behind him a wash of grudging light came through the window. Will's dawns usually arrived in *russet mantle clad* or *smiled on frowning night*. This one turned up in grey underwear and was just as grumpy as night had been.

It was time to get up but they needed sleep and without a word they lay down side by side on the heap of unused soldiers' uniforms that had been thrown through the door. She closed her eyes.

There was the sound of loud arguing in the corridor outside, the door was flung open and Frances Strange burst into the room. She must have come as soon as the message reached her. One of Cecil's men in the corridor was still talking to her.

'Too late, I'm here now,' she said, and slammed the door.

She turned to them.

'Little Lord Cecil doesn't want me to perform. Well, he can scuttle off back to his nest, because I'm going to.'

She took them in as they sat up from where they'd been lying, and gestured languidly at Ann.

'So are you my deputy witch?'

'No,' said Ann. 'You and I are Bella's deputy witches.'

Frances glared for a moment, then waved a hand carelessly.

'As long as you don't mind them all looking at me.'

Ann didn't understand why so many people wanted to go

onstage and pretend to be someone who didn't exist. As if real life wasn't trouble enough.

Frances undid her cape and let it fall to the floor, probably used to someone rushing to pick it up for her. She wore a green gown that glittered with the small purple gemstones sewn into the fabric. The fat pearls were still strung around her neck and she wore a purple and yellow hat with jewelled glass dragonflies floating above it on wires. They bounced when she tossed her head – which was often.

'So the Personage we're performing this masque for, is it the king?' she asked.

Neither of them answered. She shrugged and the dragonflies bounced.

'So, yes,' she said, peeling off her mauve gloves. 'Come along you two sleepyheads, up, up, up! We need to rehearse.' She walked over to Will and jabbed him with a long, sharp finger. 'I heard you'd been shot.'

'Where did you hear that?' asked Ann.

She ignored Ann, hoisted up Will's army jacket and lifted the bandage to take a look at the wound.

'What a small, neat hole. A wren could nest in that.'

She walked over to the desk and peered at the script he'd written.

'Well, well, well,' she said. 'So Cecil is inventing another Catholic Plot. He likes at least one a month.'

The Stranges had been a leading Catholic family but Will had told Ann that Frances Strange now called herself a loyal Protestant. It was hard to imagine Frances kneeling before anyone – she'd certainly consider Jesus the carpenter her social inferior and probably God too.

'He made the world in seven days,' she'd say. 'Oh dear, comes from trade.'

Ann turned to her with a smile. 'So now you've discovered the purpose of the masque is to blacken the name of Catholics, would you rather not perform?'

Frances's guffaw filled the stone room.

The door opened again and a huge beast of a dog leapt in, saw Ann, galloped towards her and put its paws on her shoulders so she nearly tottered backwards. Bella followed it in. It was the first time Ann had seen her for twelve years.

Ann went to speak but the dog was licking her face, panting with its warm, meaty breath.

'Stop. No…' said Bella.

The dog kept going.

'Tamburlaine. No!'

Tamburlaine? The dog was called Tamburlaine. Outrage rose in a hot wave.

'You named it after my brother's play?' she said in disbelief, trying to push the dog away. 'After you helped kill him.'

'Ann,' said Will, and reached out a hand to restrain her.

She wasn't sure if he was worried about her attacking Bella or of Frances Strange overhearing.

'You helped kill Kit Marlowe!' said Frances Strange, her eyes delighted, those glass dragonflies bouncing.

'I had no idea they were going to kill him,' said Bella.

She pulled a small morsel of meat from a bag and held it out. The dog bounded over and sat expectantly in front of her, its head as high as her ribs, tongue lolling, eyes begging.

'I have to do what I am ordered to stay alive. If I was ordered to help kill either of you, then, very reluctantly, I would do it. I would do the same to almost anyone, but, Ann, your brother was an exception. I would never have hurt him. I would have put myself in danger rather than do that.'

She gave the dog the morsel.

There was a rustle of feathers above them. Bella looked up and the crow cocked its head and looked down. They somehow seemed alike with their black clever eyes, the crow with its glossy plumage, Bella with her inky cloak and waves of black hair piled high. Now there were hollows under her eyes and her face was drawn tight with worry, yet if it hadn't been for Will's infatuation with Frances Strange, she might have been the dark lady Will glorified in his sonnets.

‘So,’ asked Frances, ‘who did kill Kit Marlowe?’
Ann and Will answered at the same time.
‘No one knows.’

WILL

The costumes Will had asked for arrived not long after Bella. The three witches wore black hooded cloaks with red silk linings which would shimmer when the explosions flashed. They had been made in under three hours.

'I should get Cecil to stage-manage my next play,' he said.

'If you ever write one,' said Ann.

Frances lit a pipe. Everyone seemed to smoke now to protect themselves from the plague. Will had doubts that it worked. He'd heard that doctors had been paid to put around that story by men like 'Rich' Spencer who controlled the monopoly in tobacco. Still most people seemed to believe it. Taverns were choked with smoke, actors puffed their pipes backstage and schoolboys caught not smoking were flogged. Frances offered the pipe to Will as she changed into her costume. He shook his head, but stared at the pipe so he wasn't looking at her in her shift. Even that was threaded with gold.

Frances went to the door and demanded they send her servant to get her apricots for breakfast. Incredibly some arrived five minutes later, God knows from where.

'Too ripe,' she grumbled as she bit into one and the juice dripped down her chin.

'Yes,' said Ann, 'there's nothing in the world I hate more in November than an overripe apricot.' He had to look away to stop himself from laughing.

They rehearsed the first words Will had written in nearly a year. Frances had watched Burbage too often and was too big and too loud. Ann was too quiet and Bella, who he knew could act, just read the words as if she was reading a letter. If it was like this, the 'Personage' would never believe they were truly witches.

Ann learnt quickly, Frances grudgingly, but Bella didn't change. He went to speak to her again, but she stopped him.

'Next time, I'll do it.'

Next time she did and she was terrifying. Something had changed in her – that barrier behind which she hid herself now seemed only a thin skin beneath which she raged and seethed.

He was impatient to see the place where they'd perform, but they didn't get to leave until mid-afternoon. Frances Strange travelled in her own coach and they were taken to a carriage which Sir 'Rich' Spencer had lent to Cecil. Spencer lent the powerful coaches, houses, ships, cooks, women, boys, and once, it was rumoured, a corpse – anything which would gain him influence.

Will, Ann and Bella sat back in the carriage with its sprung maroon leather seats, with Bella's great dog crammed at their feet. The doors of walnut veneer hid small compartments that opened when you pressed the panel to reveal small carafes of wine, silver boxes of tobacco and even a tiny bottle of laudanum. Bella took out the stopper, licked it, considered and licked it again.

'It's mixed with saffron and cinnamon and something else,' she said. She took a tiny sip and put the bottle under her cape. She saw his worried look. 'For after the performance,' she said.

They got caught in a jam of coaches and wagons by Wapping Wall. A cat skulked by, half its tail missing and patches of pink skin showing through the fur. It was near here a drunken mob had burnt an effigy of the pope that they had filled with stray cats. He could still picture the poor creatures burst screeching out of the flames. What did they have against cats? For that matter, what did they have against Catholics? But here he was on his way to feed the frenzy.

He could see what Cecil was doing. The king was bored

by policy – he needed something bright and shiny to get his attention and Cecil was providing it. If three witches told him about Catholic conspiracies then he'd listen. Will had thought about refusing, just not that hard. He'd be killed, replaced, and someone else would do it. There were so many things you could die for and this didn't seem the one.

The road stopped at West Ferry on the edge of the Isle of Dogs. It was a lawless wilderness where constables feared to go, home to every kind of rogue – rufflers, whip-jacks, priggers, prancers, dells, doxies, clapperdudgeons and plain old murderers.

The coachman handed them down. He was as pale, thin and tall as his master Spencer was red-faced, short and fat. As Will's feet touched the ground he expected the crunch of ice underfoot, but his feet sank into mud. It was less cold today and a gusty breeze rustled through a stand of poplars that marked the end of the track. Beneath the trees a regiment of the King's Guard were spread out, playing dice, or sleeping with their heads resting on their pot helmets. He heard the booming voice of Sergeant-Major Colonel Proute shouting insults at them. He was still playing soldiers. Will hoped he'd get bored soon and go off and be an admiral or something.

Frances Strange kicked at the ankles of a soldier blocking her way.

'All this lot turned up when he stayed with Dickie,' she said.

Presumably 'he' was King James and 'Dickie' the duke of somewhere or other.

'He's convinced everyone in England wants to assassinate him,' she said.

'Surely only those who've met him,' said Bella.

They walked down a narrow track next to a ditch, one of Cecil's men riding behind them. He felt something sticking to his face, brushed away some gluey threads and saw he'd broken through a web a spider had strung across the path. Now there were only low shrubs and stunted trees, dying brambles and banks of tall brown grass. Strands of sheep wool were tangled in the thorns though there was no sign of any sheep. Dark clouds were rising over Black Heath and tumbling towards them as if the sky was boiling over. A loud Welsh voice stopped them.

'Over here,' shouted Glendower. 'Can you see me?'

He stood in his spangled cape, arms outspread on top of a hillock.

'I can,' said Will.

'I don't think so,' he said and plummeted out of sight.

Glendower had done a good job in only one day. He told him that Cecil had brought in Kent miners who had worked in Flanders, mining beneath the Spanish fortifications. The trapdoor was well disguised with ivy, moss and woody nightshade. It was sprung by a cord that pulled out two long bolts, and double-hinged so you wouldn't hit the sides as you fell. The pit below was lined with wood, had a horsehair mattress on the floor and an escape hatch that led out the back of the small hill, so Bella could get out without being seen. Frances and Ann would just have to run.

The trick needed crashes, flashes and flames to misdirect the eyes and disguise the fall. Cecil's men had prepared the charcoal soaked in alcohol for the smoke, the pots of sulphur for the stink of brimstone, the squibs for the lightning and the pouches of gunpowder, all linked by a fast fuse strung from the stunted elder trees. The explosive was mixed with copper salts and powdered Bologna stones to make green and blue flames, the effect which had made audiences gasp in *Julius Caesar* when Casca had spoken of the 'tempest dropping fire'.

Will really needed to test them, but they had arrived too late to do that and have time to reset the charges. He had begged Cecil to let him use experienced stagehands from the Globe to set them off but Cecil wanted no other outsiders to know what happened, so Will had to drill Cecil's messenger boys as best he could.

Bella walked by, head bowed, fists clenched, murmuring

in Spanish or maybe Portuguese. He feared she'd been sipping from the bottle of laudanum. He had never gone into a first night this unprepared. No one in London knew it was happening so if it was a disaster he wouldn't lose his reputation – just his head.

A slow rumble turned his head to the south where forks of lightning flickered in the blackening clouds. Glendower sniffed the air.

'There's a storm coming,' he said, as if it was a prophecy.

'We'd never have guessed,' muttered Ann.

Will didn't see Lord Cecil arrive but he was suddenly beside him.

'I have told the Personage that the escaped witch was spotted out here and that she asked to speak to him.'

Will nodded, then worried that a mere nod was insufficient for Lord Cecil, but by then His Lordship had moved on.

'He will advance with me to that small clearing.' Cecil pointed to a patch of low scrub close enough to the hidden stage to hear the words, but not so close he would see through the trick.

Tamburlaine yelped and Will looked over at him. One of the boys had hold of his chain but the dog was terrified of thunder and shrank into a crouch and tucked his tail between his legs. There was a louder rumble and he ran in panic and dragged the boy into a ditch.

'Poor beast,' murmured Cecil as Bella tried to calm him. 'But we require him. The Personage expects the witches to be accompanied by their familiars.'

Three men on horseback rode up with sacks and boxes tied to their saddles. In them were two cats, a lamb, a goat, a monkey and a very angry fox. Cecil told Ann and Frances to pick a familiar. Ann chose the little black goat with a white stripe down its nose that cut through its yellow eyes. Will suggested a sleepy tabby cat for Frances but she insisted on the monkey, which one of Cecil's men said he'd bought from a sailor. It clung to her fearfully and fingered her pearl necklace which she had refused to take off.

Ann covered her in buckets of filth to disguise her, but to Ann's great disappointment, Frances thought it enormous fun. Ann only cheered up when the monkey shat on her. Will looked at them as they took their places. Witches, magicians, goats and monkeys – so this was how policy would be decided in modern England.

The sky was yellow and black to the west and just black to the south. Dusk was early and the Personage was late. The performance was meant for half-light and he would struggle to see in full darkness.

Cecil had mounted a huge white mare, his stirrups high, and was clinging to its back like one of those engravings of a demon riding a horse.

'At moments like this,' he said, with that chilling civility, 'I think very carefully if there is anything I have forgotten.'

'I don't believe we have, my lord,' said Will. 'But we need to start before the rain soaks the gunpowder.'

'Do not make excuses in preparation for failure.'

Will had always marvelled at Cecil's calm amidst chaos but now his lips were drawn back over clenched teeth and the hand holding his reins balled into a white-knuckled fist. Will knew nothing of the machinations at court but he wondered for a moment if Lord Cecil's life also hung on the success of this performance.

Thunder rumbled louder and a gust of black rooks rose up and wheeled around in a sky criss-crossed with forked lightning. The wind rose, tugging at their clothing, and ripping the few remaining leaves from the trees. A trumpet wailed half lost in the howling of the gale, and when Will listened hard he could hear the clatter and rattle of cavalry. The Personage was surely coming now.

Out of the murk, galloped a horseman with a scarlet and gold cape flying wildly around him. He pulled his horse up so sharply it nearly fell. He held up three fingers to tell Cecil the

Personage was three minutes away, and sped off in a spray of foul-smelling mud. Cecil gave Will a look, as if he was fitting him for the right-sized noose, and rode off.

Will recognised that feeling of hope mixed with terror he felt on the first night of a new play, but he'd never felt this much terror. Here they were, under-rehearsed, undermanned, drunken, drug-addled and in a raging storm. What were their chances? He looked across at the three witches. Ann was helping Bella chain a terrified Tamburlaine to a small tree beside them, while Frances glared at the storm as if it were trying to upstage her. He shouted encouragement but his words were lost in the gale.

Now the rain came, the fat first drops slapping through the twigs and bursting on his face. He ducked into a hide screened with branches that smelt of sweat and alcohol. Glendower was there holding the rope that would release the trapdoor. He yelled wildly in Welsh and, grinning crazily, handed Will the flint and steel pan to light the fuses for the explosions. Flashes of lightning were fast followed by huge claps of thunder.

Staring through the flailing branches, Will saw the flare of torches coming over a small rise. Three horsemen appeared, the smaller figure in the middle presumably the Personage. They were here.

BELLA

Perhaps she shouldn't have had another sip from the little bottle she had found on the coach. She had learnt Will's lines but they had flown away and come back all in a tangle. The laudanum was running its warm fingers through her blood but there was some other narcotic in the mix that she couldn't place – something that made her heart race and her thoughts run wild. Were opiates not enough for the aristocracy any more?

A noise carved through her head. It was Tamburlaine yelping. The poor thing was terrified of the thunder and had pulled his chain taut straining to get close to her. She couldn't comfort him now. Right now she had to – what did she have to do? Her lines, remember her lines.

Will had written in verse. She could see why. In those vile pamphlets the witches always spoke in rhyme, though wretched doggerel nothing like Will's fine poetry – the fine poetry that had fled from her brain.

The message she could remember. It was the same message Cecil had told her before – a simple message, though God knows if it would be simple enough for the king.

Still, what did she care? She saw no need to further persecute England's much persecuted Catholics. Religion was just another excuse for men to slaughter each other.

No, she must get back to – what must she get back to? A lightning strike seemed to slice straight through her, to sear her heart and leave her blood boiling. Something rankled under her skin – something rotten and wrong. It throbbed and pulsed inside her as if she was truly possessed. Now the thunder and lightning were crashing and flashing inside her skull and she feared it would shatter. No, no, no, she must control herself. She must just get through the next hour. Perhaps another sip from the little bottle was the answer.

ANN

Cecil joined the three of them and she recognised the massive shape of Sergeant-Major Colonel Proute alongside the Personage. Yellow and blue lightning flickered behind them.

Cecil pointed towards the witches, and Will must have lit the first fuse as flames ripped around them and she smelt the foul stink of brimstone. Wind rattled the branches and the rain really came, a black wall of water that nearly knocked her over. A torch carried by one of the four horsemen went out, his mount reared up, and he struggled to control it. Cecil pointed again and the horsemen walked their beasts closer – closer than had been agreed. She guessed it was so they could hear through the wind and rain. The Personage would think the storm was a satanic tempest created by the witches. It could still work if they could get the words out.

She looked across at Frances Strange who nodded. They began their chorus yelling out against the roar of wind and water.

'When shall we three meet again?
In thunder, lightning and in rain.
Where's the place? We'll meet beneath
This blasted oak upon this heath.'

He'd rewritten it at the last moment when he'd seen the storm coming.

She raised her voice and roared through the storm.

'Adder's fork and blind-worm's sting.
Lizard's leg and owlet's wing.
Eye of newt and baby's thumbs.
Something wicked this way comes.'

It was Bella's turn. She raised her hands wide, her black hair whirling around her face in the wind. She spoke, but the words were not her lines.

BELLA

Bella didn't know where the words were coming from. It was not Will, it was not the laudanum... was it her? She always shaped her speech to please those in authority, but now, speaking to the king, the most powerful man she had ever encountered, it was the truth that came tumbling out.

'You came here to look at evil,' she heard herself roar. 'If you want to find evil, go look in your own heart.'

The stink of sulphur sickened her, the gunpowder bursting in the trees blinded her, the wind and rain tried to pluck her words away but she yelled them out fiercely so he could hear.

'Everything you hear is fawning, flattery and lies because everyone you speak to fears you. No one has spoken the truth to you in years.'

She felt like she was watching herself in a dream, and wondered whether she was truly saying these things, but then in a lightning flash, she caught a glimpse of the king's face, mouth agape with shock and outrage. A river of molten rage was forcing words out of her mouth in a fiery stream. She was Zuzanka the witch, who could say things that Bella never could.

'You want me to tell you your future and I will. Your few years left on earth are insignificant but my master Satan says that soon he will welcome you to hell, where he is lord, and emperors and kings are nothing but sizzling flesh.'

She acted out a wild, crazed laugh as she thought a witch might, but then she found she was really laughing – just laughing and laughing and she couldn't stop.

WILL

Will looked across to Glendower. He stood, arms crossed, with that crazy grin on his face. Will wanted to grin too, but he didn't want to die.

He had to stop Bella if he was to save them. He'd hoped she might go back to his script, but it was too late for that now. He lit the second fuse, lunged across and pulled the rope which released the trapdoor. Bella disappeared in a huge bang and green and blue smoke rose up into the wind and rain.

King James cried something, turned his horse and rode away. Would Will and Ann be blamed for what had just happened? Surely they would understand it was only Bella who had insulted the king. He saw Cecil yelling at Proute and then Proute roared at the soldiers behind him.

'Seize her! Seize them all!'

ACT FOUR

BELLA

She pulled her bearskin cloak tighter and sang with the shepherds as the wolves circled their fire. She kissed his scar as the blurred line of camels tiptoed along the top of the dune and dusk turned the desert purple. She hugged the child in the green, green jungle where the earth steamed and snakes hung from the trees like strange fruit. She wanted to stay here in the lands of her memory but she mustn't...she couldn't. She opened her eyes and the darkness stalked her like a predator.

The trapdoor had worked perfectly and snapped shut as soon as she landed on the mattress where she had lain for what felt like hours but she suspected was only seconds. Had she taken a sip too many from the little bottle? Is that why she had spoken as she did? No, if anything, it was the fault of the dog.

For years she had locked out the world, but walking through the streets with that lumbering, affable giant had changed her. It wasn't just that she adored him. Some of the most evil men she had known loved their dogs. No, it was the way he brought her back to the world – the children's smiles, the costermongers laughing as his great wagging tail knocked apples from their stalls. She had found herself laughing and smiling too. It had made her part of humanity again, but humanity was dangerous, it made you feel the pain of others, see the world through their eyes. She had bought a dog intending to create a weapon and instead created a conscience.

She sat up on the mattress and the spinning darkness made

her giddy. She could stay there and wait for imprisonment, torture and death or she could run. She was surprised when she shed her witch's cape and hat, pushed the hatch open and crawled back into the tempest. She must want to live.

There was a truly enormous clap of thunder. Tamburlaine bolted past her in panic, his chain dragging the small tree he had uprooted. She went to follow him but he had disappeared into the storm.

WILL

Ann came out of the darkness.

'Run!' she cried. 'The soldiers are coming.'

He could make out a line of pikes and halberds appearing over the rise. Cavalrymen rose up behind them, but the ground must have been too boggy for the horses, as they turned and galloped off in another direction. Ann yanked at his arm and he followed her, head-on into the gale. The air was so full of water he wondered how they could breathe.

'God's emptying his bathtub,' Kemp would've said.

Glendower appeared out of nowhere standing on top of a hillock. He spread his arms holding his huge cloak wide to greet the tempest.

He was laughing.

'Do your worst!' he roared.

It did. The wind plucked him up and hurled him backwards into darkness. Will imagined him tumbling like a leaf across the heath, carried off down to the estuary and the North Sea, flying across its black waters, grinning all the way to oblivion.

He and Ann fled into the swirling darkness. He wondered for a moment whether he should shout in her ear and say let the soldiers arrest them. They could try to explain to Cecil that they had nothing to do with it. But he knew she'd tell him it was too late for that, and she'd be right.

He looked behind them. The advancing soldiers were battered backwards, scarlet cloaks whipped around their faces, halberds and muskets a hindrance, armour weighing them down as they slithered through the mud. He and Ann could escape, but where? This morning he had been rich, respected and comfortable. Now he was fleeing into this hell of mud, wet and cold, into this dead-ended peninsular, this blasted heath of bogs, quicksands, renegades and murderers.

BELLA

Branches flailed crazily in front of her but she caught a glimpse of a skirt swishing past. It was Frances Strange. She was walking towards the soldiers, clearly confident that she was not among the mere mortals who should be seized.

A soldier saw her and shouted, 'You, stop,' and another held out his halberd to block her way.

'Touch me with your filthy hands and I'll have them chopped off,' she said.

Her haughty voice cut through the storm.

'I am Frances Strange.'

She flicked one finger dismissively at his halberd and the soldier lowered it. The massive form of Proute barged through the black rain, and this time he must have recognised her.

'Let her go to her carriage,' he said.

The driving rain had scoured most of the make-up from Bella's face but she quickly scrubbed at her cheeks and mouth to make sure it was all gone. The world was spinning around her and she couldn't be sure if it was the drug or the storm but she hurried after Frances.

'Ma'am,' she called.

'You, stop,' shouted the same soldier, grabbing at her dress. 'Who are you?'

Bella put on a West Country accent.

'I'm yonder countess's lady's maid.'

Was the accent too much? Frances turned around and Bella

saw her cover up the surprise in her face. She hesitated for a moment then spoke impatiently.

'Hurry up, Bessie, for God's sake.'

Bella hastened after her.

LIZZIE

She tried the Cock, but the landlord told her that Mr Edgar Strange was eating at the Irish Boy on the Strand, so she made her way there, through Newgate Market, the stalls still stubbornly open in the storm. A barmaid told her that Edgar was dining in the Coronation Room and pointed up the stairs with a long, skinny arm and a wink she didn't like the look of.

She climbed a dark staircase, sticky with spilt beer, to a small corridor and cautiously edged open the only door. Fifteen or so men sat around a long, laden table. Mr Edgar Strange was on his feet making a toast.

'And may God bless our lives and our enterprise,' he was saying.

She hadn't imagined Edgar and God spending much time together, but the men banged their mugs on the table so hard the cutlery rattled. Edgar hadn't seen her through the swirl of tobacco smoke and went on, raising his voice against the noise of wind and rain outside.

'Gentlemen,' he said.

She saw they mostly were young men, well dressed in last year's fashions, not Londoners, the kind of men who stood on the edge of the crowds when they performed in small country towns.

'To health and a long life – at least for us,' roared Edgar, and they laughed the laugh of men who had emptied the many bottles on the table.

'Let us meet here again when— '

He saw her and stopped. As he looked at her the heads turned one by one.

'One moment, if you will, gentlemen,' said Edgar. He was putting on an act for these men. He edged between the chairs and a spitting fire.

A man with a big red drinker's face on a body like a sack of bricks looked at Lizzie, grinned and slapped Edgar on the back as he passed, a gesture she liked as little as the barmaid's wink.

'Hello,' said Edgar, a light arm on her waist guiding her back into the corridor.

Rain pelted against the window and water spurted through the cracks where the lead was missing and formed puddles that ran away between the gaps in the floorboards. They stood there in the cold draft. Something told her not to ask about the dinner and the toast. She wondered why she had come, but then she supposed she knew the answer to that.

'What brings you here?' asked Edgar.

'I brought you your hat back,' she said, and reached under her cloak and gave it to him.

He smiled. 'I bought a new one.'

He fitted the hat she had brought back on her head.

'That's her,' shouted a voice from the bottom of the stairs, and she saw an elderly man standing there, his jowls quivering with indignation. Behind him was a stout red-coated constable, his beard stained yellow around a black-toothed mouth. The old man wheezed up the stairs and stopped halfway to catch his breath.

'Would you like me to carry you up the last bit?' asked Edgar unhelpfully.

The man resumed his slow walk. He had big, bushy eyebrows, wiry hair sprouting from his nose and ears, but his head was bald and shiny.

'Don't try running,' he panted at her.

'No, don't,' Edgar said to her. 'He'll be after you like a greyhound.'

She elbowed him to shut up. Drips from the cracks in the low ceiling were falling on her face and running down her chin. The man finally made it up to the landing and reached out to grab her. She slapped his hand away.

'Search her for the silver teaspoon she stole from my stall,' he told the constable, who looked like a man who thought it was a waste to be in a pub without a drink in his hand. 'Arrest her and I'll reward you,' continued the old stallholder, who took out his purse and rattled the coins. The constable stepped forward.

'No,' said Edgar, 'no one searches this young lady. I can vouch for her utter and unparalleled honesty.'

The old man must have taken in his complexion.

'Says the half-breed.'

She felt Edgar tense and instinctively reached out a hand to hold him back.

The constable spoke. 'This gentleman says a woman answering her description stole a teaspoon from his stall.'

Thunder was still rumbling in the distance and the pub sign outside was creaking in the wind.

'Let's not come to blows over a misunderstanding,' said Edgar with dangerous affability. One hand was on his hip, close to his sword handle. Lizzie knew how young men liked to show off and how often it ended in bloodshed.

'What if this gentleman carries out the search in front of you?' she said, gesturing at Edgar.

For a moment he seemed reluctant to abandon the quarrel but then he smiled – that smile which carried its own danger.

'A search? Well, if you insist.'

The constable nodded his approval. He too had seen Edgar's hand hovering near his sword, and didn't want any trouble.

The old man went to object but his huffing and puffing meant it took a while for him to start.

'You had better hand me your cloak,' Edgar said to her. She did. He shook it and her needle clattered to the floor.

'See, a weapon,' said the old man.

'Which every woman needs when the streets are full of lecherous old men,' said Edgar, handing the cloak on to the constable so he too could check it. Lizzie stood there in her pale blue woollen robe.

'It'll be under there,' gasped the man, reaching for her again. She dodged him dismissively.

'Don't try and touch me again,' she said.

'Yes,' said Edgar beside her, his voice low and almost purring. 'Let's leave it at that, shall we? Life is far too short to mar it with violence.'

The constable was nodding. He wanted an easy life, but the old man didn't care. She liked him for that, but then she remembered how he'd called Edgar a half-breed.

'I want justice,' he wheezed stubbornly.

'Don't we all.' Edgar sounded sorrowful. 'But man's justice is capricious and bloody. Surely it's better to leave justice to God.'

'Damn God,' said the stallholder. 'Fat lot of help He is.'

He had the fearlessness of a man who would die soon anyway.

'You're not allowed to say that, sir,' said the Constable, taking a grip of his collar. The old man raged at both God and Edgar as he was dragged back down the stairs.

'Full of piss and wind with your long words and your fancy sword,' he shouted as the door closed behind him.

'I think that's you,' Lizzie said to Edgar.

Edgar smiled – that carnivorous smile again.

'So did you steal it?'

'Oh, surely not you too,' she said, hands on her hips. 'Will no one believe an honest young woman of spotless reputation?'

'I doubt it.'

'So if I stole it, where is it? You searched me.'

'Not very thoroughly.'

Lizzie sighed. 'Well, if you're going to be like that, perhaps you had better complete your exploration.'

Edgar's eyes fixed unblinking on hers.

'Really, must I? I'm a busy man. This is most vexatious and time-consuming.' He sighed. 'Still, I suppose if you insist.'

'I do.'

'Then hands above your head.'

She raised her arms.

He felt her shoulders, moved down and ran his hands around her ribs. She was sure he could feel how fast her heart was beating. His hands moved down to her stomach and hips, pressing lightly.

'You can see there's nothing there,' she said.

'Let's see about that,' said Edgar. 'Please turn around.'

She did and he ran his hands over her shoulder blades and down her backbone. She felt a cold finger touch her skin, and breathed in sharply.

'There's a small slash in your gown,' he said. His finger lingered on her skin. 'And the smallest of scratches beneath.'

It must have been from when she had fled the man with the sword who leapt out from the door of the theatre house. Evan had thought he had cut her. Well, that was a narrow escape. Edgar moved his hands down and around her waist. He was being very thorough, very thorough indeed.

'See,' she said, 'no teaspoon. Do you apologise?'

'It's probably hidden in your underskirts.'

'Will these terrible accusations never cease?' she said. 'Still, search away if you really must.'

'Very well,' said Edgar, 'this is extremely irksome, but I suppose I must do my bit to ensure the streets are safe.'

She hoisted the hem of her gown and lifted it so he could see that nothing was hidden there. She wore drawers that went down below her knees, so she could cartwheel through the small towns ahead of the wagon to drum up the crowds.

'I suppose you should check my undergarment,' she said.

Edgar huffed. 'Will this drudgery never end?'

He knelt in front of her like a young gallant proposing. His hands felt around her knees. He was breathing a little harder than before.

'Any cutlery down there?' she said. 'Or perhaps a small dinner service?'

'There's still places I haven't searched,' he said, and his hands slipped beneath the thick woollen fabric, ten icy fingers on her skin. She'd forgotten how calloused his hands were. She felt their roughness as they reached up her lower thigh towards her upper thigh. She was breathing harder too.

It was time to stop him. His fingertips moved forward slowly inch by inch. It was definitely time to stop him. Inch by inch. Half-inch by half-inch. It was – she grabbed hold of his hands through the wool.

'Your search must surely be complete.'

'Very nearly.' His words were stretched out between clenched teeth.

'And are you satisfied?'

He looked up at her. 'Not entirely.'

He removed his hands and stood.

'I will be finished with the dinner in an hour or so. You could join me afterwards, perhaps for a small bowl of syllabub? I believe you've brought your own teaspoon.'

He lifted off the hat and pulled the teaspoon from where she had hidden it in her hair, and handed it to her.

'And when did you realise it was there?' she asked.

'Some time ago.' He grinned. 'Is it fun to steal?'

'Have you never stolen?'

'Only hearts.'

She groaned. 'You were doing well until then. I suppose the ladies at court go for all that clever talk.'

'It's not what you think,' he said. 'Since Shakespeare's play came out they call me Othello. "Oh, here's Othello," they say, but I'm just a passing fashion who'll always be beneath them.'

'So you've found a girl from a magic show who you think is beneath you.'

'No, no, no,' he said quickly. If this was acting he was good at it. 'I'm not sure anyone's beneath me.'

His face was close to hers. His lips. Was he hoping for another kiss?

'What is your stage name?' he asked her.

'Cordelia. Glendower chose it.'

'So will you come and see me later, Cordelia?' he asked.

She remembered the grin from the landlord of the Cock and the wink from the barmaid below as if she was one of a string of visiting girls. She remembered the backslap from the red-faced man.

'Not tonight,' she said. 'Another time.'

To say yes too quickly was to be a whore and too slowly was to be a flirt. Men didn't have this problem.

'Will you tell me where you're staying?' he asked.

Should she tell him of the room the Widow had found her? Damn it, she'd come here, hadn't she, and she knew what he was, and she knew what she wanted, and it wasn't a good-hearted, fresh-faced country boy. The door handle was turning and someone was about to come out of the dining room. She quickly told him where she was staying and he repeated it twice to remember it.

A big man came through the door.

'Everything alright out here?' he asked Edgar.

She hadn't spotted him when she had scanned the faces in the room, but he wasn't one of the young gentlemen. He had a face scarred by burning and strange eyes that had no colour. This man was the killer Ann had described. Her heart raced again but now with a crazed and ragged beat. Why was he here with Edgar? She went to take a step back away from him but stopped herself. He surely couldn't hurt her here in a busy tavern with Edgar standing next to her.

'Will you introduce me?' she asked Edgar, hearing the tightness in her voice and hoping the man hadn't.

'This is Mr John Johnson. This is Lizzie.'

She moved her face into a smile.

'Pleased to make your acquaintance, Mr Johnson.'

He fixed those eyes on her face.

'Lizzie, I hope we meet again.'

She couldn't tell if he was trying to put her at her ease or terrify her. He stood very still for a moment as if he was deciding what to do, but then he stepped back into the room.

Another man, young and handsome, came out the door, smiled at her then stopped smiling abruptly. She recognised him as the priest who had been hiding in the country house where they had performed, only now he was disguised as a young gallant. He looked terrified to see her and she realised he must be fearful she would give him away. How could she reassure him?

'I will see you again, Mr Strange,' she said to Edgar, but then turned to look at the young priest, 'for I am a woman who always keeps the oaths I swore.'

ANN

She didn't think she'd been this cold, even when she'd fallen in the icy water of the Thames. Half their clothes had been torn off them by the tempest or shredded by the brambles. She looked behind them and saw only the low trees thrashing in the wind and rain. If the soldiers were still pursuing them she couldn't tell. Lightning flashed jaggedly and a roe deer leapt between them, black eyes wide with terror.

She smelt burning leather and saw a tree that had been struck by lightning, its branches shattered, its stump still smouldering. How could anything be on fire in this rain? How could there be so much water in the sky?

She remembered the Saint Guinefort greyhound ring she wore. Wasn't that supposed to protect you against lightning? She looked down to see if it was still on her finger, tripped over a looped root and hit the ground hard. She found herself face to face with a small, trembling animal. She thought she was imagining it, but there it was, a black nose twitching, wet fur standing on end, big scared eyes. It was the sailor's monkey that Frances Strange had been holding. Perhaps it only knew humans and had followed them. She tried to tell Will but now her voice didn't work either. She felt him pulling her to her feet and he dragged her forward.

And so they stumbled on, teeth chattering, bodies trembling, shoeless, hopeless, scratched and torn. The moon came out for the first time since the storm and the marsh stretched out ahead of them, a flat expanse of nothing, dotted with stunted trees. A figure rose up from the shrub ahead of them holding a lantern. It wasn't a soldier. It wasn't Bella or Glendower. It was a portly man with a mass of bushy white hair sticking out on either side of his big, round red face. So much of her was numb she wondered if she was dead already and this was heaven. He stood there beaming, his big belly a rosy red, his arms spread wide. He was stark naked.

'Friends,' he boomed. 'Welcome!'

'Bloody hell,' she thought. 'Saint Peter has really let himself go.'

BELLA

'Well,' said Frances Strange. 'What fun that was.'

The coach bucked and bounced as they took a corner at speed and the thoughts in Bella's head were thrown this way and that.

Why had she shouted those words at the king? When she was a little girl they had told her that the world was flat and she had run away from the orphanage so she could jump off the edge to see what was there. Now all these years later it was as if she had finally done it, thrown away caution and constraint and leapt into the abyss.

'Of course,' said Frances, 'the trouble with the king is that he's really a touch common. Go back a bit on his father's side and they were just cattle thieves.'

Frances's hair was still full of muck and she pulled back the curtain, lowered the carriage window and stuck her head out into the pelting rain. She brought it back in and shook her long black hair so vigorously she sprayed Bella with water and dirt.

What should Bella do? Before she could complete a thought, new ones came swirling in. Survive. She should survive. That was it.

'So, Bella,' said Frances, 'talking of heritaged, I believe you have two sons.'

'No,' said Bella.

'Come along, Bessie,' said Frances, and in the maid's name Bella recognised the threat to unmask her. 'I know about Charlie, your bastard.'

‘I’ve only one son and I’ve lost him,’ said Bella, and saying it she felt the sharp hurt of the child who had abandoned her.

The carriage stopped, and Bella could see through the blowing curtains that they were at a fork in the road blocked by a cart with its axle snapped. In the middle of the junction knelt an old beggar woman, still out in this raging storm, her body held together with nothing but skin and gristle, her face puckered tight over her skull. Frances Strange pulled the filthy costume off over her head, shouted, ‘There you go,’ and threw it out the window at her. It hit the beggar woman and knocked her over. ‘Oops,’ said Frances.

Bella hoped the old woman would have enough sense not to put on a witch costume.

Frances unrolled her hose, chucked it on the floor with a wet splat and started to unbutton her petticoat.

‘I think you’re lying, Bessie. What about the bastard you had with my father, the beau going around London telling everyone of his heritage?’

‘I never had a child with your father,’ she said.

The coachman yelled at the horses and they moved off.

‘Why should I believe you?’ said Frances Strange.

‘Did you see of much of your father?’ asked Bella.

‘Of course not. We’re aristocrats.’

Frances Strange was only wearing her shift now. She went to take it over her head but it was so soaking it clung to her neck and shoulders.

‘Help me,’ she called from beneath it. ‘After all you are my lady’s maid.’

Bella yanked at it and hauled it off.

‘Your father,’ she said, ‘had no interest in sex, except as a necessity to continue his bloodline. He only cared for power. He never touched me. I’m sure you have the money and influence to make enquiries, and you will find that I am telling the truth.’

Frances sat there, pink-skinned and naked. Now would be the time to jump from the carriage.

'So Edgar Strange is lying,' Frances said. 'Well, well, well.'

EDGAR

'You're very chummy with the new girl you were told to kill,' said John.

'I could hardly stab her here on the landing.'

John shrugged as if to say, *Why not?*

Edgar had liked it better when he'd been in command, back before he'd been chosen from among all of them to carry the secret letter from King James, back before he'd been betrayed and everything had gone wrong.

John peeled a scrap of dead skin from his face, where he'd been burned, and examined it.

'It all needs to be finished by tomorrow. Do you know where the girl is staying?'

Edgar shook his head, fearful those pale eyes could see his lie.

'Do you?' he asked John.

'We can't tail her. She runs everywhere.'

Edgar felt himself smiling and had to turn it into a grimace. He loved Lizzie's swift-footed assurance. He loved her bravery, her effrontery, her larceny. Perhaps he loved her. Was this what this feeling was – the way his stomach melted and his heart beat faster? It was very like fear.

At least, she should be safe. They wouldn't find her and tomorrow there'd be bigger things to worry about. The gale blew out one of the small panes in the window and it smashed onto the floor.

'So what's she doing now?' asked John.

'Hiding.'

'Hiding,' John repeated, no expression on his face, no expression in his voice. That's when he was dangerous. 'And the Widow, she still seems to be alive too.'

'I was waiting for the salt to be delivered, but yeah.' Edgar tried to sound gruff and businesslike. 'We can get rid of her now.'

John peeled off another piece of burnt skin and held it up in front of his face. For a moment Edgar thought he was going to eat it but instead he sniffed it and dropped it on the floor.

'Why do they all need to die?' Edgar asked. He thought he might as well try.

'Because I told you they do.'

There was a racket in the dining room. A lot of the young gentlemen couldn't hold their drink.

'You need to get back in there,' John said, 'Littleton and Tresham are getting nervous.'

He kicked the broken glass into a corner and headed down the stairs.

'Use your charm.'

He made 'charm' sound like it was a disease. He walked out the door into the storm and the wind slammed the door behind him so hard that another pane fell out of the window.

Edgar reached for the door to the dining room, but heard someone coming down the narrow stairs that led up to the top floor. It was Dogface. Men like him weren't permitted to carry swords but he carried a long leather bag and Edgar knew what was in it.

Dogface had come with John. Small, wiry and sunken-faced, he'd originally been called Ferret and crawled down the cramped tunnels to set the gunpowder under the enemy walls. He'd become Dogface after he'd gone off on a drunken binge for two days and came back with his teeth filed to points, though no memory of how it had happened.

He winked at Edgar as he walked past.

'Where are you off to?' Edgar asked him, trying to sound like he was in charge.

'Down to Blackfriars Stairs. Job out east.'

'Will the boats be running in this storm?'

'I'll find something.'

He pulled the hood of his cloak over his head, ready for the wind and rain.

'So the skinny Dutch bint,' said Dogface. He hated the Dutch. 'Did you give her one to take with her?'

'Take with her?' asked Edgar.

'Yes, to hell,' said Dogface. He was enjoying himself. 'John's gone to kill her seeing as you're a bit slow.'

Was he bluffing to get a reaction?

'We don't know where she lives,' said Edgar.

'We didn't until I told him.' He grinned a pointy-toothed grin and tapped the wooden ceiling above their heads. Edgar looked up. Water dripped through the big gaps between the planks. From up there you would hear everything said in this corridor. Dogface had been up there when Lizzie had told him where she was staying.

'Your big aristocratic brain worked it out now?' Dogface asked. 'That's why John doesn't like women. Nasty, sticky traps the lot of them – make you betray your mates.'

Edgar didn't stop to get his coat and leapt down the stairs in three bounds. Dogface laughed at him.

'Too late, lover boy.'

Was he? Lizzie's place was five or six minutes away and Johnson had left a couple of minutes before him. He threw himself out the door into the storm.

WILL

The naked man picked up Ann and tipped her over his shoulder like she was a sack of coal and, before Will could say anything, walked off up a low rise into the moonlight. Will could do nothing but stumble after him, gasping to keep up as he headed towards another hillock. The hillock turned out to be some sort of shack covered in turf. It was only when the naked man pulled open a door made from a broken rowing boat that Will's mind started working again and he remembered.

It was the crazed Friar whose expertise had helped them find out how Kit Marlowe had been poisoned. He beckoned Will in and shouldered the boat door closed behind him.

'Never wear clothes in the rain,' he said. 'They only get wet.'

If anything, he'd become even crazier.

He pulled the white robe of a Capuchin monk over his head, lit more lanterns and threw them some blankets so moth-eaten there were more holes than blanket. They wrapped themselves up, and crouched close to his smoky peat fire.

'I know you two, don't I?' he said 'You have graced me with the honour of a visit before. Did we not dig up a corpse together? That playwright who was poisoned.'

Will nodded, his teeth chattering, his body more convulsed with trembling now than when he'd been outside.

'Cold?' asked the Friar.

'Just a little,' Will said.

The Friar walked over to a couple of blackened cauldrons bubbling above the fire.

'Some broth will warm you,' he said.

Will found it hard to hear, his teeth were rattling so loudly. He and Ann huddled closer to share what little warmth their bodies had left. The Friar found two filthy bowls and wiped them with the even filthier sleeve of his monk's habit.

Will glanced at Ann and saw she too remembered how the Friar had tested hallucinogenic potions on them, but she shrugged. They were too cold and hungry to care.

'Who wants fish and who wants meat?' asked the Friar.

Ann chose fish and he chose meat and the Friar scooped out the thick, lumpy liquid. Will spooned some into his mouth.

'One moment,' said the Friar. 'Grace.'

They stopped eating. The Friar closed his eyes and held his arms aloft.

'Bless these bountiful gifts of food and fellowship Thou hast bestowed on us, O Gods.'

Will decided it was best to ignore the plural and started to eat again. He bit on something crunchy.

'Careful of the bones,' said the Friar, as Will pulled a suspiciously tiny backbone from his mouth. He went to ask what meat this was but decided it was better not to know.

'Newt,' said the Friar.

Oh, well, that was just about meat.

'The Minoans considered them a delicacy,' said the Friar.

The Minoans – hadn't they become extinct? He hoped it wasn't because of the newts.

The room still contained the glinting jars of potions and small animals, some floating lifeless, some wriggling and squirming, but unlike before, it was all in disarray. Many jars were cracked, broken glass stuck out of the mud floor and a vile odour hung in the damp fug. Water streamed through the turf ceiling and the smoke swirled in slow circles as if the chimney was blocked. When Will went to rest his bowl on a small table it sank into the rotten wood.

The Friar too had fallen into disrepair. He was still big-bodied and round-cheeked, but his eyes were sunken, his skin blotched and his hands swollen a mottled purple. Will wondered whether he still held sway among the thieves and killers who hid in this swamp. Will took a handful of coins from his purse and held them out.

'Would you do the kindness of sending someone to find a wherry that could pick us up from the nearby shore?'

'I take no payment from my friends,' said the Friar, waving away the coins. 'And certainly not from the man who wrote *Love's Labour's Won*. That's my favourite.'

For a madman he had excellent judgement. It was far better than *Love's Labour's Lost*, and certainly his finest comedy. Perhaps that was the play he'd be remembered for.

'How was the gu?' the Friar asked Ann as if this thought naturally followed.

She looked perplexed.

'The what?'

'You said you wished to try out that most powerful of poisons, so I gave you some to take away.'

She shook her head.

'Not me.'

He chuckled.

'I see. Tell me how it worked when we are alone.'

Will wondered whether this was just some wild imagining or whether the Friar had mistaken Ann for someone else.

ANN

She hadn't expected that question but she hoped she hadn't shown too much surprise and made Will suspicious. Thankfully the Friar's brain wandered off somewhere else.

'I expect you wonder how I escaped punishment after they came upon me digging up Christopher Marlowe's coffin.'

'Yes, I do,' she said.

'They took me to a dungeon in the Tower of London. Have you been there? It's intriguing. There are some fascinating moulds on the walls – a pink one very like ear rot, but iridescent – when you snuff out a candle, it continues to glow in the dark.'

'Fascinating,' said Ann.

'I'd have liked to study it more but they let me go,' said the Friar, vigorously scratching one armpit. 'They let me go because I taught them how to make a potion which makes men tell the truth.'

'Does it work?' she asked, gulping down more warm broth.

'Oh yes. It's so powerful that it even works on lawyers.'

He chuckled at his joke.

'They tried it on a witch who had revealed nothing though they'd made her a foot longer on the rack. But dosed with my elixir, she told them where the devil slept when he was in England.'

This madness again. And yet she had to ask.

'Where was it he slept?'

'I believe somewhere near Croydon.'

Something squirmed close by and she realised she was resting her arm on a large jar full of a knot of twisted grey snakes. One seemed to be trying to kill the others.

'You didn't put any of your truth potion in our broth, did you?' asked Ann.

'No, no, no, it's far too rare and valuable for that.'

He puffed up with pride, rotund, pink and steaming in the heat.

'Only last month, they sent an emissary in an ermine cape with three armed guards to fetch a vial, said it was required for great matters of state.'

Surely this was one of his hallucinations, but it was hard to be sure. Will asked about the boat again.

'As soon as it's dawn, I shall send a message to Boneyard Billy to bring his waterborne conveyance here,' said the Friar. 'I provide him with certain restorative tonics so he will do as I ask.'

Was everyone on the Isle reliant on the Friar's narcotics? They were in the middle of a swamp full of drug-crazed criminals.

'Now, sleep,' said the Friar. 'Sleep heals the wounds of daylight. It is a far better medicine than I can provide.'

The storm had either passed, or the sod walls were so thick they couldn't hear it.

Ann felt her eyelids pressing down.

'Sleep, my children,' said the Friar, 'sleep.'

It was as if the words were drugging her. She was jolted awake by a violent rustle beside her as the snakes fought again.

'I think we shall remain awake, thank you,' said Ann.

'I don't think you will,' said the Friar.

EDGAR

The street was a river running over the cobblestones, the shop signs above creaking and swinging wildly in the gale.

He turned left and right and hoped he was in Ave Maria Lane but Newgate Court was on his left and not his right which meant – what did it mean? Had he gone too far east? Something fell and shattered next to him in the street – a chimney pot. If he could just find Pilgrim Street he could find Pilgrim Court.

A prostitute stood in an open door still holding a lantern that had blown out.

'I'm looking for a girl of about eighteen,' he said.

'I could pass for twenty if we just light one candle.'

'No, no,' he said, not sure if she'd been joking. 'She's wearing a blue cape. Has she passed this way?' She looked blank. 'Or a big man with a scarred face?'

She shook her head.

'Then how do I get to Pilgrim Court?' he asked.

'Now you're asking a question I can answer. It's right behind me,' she said, pointing at a brick wall. He could hear the desperation under her jollity. 'But to get to it you go to the end, turn left, left again, then it's on the left just past the pork butcher.'

He wanted to give her a coin, but he couldn't bear to waste the five seconds that would take.

'I'm Jenny,' she shouted wearily after him. 'Always here, rain or shine.'

He got up and ran on, each gasping breath sucking in cold rain. He slithered on a loose cobble at the corner and sprawled with a splash into a puddle. Ahead of him the whole street was awash, but he ran on, and there it was, the cut-out sign of a pig swaying wildly on its metal frame. He ran into the alley beside it. At the far end, Lizzie had said. He banged on the door there but no one answered. What if John appeared now? He'd fight him he supposed. He battered on the next door down but again there was only silence. Who'd open their doors to a stranger on a night like this? Lightning flashed and he saw there were a couple of smaller side passages off the alley, so he squeezed down the one nearest the end.

A light was flickering behind one window, so he stood on tiptoe and wiped a pane of glass with his sleeve, and there, miracle of miracles was Lizzie, asleep, her face lit by a candle on a saucer next to the bed. He tapped on the rain-smeared window but, as he did, the thunder came rumbling and made more noise than him. He went to bang on the window again, but before his fist hit the glass, a large, dark figure strode towards Lizzie, an axe in his hand. Edgar opened his mouth to scream but John Johnson smashed the axe down on her head.

WILL

Will dreamt of Kemp, though it felt more than a dream, more as if Kemp was back from the dead and walking around in Will's head.

'I'm sorry,' said Will. 'I'm sorry I deserted you.'

'I'm dead,' said Kemp. 'I didn't know you had.'

'I swear, I'll avenge you,' said Will.

'You?' said Kemp. 'Come off it.'

They were upstairs at the Mermaid, Kemp's favourite tavern, where he flirted with the landlady and got them free drinks by doing his act. Webster was there, a long wisp of misery, and Ben Jonson, square, loud and drunk, trying to get Kemp to do his King James impression. Kemp said it was too dangerous as he always did, and then, as he always did, went and performed it anyway.

He stood on a table, stuck a lump of bread roll in his mouth to mimic the king's spluttering diction and put on an absurd Scottish accent.

'Och aye, I'm by far the cleverest man in the whole wide world from the Great Wall of India in the east to that other place across the big wet thing in the not easterly direction.'

He'd filled his mouth with beer too before he'd started talking and sprayed it across the room as he spoke, cruelly mimicking the way James drooled.

'Yes, my wit is so huge it's even bigger than my tongue. I'm an enormous wit.'

He turned to the woman sitting below.

'No, madam, not "twit", "wit".' He spelt it. 'W – i – erm,

and that other alphabet thingy. But listen, I'm so witty that the second greatest wit in the world is my arse.' He turned around, dropped his breeches and farted. Everyone laughed. 'See, I told you my arse was funny.'

Will couldn't help laughing; could you laugh in dreams? Well, it seemed so.

But when he looked back to Kemp he was swinging from a rope. He stared pleadingly at Will, though when Will tried to run to him nothing happened and when he looked down he had no legs.

MONDAY

ANN

When Ann woke the sun was shining through the holes between the stacked peat, sending cones of light through pots and jars so the muddy hovel was lit with a dozen shades of green, ochre, amber and blue. Next to her head was a bright red jar with some small beast wriggling happily in the liquid inside. The fire was out and the Friar was gone.

Her body felt so weak that it barely existed, but she floated around pleasantly without it. Sweet birdsong rippled in her head and mixed with the tinkling trickle of the nearby river. The swish of the tall grass calmed her and everything smelt fresh from the rain. She remembered the broth the Friar had given them the night before. What had he put in it this time? Whatever it was, she wanted more.

She turned to watch Will sleeping. His eyes were sunken and red-rimmed, his face scratched and gouged, his head covered with as much mud as hair. Yet what a miracle he was, what poetry, what stories had come out of that skull. What amazing phrases where words leapt unexpectedly together.

Staring at his face she saw tufts of white hair in his beard which hadn't been there before. So he had dyed his beard, but the river or the rain had washed it out. In some ways it was so unlike him but, of course, he'd changed. She found Will's new vanity touching. She wanted to reach out and stroke those little white patches.

His eyes fluttered open as if her gaze had woken him. The Friar must have thrown an animal fur over them to keep them warm, and as Will sat up, small insects flew up out of it into the beams of light, a host of tiny angels to protect them. He smiled at her.

'How did you sleep?' she asked.

There was a moment as something came back to him. The smile vanished and he shuddered.

'What?' she asked.

'Dreams,' he said. 'They seemed so real.'

'What about?'

'The dead. Kemp, Kit.' He hesitated, but she could see he wanted to tell her. 'My son.'

He reached for her hand and clutched it. Or had she reached for his? She wasn't sure. How long ago had his boy Hamnet died? It must be seven or eight years.

'He was sitting at dinner, but he was dead and only I could see him. They told me not to be a fool because no one was really there.'

She squeezed his hand.

'And then they were all there,' he said, 'Kemp, Kit, Tom Kyd, all the dead.'

He looked as if he was still seeing them now. Perhaps the Friar had added something different to Will's broth.

Will turned to her. 'Do you still dream of your children?' he asked.

The safe, fuzzy world she had woken up in turned hard and brittle.

'Sorry,' he said. 'You don't have to answer.'

She knew she did.

'I used to,' she said, 'all the time.'

Her two had both died before their second birthdays around the same time she'd heard that Will had lost his son.

She could see he wanted to ask another question and she nodded to tell him that he could.

'And when you dreamed of them, did you know they were dead?' he asked.

'No,' she said.

It had been terrible to wake and remember again that her two babies were gone. Each morning she had to throw back the eiderdown and swing her feet onto the floor to steady herself, feeling full to the brim with tears she couldn't cry. Yet every night she was still always eager to fall asleep so she could be with her children again for a few moments, to hear them giggle and see them smile, even though she knew the price she'd pay when she woke. When she told her husband John, it made him angry, as if she was wilfully conjuring them out of the darkness, as if she was making her pain go on longer when she should just be washing his breeches.

'And do you now?' asked Will.

'I don't dream.'

'Of them?'

'Of anything.'

Her nights were a blank, a gap between falling asleep and waking. She looked forward to them.

'I think you must dream,' he said, 'but just not remember.'

Was that true? Did she drift off to a place in the past where her babies were alive, was her mind kind to her, had it found a way to forget so she didn't always wake to that grim shock? If only she could be in that world of dreams all the time and never have to come back to face the truth.

'And you?' she asked. 'Do you dream of him a lot?'

'All the time, but I always know he's dead.'

'You mean like a ghost?'

'No, he's just a boy being a boy, but I know that he's really dead.'

That seemed crueller than her dreams.

'Do you think of him much when you're awake?' she asked.

He shook his head. 'If I do I can't stop. It's too…'

Will Shakespeare couldn't find an adequate word.

'Then perhaps that's why he comes to you in dreams,' she said.

'I think it's my punishment for being a bad father.'

It always came back to this with him.

'Most of the theatre people leave their families and come to London,' she said.

He smiled at her attempt to let him off the hook.

'And you know what it's like between you and your Anne,' she went on. 'You two could never live together.'

'We couldn't,' he said, staring into the coloured light alive with dust and small flying creatures. 'And yet, you and I, do you think we could?'

He'd caught her by surprise. She wasn't ready for this.

'Can we go back to talking about dead children?'

He seemed shocked for a moment, then he laughed.

'Only you could say that.'

She shrugged.

'Why do you say this now?' she asked.

He hesitated. He struggled for an answer. 'Because by tomorrow we might be dead.'

'Then there's no point talking about it.'

She was being hard because one of them had to be. What was the point of talking?

What was the point of telling him that he was the only one in the world who made life bearable – the only one left alive whom she cared for more than herself? Her thoughts shocked her. Where had all this come from? Was it even true? Perhaps it was just the Friar's broth. Well, it didn't matter either way. They'd said all these things before and look where it had got them. It wasn't enough.

She was still squeezing his hand but it felt wet. She looked down and saw her cut hand was bleeding again. She let go of his and wiped hers on a corner of a blanket.

The boat door creaked open and the Friar's broad, beaming face appeared, his bushy white hair lit by the sun like a halo.

'I've brought you a little breakfast,' he said, and held out a bowl of cobnuts and a small sack in which something squirmed.

'Just the nuts for me,' said Will.

Ann remembered the last time she'd eaten a nut and it had nearly killed her. There were still three or four of them in the small bag around her neck, which had somehow survived the river, storm and swamp. She got one out and showed it to the Friar and told him how a couple of them seemed to have poisoned her but no one else.

'Ah, yes, I've heard that there are people whose peculiar humours act on some foods, to poison their own blood so it attacks them. It's often nuts, I've heard of it but never seen it.' He looked excited. 'Would you eat one now and show me?'

Her face must have answered that question.

'Perhaps just half a nut then,' he pleaded hopefully. 'It's for science.'

'I'd rather not die if it's the same to you.'

He cocked his head to one side. He had heard something they hadn't. 'Ah,' he said, 'I'm dreadfully sorry about this, but he insisted.'

The boat door scraped open and a grin appeared – a grin full of filed pointy teeth.

WILL

Dogface had a long sword in his hand and a twisted smile on his lips. He was muttering that incantation of his. He shut the door, shoved the Friar out of the way and stepped towards them. Will tried to throw off the blankets but one arm got entangled in a hole. Dogface was nearly on them. Will reached out with his other arm and swept a jar towards him. It hit him at knee height and smashed. The Friar yelped in distress at its loss but Dogface just sneered at such a useless attempt to stop him. He raised his sword. Then he saw the writhing mass of snakes at his feet, wriggling among the broken glass. His mouth opened, he gasped and froze. He jumped back and slashed at the nearest snake with his sword and cut off its head.

'Oh no,' said the Friar, 'not Penelope.'

Dogface was clearly terrified but Will had only bought them a moment because soon Dogface would kill the rest of the snakes, and he still blocked the door and had the only weapon.

Will was kneeling now. He reached out for the nearest squirming snake and grabbed it behind its head. It hissed and flailed crazily and tried to strike him but he chucked it at Dogface.

It landed hissing on his chest and looped itself about his neck. Dogface made a wet, choking noise, dropped his sword, turned and clawed at the door. Will and Ann reached for the sword at the same time but Will got there first.

'Kill him,' Ann yelled.

He raised the sword, meaning to run him through, but nothing happened.

'Go on,' she shouted.

He couldn't do it. He wanted to, but his arm wasn't having it. Dogface had finally heaved the door open.

'Give it to me,' screamed Ann, and reached for the sword's handle, but he moved it away from her. That enraged her, and she got hold of his arm and prized the weapon from his grip, but now there was just an open door and Dogface was running away through the reed beds.

ANN

She rushed through the door into the cold sunshine, her bare feet squelching in the mud. Dogface was heading towards the river and already twenty yards ahead of her. He leapt over a small rise and disappeared. She kept running but her legs were so weak she felt there was nothing between her and the ground. Will caught up with her.

'Ann, we won't catch him,' he said.

Of course he'd say that. She didn't waste breath replying.

They crested the ridge and there he was on the muddy river edge, pushing a small rowing boat out into the river. He must have used it to get there. She gasped in air for a last spurt, somehow jumped a ditch, tottered as she landed, nearly dropped the sword, but made it onto the mud. Dogface was only a couple of yards from the shore, pushing the boat out into the deeper water. She tried to get to him, but the thick, claggy mud clung to her feet and ankles. There was a rope that dragged behind the boat and she switched the sword to her left hand and tried to grab it but missed. Will dived past her, made a lunge and had the very end of it in his hand. Oh, so now he wanted to stop him.

Dogface gave the boat another heave and the rope slipped out of Will's grasp. He clambered into the boat, got the oars in the rollocks and took a panicky stroke but it was enough. He was out of reach. She went to throw the sword at him but stopped halfway. It would be useless. He was muttering that same Latin phrase again as he rowed away. She felt the freezing clamp of the water on her feet and ankles, and her legs started to give way. Will reached to steady her but she batted his hand away and stumbled through the sticky mud and back to the reed beds. She shouted in Will's face, 'Why didn't you kill him?'

Behind him, Dogface in the boat waved at her, grinning.

'How many times has he tried to kill us?' she yelled. 'He probably killed your friend Kemp. Remember Kemp who you wanted to avenge?'

Will went to speak but his voice didn't work, just like his arm hadn't when it held a sword.

'We could have taken his boat and got away from here.'

Her legs gave way and she tottered and he again tried to take her arm but she just had the strength to knock him away. She felt a small hand reach and clasp her other hand. Confused, she looked down. It was the monkey, big eyes looking up at her, its hair in muddy spikes. The hand was shivering. The sight of it took her anger away and she felt like crying. The poor thing had probably been snatched from its mother. It grasped at her skirt with its other hand.

'It wants to jump up,' said Will.

Oh, so he could talk now. She pulled up the hand and it jumped up and put its arms around her neck.

'I'm sorry,' said Will. 'I couldn't do it.'

She said nothing.

'Could you have killed him? Could you kill someone?' he asked.

'Watch,' she said. 'I'm going to kill that double-crossing Friar right now.'

A voice came from behind them.

'I'd rather you didn't. I've a coracle you can have to get back to London.'

She wasn't going to kill the Friar, but she thought it was worth making him think she might.

'The emissary who came for your truth potion. Who was he working for?'

The Friar made a lot of *er* and *um* noises. 'Didn't say. No clue. Thought best not to ask.'

She stuck the point of the sword up against his throat so it made a small indentation but didn't break the skin.

'This is my truth potion,' she said.

He spluttered and stuttered. She pushed the sword a fraction further.

'No, no, don't. If I recall correctly, as they were leaving one of them said, "Do you reckon His Lordship will give us a reward?"'

A drop of sweat fell from his nose and burst on the sword blade. He gazed at her pleadingly. This was all she was going to get.

She pulled the sword back, turned and shooed Will towards the coracle.

'Could you truly kill someone?' he asked again.

'I could,' she said. 'I killed Lord Strange.'

WILL

He knew her better than anyone else – how could he not know that? Was it even true?

'Wasn't Lord Strange poisoned?' he asked.

'Who do you think poisoned him?' she said, stumbling as she dragged the coracle towards the beach.

He hurried to help her.

'He'd killed Christopher and he was going to get away with it,' she said, swatting loose hair away from her forehead. Her cut hand had started bleeding again and she left a smear of blood above one eye. It didn't seem the right time to tell her that. He went to ask more about Strange but she cut him off. 'What do we do now?'

That question again. At least she'd stopped talking about how he'd let Dogface escape.

'I'm sure you let Dogface escape because you had a plan,' she added.

She hadn't.

'We could find Lizzie. Or we could still look for Berrycloth and find out if he was the man with the black eye.'

'So that's it?'

That was it. It didn't seem like much and he'd promised Kemp in his dream that he would avenge him. Did promises made in dreams count?

'It's too dangerous taking the boat into London,' he said. 'Cecil's men watch the river. We should go downstream to Deptford or Greenwich and make our way by land from there.'

They pushed the coracle out into the river and the Thames, like God, laughed at their plans.

The racing tide flung their flimsy boat upstream towards London and there was nothing they could do about it. They tried to paddle but only spun in circles, spun helplessly towards Cecil and the Tower. The Friar seemed to have forgotten the sword pushed into his throat and stood beaming on the shore waving goodbye like a jolly aunt.

'Don't be strangers now,' he shouted.

'Was that what the Friar was talking about?' Will asked. 'The poison he said he gave you twelve years ago, the... something.'

He couldn't remember the name.

'Gu,' she said.

Will and Ann had made two visits to Lord Strange after his attempt to depose Elizabeth and become king in her place had been discovered. He had escaped punishment because it somehow suited Cecil to keep his role quiet. On the first visit Strange had gloated at how he had escaped justice. On the second he had vomited black blood and collapsed. On the first visit he had offered them wine...

It was as if Ann tracked his thoughts.

'Yes,' she said, 'I put poison in his wine.'

Well, she had always sworn she would kill her brother's killer. He had thought it bluster, but he should have known: never underestimate a Marlowe. He went to ask her more questions but she cut him off.

'Paddle harder.'

They did their best but they were carried upriver along with the broken spars, uprooted trees and dead animals that the storm had swept into the Thames. His oar caught on something. It was a body, a woman, a fan of fair hair around her head. He pushed it away but it clung stubbornly to the coracle until an eddy spun the boat around and it floated off, one pale arm still reaching out towards them.

The monkey clung to Ann, one hand grasping a hank of

her hair. The Friar had offered to 'look after the little fellow' so they'd had to take it with them. It blinked and looked at him over Ann's shoulder – those big liquid green-brown eyes seemed more human than a human.

They passed flooded fields dotted with swans and by the time they swung past Limehouse the Thames had got busy. They paddled furiously to avoid the maroon-sailed Thames barges, the dung boats low in the water, the brigantines, ballingers, galleons and galleasses that criss-crossed the river. Sailors knew a lot of swear words and shouted most of them at the piece-of-shit, half-arsed, sodding whoreson of a basket that they knelt in.

'Why didn't you tell me before that you killed him?' he asked her.

An eddy swung them around and threw them into the path of a fat black cog. They paddled frantically to get out from under it, but the coracle touched its side, lurched and nearly overturned. The ship's captain at the tiller swore in guttural Dutch and spat a stream of black tobacco at them.

'Why would I?' said Ann. 'I didn't suppose you held with poisoning the nobility, now you're nearly one of them.'

They were passing the village at Wapping where the three ships were being loaded for the Virginia expedition.

'I'm glad you did it,' he said to make peace, then realised he meant it.

He was glad she'd killed Strange. He was glad Bella had spoken the truth to James, and not the words he'd written inventing a Catholic conspiracy. He was glad he'd never be a 'sir', and almost glad he was in this piece-of-shit, half-arsed, sodding whoreson of a basket with this bloody-faced, murderous woman clutching a monkey – this extraordinary woman who despised him.

ANN

She'd thought that Will must have worked it out long before that she'd killed Strange, how she'd slipped poison into that royal blood in which the heritage of Henry the Seventh and Henry the Eighth mingled, how she'd watched him dying, indignant that Death had the impertinence to come calling on such an exalted lord without making an appointment.

She didn't regret it. It might be the only thing in her life that she'd never regretted. And yet… And yet there were times when she walked among the crowds at Buttermarket that she felt she was somehow marked out, that she was a stranger in her own town, that she wasn't like everyone else because she had killed another human being. And there had been times when she bathed her babies, when even as they'd splashed and giggled she'd felt that she shouldn't be touching them with the hands that had poisoned a man. And when they cried, when she was exhausted, when she couldn't think straight, there were times she felt that somehow they knew, in the way animals knew things, that their mother wasn't like other mothers, that she was cursed, that she was evil.

She told herself to stop it, not to be so dramatic, that she was nothing special, that her life had gone on exactly as it would have if she had never killed anyone. Will had fallen out of love with her, and here she was, just another woman growing old in a bad marriage. And yet, when things were at their worst between her and John, there were times a small voice told her that she wasn't allowed happiness after what she'd done, and, yes, after her babies had died, when she was alone late at night, and the last candle flickered out, yes, sometimes she knew that their deaths were her punishment for being a murderer. She knew it at the same time as she knew it was all bollocks.

But that didn't seem to help. Good God, if she felt this for killing Strange, what would she feel if she had killed someone innocent?

It wasn't as if she wanted Will to suffer as she had so she shouldn't blame him for refusing to kill a man. Yet he'd had even more justification than she had. It had been in a fight. Dogface had been about to kill them, so it had truly been self-defence. And being a playwright was no excuse – her brother and Thomas Watson had killed a man in a fight, and so had Ben Jonson, so why couldn't he? At least, it would give him something to write about.

They paddled hard for Queenhithe and the north shore but the current swept them towards the south bank and they fetched up near Bear Garden Steps where all this had started.

At least no soldiers came running so perhaps Cecil's lookouts had missed their strange basket.

'We should go to the Globe,' he said.

'They'll be watching the Globe for sure.'

'I know, but we can wait outside for someone we can trust.'

'And who can you trust?'

She didn't like the pause as he thought.

'There's a few,' he said.

At least they were disguised. Their faces were grimy and scratched and in the Friar's shredded blankets they looked like vagabonds.

'We can pretend to be beggars,' she said. 'No one sees beggars. And the monkey helps.'

They found an alley from where they could see the street in front of the Globe, and sat down propped up against a wall.

A stout man with jam in his beard rolled a barrel towards them, humming the same soldiers' song as the big man who had chased them across the Thames. He rolled the barrel past without ever looking down at them.

'Have you got a couple of farthings?' she asked Will.

'Why?'

'Beggars always put some coins in their hats. It makes passers-by more likely to give if they think other people have been kind.'

He reached for his purse, but it wasn't there. He'd lost it somewhere. She wished she'd taken a chance and kept the sword to sell. Now they really were going to have to beg.

She held out the blanket to some women coming back from the communal bread oven but they walked past chatting about a talking sheep that had been discovered near Hemel Hempstead.

'We should pretend to be blind,' she said, 'you get more that way.'

He looked baffled.

'I had an uncle who used to run the beggars in Rochester.'

She missed jolly Uncle Hal. They'd found his body floating in the Medway. His head they'd found outside a pub in Chatham.

'You just half close your eyes and stare into the distance,' she explained.

Will did his best but Uncle Hal wouldn't have been impressed.

Burbage walked by chewing a big lump of cheese. She looked across at Will to see if Burbage was one of the people he trusted, but Will pressed himself back against the wall. Burbage never looked at their faces, just chucked them the cheese rind as he walked off. She tore it in two and gave Will half. He hesitated for a moment and then scoffed it.

'Does anyone know that you killed Lord Strange?' he asked, still chewing.

'No one. Apart perhaps from Cecil who knows everything.'

'Could all this be revenge for his death?' Will asked.

'Perhaps someone knows he was poisoned but doesn't know which of us did it.'

'And who is seeking revenge?' she said. 'His raven-haired actress daughter?'

'Frances Strange?' said Will. 'It's possible, I suppose.'

She could hear from his voice that he didn't believe it but was pretending to consider it so as not to set her off.

'I don't see how she could have known about it though,' he said. 'When it happened she was just a young girl living on their estate in Lancashire. Cecil didn't want Elizabeth to look weak so he hushed it all up and made Strange out to be a hero.'

The picture of Frances Strange kneeling over her with a knife in her hand flickered in her head for a moment.

'You were going to let her stab me in the throat, weren't you?' she said.

'God, no.'

For a man who made things up for a living, he wasn't a very good liar.

'William Shakespeare,' she said, shaking her head.

She knew he was wondering if he'd lied too much to back down now, and it made her want to smile. Finally he blew the air out of his cheeks and all of him seemed to deflate a little.

'I nearly did,' he said, 'but she was going to open up your windpipe so you could breathe.'

'Oh yes,' she said, 'isn't that what they said to Ann Boleyn on the block?' They sat there for an hour and a half and collected three farthings, a button and a carrot. Someone had thrown them a crust of bread but the monkey had grabbed it before they could. She picked up the carrot.

'Eat half then hand it over,' she said.

'No, you go first,' he said.

'What a gentleman,' she said. 'But then you are almost a knight.'

'Ann, Will,' said a voice above them.

They looked up. It was Lizzie.

WILL

Lizzie told them breathlessly how she had told Edgar Strange where she was staying, but then had doubts that she could trust him, so she'd left a pile of old clothes under the blankets in the bed and placed the plaster head of her from the magic show sticking out. She had kept watch on the alley and sure enough he had sent the man who tried to kill Ann to kill her. The man's name was John Johnson.

'And what are you doing here?' Will asked her.

'I was waiting for that playwright.'

'Which one?'

'He's always drunk.'

That didn't narrow it down much.

'He looks like he's dead.'

'Webster,' said Ann.

'Why are you waiting for him?' Will asked.

She told them about Evan, the bottle boy with his black eye who had been to Kemp's, and how, if he could be believed, there had been a coach waiting outside with four black horses with black plumes and a white-faced coachman and how she had thought of the tall, pale playwright who talked so much of death. She had come here to find him though she didn't know what she would do if she did.

'So it wasn't Berrycloth with the black eye,' said Will. Their one slim clue had just vanished to be replaced by another.

Lizzie had so much to tell them she never stopped talking. She'd got some money from somewhere – probably best not to ask where – and they found a stall and bought three steaming bowls of pease porridge.

An elderly woman with two cats stuffed in her jerkin, and who had given them a farthing, saw them stuffing down the bowls of porridge.

'Beggars, are you?' she said disgustedly. 'Eating food I can't afford. I bet you're not even blind.'

Lizzie offered to buy her a bowl but she wafted a gnarled hand at them and walked away muttering complaints to her cats.

Lizzie suggested they go to the house where the Widow had gone to hide. Louise, the other widow who had stayed at the shop, had told Lizzie where to find her. Anywhere warm seemed a good idea so they headed back towards the river.

The coracle was still there though the sword had gone. The tide was starting to turn and the current slower but the little boat still only made it across the Thames after a ferryman took pity on them and told them to grab on to the back of his wherry as he rowed.

He called to Lizzie as they reached the bank, 'My father owns a house and he's about to die. I'm going to inherit it so I'm a good catch. Want to marry me?'

'Tempting,' said Lizzie. 'Get back to me when he's dead.'

'I'm Sam Barebone,' he called after her. 'All the boatmen know me.'

They cut through Billingsgate market hoping they'd be harder to spot in a throng of people.

'Mrs Barebone,' said Lizzie. 'That is actually quite tempting. And, oh, oh...'she said remembering something else. 'There was a priest at the dinner disguised as a young gentleman. I knew because—'

Ann cut in. 'The coachman!' she said so loudly the monkey hid its head. 'The pale-faced coachman, the black horses with the black plumes, that's the coach that Cecil put us in to take us to the Isle of Dogs.'

She was right. He could see that long, pallid face beneath his black hat.

'It's not Cecil's coach though,' he said. 'It belongs to "Rich" Spencer.'

Spencer was not to be underestimated. His obsession with witchcraft made a very clever man seem foolish. He had first made money when the plague had wiped out nearly half of Venice. He had sent a ship and bought up the bedding of the dead for almost nothing, then when the plague reached London, had cut it up and sold it as shrouds. He moved into medicine – mercury, antimony, opium and wormwood, and then into everything else. He bought the docks where his goods landed, bought the carts and ships that carried them, and bought the shops that sold them.

He bought herds of cattle and the pie shops where they ended up, installed public latrines where the pies ended up, employed night-soil farmers to empty them and take the cess to his dung boats which carried it to his fields where it fertilised his grain which fed the herds of cattle.

He bought and bought and bought, goods, houses, men, respectability, but it was meagre respectability, given only to his face, for those born with riches thought him vulgar to seek what they already had. Who knew what secret anger seethed in him? Could he have lent his wealth to some plot? Was he somehow responsible for Kemp's death?

LIZZIE

All these strands and threads – she felt something was starting to take shape but she couldn't grasp it. Nothing quite made sense to her, especially Edgar Strange. He could have killed her up there on the tower, but when she'd felt the rotten rail giving way behind her, he'd pulled her back. Yet only he knew where she was staying so surely it must have been him who'd sent Johnson to murder her. And yet, why had he come running himself only half a minute after Johnson? She'd seen him sprint breathlessly into the alley when she'd kept watch in the rain and darkness.

She went back over the moments between them, those moments where there was that precipice of excitement as they waited to hear who'd say what next, those moments when her body didn't feel quite solid and her heart thumped against her ribs as if it wanted to be let out. Was he just playing a game with a silly girl, was he just acting? It didn't seem like acting but, of course, that was the point of acting. What could she be sure of? That he seemed reluctant to kill her. There'd been better starts to romance.

She heard Dutch voices and saw a labour gang of refugees ahead of them hauling away a donkey killed by a falling gargoyle in last night's storm. They turned right down a side street to get round it but when Lizzie looked back she glimpsed a cloaked figure turning the last corner as they turned the next. She told Will and Ann to turn right again so they were heading back the way they had come. When she looked behind them she saw nothing but when she looked in the shop windows she caught a fractured reflection of a dark shape very like the first one. She feared that if they were being followed that they would lead their hunter to the Widow. She told Will and Ann to continue their circular route, sprinted off ahead of them, then doubled back through the alleys so she came out behind them.

Her heart was beating at the speed she liked. She wasn't a fool, she knew all this could end with a blade stuck in her guts, but escaping coffins and dodging death from a falling axe twice a day had got boring and this wasn't, at least not yet.

'You should have been born a man,' Glendower had said to her once.

'Why?' she'd said. 'Why not a tiger?'

And there it was, the cloaked figure, sheltering behind passers-by, keeping its distance behind Ann and Will. She couldn't see the face but she didn't need to. She knew that walk. She stepped up behind it and tapped it on the shoulder.

'What are you doing?'

Evan's face jolted around in surprise.

'Um... following you,' he said.

'Doesn't look like it, does it?'

He shook his head.

'How did you find me again?'

'I waited around outside the theatre.'

She cursed herself for not having spotted him watching them. He'd learnt more from Glendower than she'd realised.

'I'm protecting you,' he said. 'I'm your guardian angel.'

She didn't want a guardian angel, but what was it she did want? The man who kept trying to murder her? Oh well, the course of true love never did run smooth. Was that one of Will's? The best ones usually were. She supposed her guardian angel might as well come with them. He was one of the few people in London who didn't want to kill them, at least she hoped he was. She wondered for a moment, if he'd followed them from the Globe, how he'd found a way to cross the river, but Evan had his skills. They hurried to catch up with Ann and Will.

'The coach you saw,' she said to Evan as they walked, 'can you remember anything else?'

'The horses had black plumes.'

'You said that before. Try and picture it.'

He closed his eyes, clenched his fists, and strained to do as she asked.

'It was low on its springs,' he said, 'as if it was full.'

Full, she thought, *or with one enormously fat man inside*.

ANN

The Widow found some food for Evan, who was ravenous but still shared it with the monkey. She found a fresh gown for Ann and was about to hand some men's clothes to Will when Ann stopped her. People knew Will Shakespeare's face. Wearing everyday clothes he'd be recognisable in a way he wasn't in beggar's rags. It was the Widow who suggested that they could dress him in women's clothing.

'That won't work,' said Will, and the three women laughed.

'So why do you keep doing it in plays then?' Ann asked him.

In the end he agreed.

Ann soaped Will's face, took the razor the Widow had given her and shaved away his beard. She did her best to be gentle where his face was bruised or torn, but she could see him wince.

'Sorry,' she said, but he just shook his head to say she didn't need to apologise.

As she scraped off the soap she saw the lines that had appeared and the shadows that had deepened. Without his beard he looked naked and vulnerable. Her rage at his uselessness back on the Isle of Dogs had faded. She felt most tender towards him when they did simple things for each other, these small acts of kindness.

She thought of her life with John and how such moments never happened. He wasn't a monster like her father. He'd never raised his hand to her – well, he'd raised it but he never carried through with it, because he never carried through with anything. He'd given up on the cobbler's business, and taken over a pub which he'd said was a little gold mine but which he'd turned into a big plague pit.

John gave free drinks to councillors, to the committee men of the local guilds, anyone who owned a gold chain. He dropped heavy hints about being made a Sergeant at Mace. They nodded and asked for refills. It wasn't that she scorned his ambition, she scorned how narrow it was. He scorned her for everything.

Lizzie was telling the Widow everything she'd told them and the Widow remembered that Edgar Strange's associate, who'd bought supplies for the Virginia expedition – a big man with pale eyes – had been called Mr Johnson.

'He bought forty faggots of wood, which was a lot, and had it delivered to West London,' said the Widow, 'I think a house in Prince's Chambers, but I can check.'

'But the ships for the expedition are in the other direction,' said Will. 'They're down the river in Wapping.'

'Even if it's not for the expedition, it's strange he bought it from us,' said the Widow as she fitted a bonnet on Will. 'There's merchants much closer to Prince's Chambers and that's a lot of wood to cart across London.'

She tied the bonnet under Will's chin.

'This Mr Johnson came back a second time too. He bought pickaxes and shovels, for the expedition he said, but this time they were delivered to a house across the river in Lambeth.'

'Is that the same one where Edgar Strange sent the salt?' asked Lizzie.

As she mentioned Edgar Strange, Lizzie flushed pink and Evan, seeing it too, glowered darkly.

'I think it was,' said the Widow.

'So again the wrong direction for the New World Expedition,' said Will.

'And I think he bought some charcoal from Allfarthing's up near Aldgate,' said the Widow. 'And from Wentworths in

Tooley Street and somewhere else down there in Southwark. You're asking why he'd go to so many different places, aren't you? I think he was trying to stop anyone finding out how much he was buying. He probably doesn't know how the merchants all talk to each other. I think he didn't want anyone asking questions.'

The monkey poked a long finger up Evan's nose, but he didn't seem to mind.

'I'll tell you something else about John Johnson,' said the Widow. 'When he first came in, that wasn't his name.'

'What was it?' asked Will.

She strained to remember but shook her head.

WILL

The Widow pulled some pots and bottled lotions out of the cupboard and pointed at Will.

'Shall we give him a bit of make-up?'

The three women all stared at Will's face.

'Perhaps not,' said the Widow. 'We don't want him looking like a prostitute.'

'Or just really desperate,' said Ann. She put on a man's voice. 'She's not got a wedding band. Her age and not married, it's sad. Though you can see why.'

Lizzie tried not to laugh and failed.

'I'd swive her,' said the Widow, now putting on a man's voice too. 'You don't look at the mantelpiece when you're poking the fire.'

'Not me,' said Ann. 'I like a bit more meat on their bones. Make them go on top in winter and keep you warm.'

She nudged Lizzie to join in.

'I'd give her a tumble,' she said in a northern accent, 'the ugly ones try harder, bless them.'

Now they were hooting, Will too, all laughing a bit too much after all they'd been through. Still, it was better than drowning in icy rivers.

The Widow couldn't find the exact address in Lambeth where the salt had been sent, but she said that Louise, the other widow, would know.

'She knows everything,' she said fondly, 'and if she doesn't, Little Marie will know. Her memory is amazing. '

They sent Evan on ahead to check it was safe, then walked

there briskly, laughing anytime Will tripped over his gown. They heard Holy Sally in the next street.

'He is here amongst us,' she shouted.

It was odd. She had said nothing but 'I have seen his face' for years.

A constable came around the corner, but he was just using a long rod to make sure people kept their distance because of the plague. Although those regulations had ended, some petty officials still loved bossing people around. Anyone who was too close he poked with the end of his stick. Their group stepped apart to keep the man happy as they walked up to the shop.

Evan told them it looked safe but when the Widow went to open the door, it was bolted even though the shutters were pulled back to show the shop was open. The Widow called out to Louise, but she didn't answer. They looked around them nervously. A man dragged a narrow cart stacked high with chairs, but nothing seemed out of place. The Widow's shouts were getting panicky.

He and Ann looked at Lizzie at the same time, both thinking of her housebreaking skills. Lizzie asked the Widow if there was a yard at the back and, when she said yes, squeezed past the cart and ran to the end of the street. Will picked up his skirts and hurried after her. He reached the corner in time to see her running along the top of the wall that separated the yards, arms outspread for balance. He hurried back to the shop door, where Ann and the Widow were talking to a couple of neighbouring shopkeepers. A woman fishmonger, still carrying a knife and a large, wriggling crab, was talking.

'And he asked where to find you – weaselly little bloke, had these pointy teeth.'

Will felt a lump in his throat that stopped him breathing. Lizzie opened the door from the inside, leant out into the street and retched. She was crying.

'Don't go in there,' she said.

Ann went to hold back the Widow but she shrugged her

off and ran into the shop. They dashed in after her. Everything was in place but the Widow ran on through into the back room. She screamed a horrible scream. He and Ann followed. Ann was slightly ahead and he heard her gasp. The Widow knelt on the floor in the middle of the bloody bodies of Louise and the two children.

'All my pretty ones,' she sobbed.

Ann turned to him and made a choking noise as if something fierce inside her was trying to escape. She said nothing but he knew. She blamed him for letting Dogface go.

ANN

Ann told herself that she must do something useful and stop going over what had happened in that bloody room but her mind wouldn't obey her. Had he killed the children first so Louise had to watch them die? Or had the children had to watch him stab their mother to death, knowing the same thing would happen to them? No, no, no. She mustn't keep picturing it. She must find some way to help Agnes. But what could she do? Agnes was sobbing and howling. Lizzie held her hands so she didn't tear at herself. Will stumbled out of the back room, his face grimly set, his shoes bloody, looking absurd in his women's clothes. He'd come dressed for a comedy and found himself in a tragedy.

In the street, a raven held down something wriggling with one claw and pecked at it unhurriedly.

Rage pulsed inside her. For twelve years she'd lived with the guilt of murdering Strange, but Will, he was too pure, he was too important, he was too much of a gentleman to get his hands dirty. He wrote about murder, but given half a chance to do something about it, to stop murder, what did he do? Stand there, a sword in his hand, and do nothing.

No, she must stop thinking about that too, busy her mind so it stopped dragging her back into that bloody room, find something useful to do. She went over to the crowd of shopkeepers who'd gathered and asked them what they knew about John Johnson. She heard the words come out of her mouth as if it was someone else speaking. A man said that he'd heard how, back in the summer, Johnson had bought saltpetre from a wholesaler down in Limehouse, and that too had been shipped down the river to a house in Fore Street in Lambeth. There was a voice behind her.

'You need to go before the constables get here.' It was Evan. He had some sense after all. She knew what they should do. They should go to that house in Fore Street. They needed to find out what was going on. They couldn't just wait around to be picked off one by one, never knowing why or what it was they'd done.

They tried to get the Widow to come with them but she wouldn't leave her loved ones. The band of tradesmen and women who'd armed themselves with billhooks and cudgels took her back into her shop and swore they'd protect her. Evan was arguing with Lizzie about something and he shouted at her and sulked off, taking the monkey with him.

So Lizzie came with them, pale and silent, shivering as if she was feeling the cold for the first time. Leaden clouds sagged in a sky the colour of pewter and a cold drizzle seemed to just hang in the air. They walked west through crowds of strangers who were thinking of buying warmer gloves or what they were going to have for dinner, and not a butchered family. Will lagged behind, head down, walking as if he'd only just learnt how.

She'd told herself that she was sick of him back when she'd found out he was trying to buy a knighthood but it was as if God had called her bluff, because when he'd fallen through the ice, it turned out she'd wanted him back. Well, now it was different. She was stuck with him until all this was sorted out but once it was over God could chuck him in a river or a plague pit or anywhere He liked. He'd see. This time she was really done with him.

Tiny feathers fluttered down in front of her face and for a moment she thought God was somehow answering her, but looking up she saw a woman leaning out of a window beating a bolster above her.

When she looked back down Will was gone. She turned

to see him running off down a narrow side street into the Syrian market, where men with bright robes and gold teeth sold whips, belts and bags.

She called after him, but he ran on without looking back, stumbling into a man supporting a stack of baskets on his head. Further along the street she saw what he must be heading for – an ornate sedan chair was moving away from them carried by four men in scarlet and gold livery. A short, self-important man with a gold mace was ahead of it, shouting at someone. He wore fashionable shoes with a three-inch-thick sole designed to raise you above the muck in the streets.

Another sedan chair was coming the other way and the street was too narrow for them to pass. A herald ahead of the advancing sedan chair was yelling, 'Back up. A marquis takes precedence over a mere knight.'

The short man with the mace laughed theatrically.

'Not if the marquis rides in a chair that the knight lent him.'

Both chairs had now stopped and Will reached the nearer one, stepped alongside it, ripped back the curtains and grabbed at the man inside. The man with the gold mace came back and tried to stop him, but Will shook him off. Ann saw who it was inside the chair – Sir 'Rich' Spencer. For a moment she thought Will was going to try and kill him but of course he wasn't. He shouted in Spencer's face. 'Why did you take your carriage to Kemp's house on Thursday?'

Spencer bellowed at the man with the mace, 'Hengist, get this mad whore off me,' and flapped at Will with a bejewelled sleeve.

Hengist had a red face and a ridiculously wide, waxed moustache. He lifted the mace over his head to bring down on Will but, as he swung it back for the blow, Lizzie took hold of it from behind him, and he toppled off his shoes and fell over.

'Did you go there to kill Kemp?' Will yelled in Spencer's face.

The sedan chairmen were all big men – they had to be to carry Spencer – but they weren't sure what to do.

'Don't just stand there!' Spencer shouted at them. 'Get rid of her.'

They put the chair down and advanced towards Will. Perhaps he'd be able to find something out. She tried to buy him some time.

'Please leave her,' said Ann. 'She's caught the plague and it's driven her mad.'

The men stopped and backed off.

Spencer had squashed himself on the far side of the chair to get as far away from Will as possible, but it left a gap. Will opened the door and squeezed himself onto the bench beside Spencer.

'Why were you outside Kemp's house on the day the gunpowder factory blew up?' said Will.

Spencer stared at him with his small, squashed eyes and Ann saw it dawn on him who it was.

'Why in Holy God's name are you dressed as a woman, Shakespeare? Have you gone mad like Homblet?'

'Hamlet,' Will corrected him.

'I've put money into your theatre. I can take it out, you know?'

'Why were you there?' said Will, and actually poked him with a finger.

'Tell him and he'll leave you alone,' said Ann.

'And who the hell are you?' said Spencer. 'Are you really a woman or another theatre batty boy dressed in women's clothes?'

Anger ripped through Ann.

'Christopher Marlowe was my brother, your son's dead lover.'

Spencer spluttered and his red face got redder.

'Why were you there?' Will asked again.

A haughty voice yelled from down the road, 'Tell him, Spencer, then we can all get where we're going.'

The marquis had stuck his long neck out of his chair.

Spencer made more furious grunts but finally turned to Will.

'I'll tell you if you get out of my conveyance.'

'I'll get out of your conveyance if you tell me,' said Will.

'For God's sake, Spencer,' shouted the marquis. 'Tell him.'

Spencer spluttered some more but finally capitulated.

'On Thursday, I was playing dice all day,' he said. 'At the residence of Lord Gilbert Talbot the seventh earl of Shrewsbury.'

He was furious but not too furious to boast of his acquaintances.

'You can ask him,' said Spencer, 'not that he'd let you on his estate, except to dig a new latrine.'

Everyone knew Talbot only let a merchant's son like Spencer on his estate because Spencer deliberately lost huge sums at cards and dice.

'So why was your carriage outside Kemp's?' Will went on stubbornly.

'Come along, Shakespeare,' the marquis cried. 'Off you trot, back to your scribbling.'

'You trot off back to your pox doctor,' yelled Will.

Not his finest line, but he no longer sounded like a man seeking a knighthood. Nor would he give up with Spencer.

'Was it Cecil you lent the carriage to?' he asked.

Spencer laughed scornfully.

'Oh, someone more important than that.' He waggled a finger stuffed into several bejewelled rings at his men. 'Earn your wages. If he doesn't get out of my chair in five seconds, kill him.'

Hengist pulled out a knife and the chairmen stepped up behind him. The marquis must have spoken to his men too because they hurried across to help.

'Get out,' said Ann to Will.

Will hesitated so she grabbed his arm and yanked him out.

The constable with the measuring pole was hurrying towards them from the far end of the street. They ran.

Will was trembling with rage.

'I should have killed him,' he said.

No, thought Ann, *you should have killed the man who killed the Widow's family when you had the chance*.

The argument about precedence had started up again between the two sedan chairs and no one was chasing them.

'Do you think Spencer was telling the truth?' asked Lizzie.

His boastfulness had made Ann think he was.

'Yes,' she said. 'But who is more important than Cecil? God?'

LIZZIE

No one answered when they knocked on the door of the house in Fore Street where the saltpetre had been delivered, so Lizzie shimmied up a cherry tree, forced a window and unbolted a side door.

They searched the basement to see if any of the goods that had been delivered were down there but it was empty. Maybe they really had sailed it back up the river to those ships at Wapping. Ann sniffed the air.

'It's the same smell as when you lit that barrel during the performance.'

'Brimstone,' Will said. He was still grim-faced and barely speaking.

In the drawing room, there was a portrait on the wall of a dashing young gentleman. It was good. His face looked straight out, set fiercely, as if daring the watcher to take offence, his hand on the hilt of his sword as if ready to draw. Will and Ann rifled through a desk but she stayed staring at the portrait. She knew him from somewhere.

'Yes,' she exclaimed, and Will and Ann turned around. 'He was sitting next to Edgar at the dinner.'

She worried that sounded too familiar.

'To Edgar Strange,' she corrected herself. Edgar Strange whose pale brown eyes hid his purpose, whose dark lips had lied to her. Edgar Strange whose hands were stained with the blood of Louise and her children. Edgar Strange who shouldn't be in her head.

She didn't want to be the girl who couldn't stop mooning

after a murderer. She pictured Louise and the children and it filled her with thick horror. And yet, and yet, Edgar Strange still wouldn't go away.

She imagined him hanging from the gibbet where he belonged, but even then, he just winked at her. She felt herself a thing beyond her own control, a drop of quicksilver in an alchemist's palm. Constables, soldiers, men with swords, she could outrun. Love was more relentless.

She went back to staring at the portrait. She wondered for a moment if he was also the man with the sword who'd nicked her back as she ran from the theatre's safe house, but then she thought he wasn't.

Ann and Will unbolted a door that opened onto a yard which led directly to a private dock where a large rowing boat was tied up. Will looked out across the river and pointed.

'That's the other house over there.'

'What are you talking about? Which house?' asked Ann.

'Prince's Chambers, the house where the salt was delivered.'

They decided to steal the boat and cross the Thames to have a look at it. Will and Ann took an oar each and she watched them row in circles until she lost patience and took over. Ann rubbed her forefinger on the bottom of the boat and it came away with a sticky residue. She sniffed it.

'Brimstone again,' she said.

'And the Widow said they delivered charcoal and saltpetre,' said Lizzie.

Brimstone was another name for sulphur, and Lizzie knew from the magic show.

'Mix saltpetre, sulphur and charcoal,' she said, 'and you get gunpowder.'

ACT FIVE

EDGAR

God, she was bold – the plaster head in the bed. It was as if she'd played a practical joke on them even as she fled for her life, thumbed her nose at them and ran off into the night. But now she must think it was him who'd told them where she was staying. When it was all over, perhaps he could find her somewhere and explain it to her. He was good at talking people round but this time it would be hard. He pictured her face, knitted and fierce, that weapon of hers clasped in her fist. She'd chew her lip in that way she did as she thought about it, but then perhaps her face would soften, and she'd lower that little spike and, in the end, perhaps she'd kiss him as she'd kissed him on the tower. The trouble was that he couldn't explain it to her. They'd never told him why they needed the five of them dead.

He locked the doors and headed back to his room to get some sleep. His hands were scratched and sore from carrying the wood, but he'd got used to all that during the Siege of Ostend – the University of War, they'd called it. He'd still probably be there attending those bloody lectures if he hadn't been chosen to carry that secret letter from King James, if he hadn't been betrayed and the Dutch hadn't handed him over to Cecil's men. Since then, he'd just tried to stay alive. Still, if it all worked out he'd step into a new world where he'd have power and money. He didn't think Lizzie would care much about that, but at least he'd be able to protect her.

You don't need to go back to your magic show, he'd say, *because from now on, it'll be you and me making the magic.*

And she'd groan and shake her head, and loose strands of hair would fall over her eyes, and she'd shake them away and call him daft but maybe she'd also smile.

A shout made him look up. A carriage drawn by four bay geldings clattered towards him and the coachman, stuffed into an absurd purple and gold uniform, yelled at him.

'Out of the way, you bastard.'

'I prefer "love child",' said Edgar, mostly to himself.

The coachman cracked his whip in Edgar's face and the carriage came at him, filling the narrow street so Edgar had to step back into a gutter deep in filth. It rumbled by, inches from his face, the horses snorting, their harnesses creaking, its polished panels smelling of fresh paint, its black curtains drawn, a lord's coat of arms embellished on each.

Well, thought Edgar. *I wonder if you'll be alive by tomorrow evening*.

LIZZIE

She couldn't get into the house in Prince's Chambers. The front door and the double door that led to the cellar were both locked or bolted, and it joined directly onto the other houses in Palace Yard on one side and the Palace of Westminster on the other. As they stood staring at it, a woman came out of the house next door, wearing an apron, her hands covered in flour.

'Can I help you?' she asked.

Lizzie had learnt long ago that this was what people in England said when they didn't want you there. She watched as Ann forced a smile.

'I'm from the Widow's chandlers. We've delivered a lot of materials here but we've not been paid.'

'Materials for the building works?' the neighbour asked, slapping her hands together so the flour made a small cloud in front of her.

'That's right,' said Ann.

'Hellish racket all autumn.'

'We mostly delivered to a house across the river,' said Ann.

'Yes, they rowed it across. Woke us up dragging it in there.'

So they did it at night.

'Workmen?' asked Ann.

'Mostly gentlemen doing the work themselves.'

Lizzie remembered the callouses on Edgar's hands.

'Not gentlemen who settle their bills,' said Ann. 'When women run a business they think they can get away with it.'

Ann's grumbling was very convincing and the neighbour was nodding sympathetically.

'What work have they been doing?' Will asked.

He was using his normal voice and must have forgotten he was a woman.

The neighbour's head jolted around towards him but she answered.

'Repairs, that's what they say. But it's my house that needs repairs now. There's cracks in my walls.'

'Is it a Mr John Johnson who's been working here?' Ann asked.

'Not heard that name. It's a Mr Percy who rented it.'

'So you haven't seen a big man, very pale eyes, he burnt his face a few days ago.'

'Oh him, yes,' she said, 'he's less of a gentleman and he's not called Johnson. My cousin knew him back in the Old Queen's reign.'

'What is he called?' asked Ann.

She took a moment to remember.

'Guy Fawkes.'

WILL

The neighbour went off to check on the saffron cake she was baking and as soon as she was gone they all started talking.

'Are they really going to blow up Parliament?' said Ann.

Will started to say that surely that wasn't possible but stopped – what else could it be? A group of Catholic gentlemen had bought the components of gunpowder, rented a house next to the Palace of Westminster and spent the autumn tunnelling beneath it. In a few hours, the king, his sons and all the lords in England would meet there to open Parliament.

Will had thought himself caught up in some grubby murder plot, yet here he was in the middle of something so bold, so huge, that it would shatter the course of English history.

Dread and horror swept away his exhaustion.

'We must go to Cecil,' said Will.

'Yes,' said Ann. 'He'll surely forgive anything else he thinks we've done.'

'I'll meet you at the Widow's shop later,' said Lizzie.

'Where are you going?' Ann asked, but she was gone, running with her long strides down the street.

They turned to go too, but saw the neighbour coming towards them carrying a plate with three slices of cake.

'Caught it just in time,' she said, holding it out towards them. 'As long as you like it crisp.'

Politeness made him pick up a slice and take a bite. It tasted of burnt sugar.

'Oh, here they come,' said the woman, looking over her shoulder. 'Good luck getting any money out of that lot, mind.'

He turned to see Johnson, or Fawkes, or whatever he was called, walking towards them with Dogface and two gentlemen. One was the man from the portrait where he'd had one hand on the hilt of his sword. Now he was drawing it. The four of them recognised Ann and Will and broke into a run.

He and Ann turned and fled, Will choking on his mouthful of cake and spitting out blackened crumbs as he ran.

'There's gratitude,' he heard the neighbour grumble.

Will glanced behind him and glimpsed the four men split into pairs, the two gentlemen coming after them and Fawkes and Dogface heading out of a gate on the north side of the yard.

'There's sentries at the Royal Quay,' he said, grabbing Ann's hand.

If they could make it there, they'd find protection, but the men chasing them were quick and running in skirts was hard.

They turned a corner into Cutter's Yard past a couple of workmen putting up barriers for the opening of Parliament. Could he appeal to them, shout that there was a conspiracy? Would they just think he was mad?

'Stop, thieves!' yelled one of the men behind them. It put paid to that idea.

He ran on, gulping, heart thumping, lungs shrieking for air. When he was younger it was his legs that gave out when he was running, now he just ran out of breath.

They turned into a narrow street of shops that ran towards the river, the quay and the soldiers.

'Nearly there,' he gasped to Ann.

Fawkes and Dogface came out of an alley ahead of them and blocked the street. The gentlemen with their swords drawn were behind them. They were trapped.

'In here,' gasped Ann, and led him through the door of a tavern.

It was crowded with workmen and they pushed their way

through, still fighting for breath. Drunken singing echoed through the low stone rooms. Will looked behind and saw Dogface and the two gentlemen coming in after them, while the silhouette of Fawkes blocked the door. At least there were enough women in the tavern that they didn't instantly stand out.

Will tried a door that looked as though it might lead to some stairs but it was locked and so they kept going towards the back. There was room after room, each lower, louder and smokier than the last. Will thought again of trying to get the crowd's attention and telling them of a plot to blow up the king, but you couldn't take a step in London without someone telling you about some daft conspiracy, and who would the crowd believe, a man dressed as a woman or the two gentlemen? He and Ann ducked through a low arch and down a couple of steps into a dark vaulted cavern that reeked of beer, sweat and smoke. Drunken men, arms linked, sang a song in a language he didn't recognise. They edged past them. The room ended in a wall, no back door, no window, no escape. They were trapped again.

He looked back. The three men were checking each room thoroughly so they would take a while to reach them.

'Hello,' Will shouted at the nearest singer. The man smiled amiably.

'No English,' he said, closed his eyes and tilted back his head, lost in the song.

He and Ann stepped into the darkest corner beneath a low arch and felt for any gaps, but the wall was solid stone.

'Stay here,' said Ann, tearing off the brown cloak she wore and rolling up the sleeves of the grey gown the Widow had given her. She looked different but not different enough.

'That won't fool them,' said Will.

She reached inside the small bag around her neck and brought out something she held between her thumb and forefinger. It was one of the nuts that had nearly killed her.

'No,' shouted Will, and reached out to stop her.

She put it in her mouth.

ANN

This time she knew it was going to happen and again it was quick – the hot, scary rush taking over her body, spreading to the tips of her fingers and toes. She spoke quickly to Will because she could feel the choking starting.

'Hide in the arch, I'll get the sentries.'

Already she was fighting for air and her eyelids had puffed up so it was hard to see. Would it work as a disguise? Will had said last time that her face was so red and swollen that she looked like a different woman so it was worth a go. She shovelled her hair under her bonnet and sucked in as much breath as she could get down her throat. Now she just had to walk. She made it up the three steps into the next room, and gasping, sweating, tottering, trembling, moved forward, one arm scraping along the wall to steady her. Everyone would just think she was drunk. The panic rose. That was what had happened before, the lack of air, the fist grasping her windpipe, but this time she at least knew what it was and could try and fight it. Through another door – stagger, stop, step forward again. There they were, she saw them through her half-closed eyes, the two gentlemen and Dogface scrutinising the faces.

She hoped it wouldn't be Dogface who checked her because he knew her best. It was. It would be so easy to kill her here, brush against her, twist a dagger up under her ribs and walk away. Another drunk woman falling over. He was staring at her. Did he know her? She was swaying, the room slowly spinning, and here he was, the rotting-meat stink of his breath, his spiky grin looming in front of her face. He reached a hand towards her, the mad-dog mouth close to her, spittle and black gums. His hand squeezed her breast. Good God, he'd seen a drunk woman and knew he could get away with a crafty grope.

Disgust, relief. She was past him, now she had to keep walking, one step, then another, heart pulsing crazily, she just had to get to the rectangle of light that was the street door, her mind without enough air to think, only holding on to that one thought, then there she was at the door not really knowing how she'd got there, the big one blocking her escape, Johnson, Fawkes, he knew her best of all, had remembered her from twelve years ago – *cunning bitch*, he'd called her. He stared at her. She twisted her swollen face into a grin, managed a cackle and made a lunge at his crotch. If Dogface could grope her, she could do some groping too. He recoiled disgusted, called her a 'drunken whore' as she lurched past him, but she was past him. *Cunning bitch*, she thought, *that I am*.

Her breathing was coming more easily, she could walk further without a rest. On she went, ten yards, twenty yards, and then like before she suddenly found herself there, standing in front of the sentries, two with halberds guarding the entrance to the pier, more playing dice sat on a bench at the side. They'd think she was mad or drunk or both. She had to get this right and she had to be quick.

'I'm a spy for Lord Cecil. There's four men in the Angel who are planning to blow up Parliament.' She gasped for breath. 'You may not believe me, but just think what'll happen to you if I'm telling the truth and you do nothing.'

WILL

He could see them but they hadn't seen him yet. He stripped off the dress. He was wearing a dark cambric undershirt and knee-length hose, but at least he no longer looked like a woman. The pointy-toothed one they called Dogface pushed his way down the steps into the last room. Calling him Dogface was a slander on dogs.

Will stepped out of the dark corner and put an arm around the man he'd tried to speak to. He didn't seem to mind. Will put his other arm around another singer. It wouldn't fool them forever but it would give him more time. He didn't think Ann would get the soldiers to come but perhaps, at least, she'd escape. He'd hold on to that thought, her walking free, walking out of this mess, living her life and finding some happiness.

It was a sad song full of yearning, and Will joined in, oohing and aahing to the tune so he didn't stand out. The two gentlemen joined Dogface and moved slowly, methodically, through the crowded room looking at the faces. Will sang. What else could he do? He howled along to that sad song, head tilted back like the man beside him, singing of a lost love or a lost land, he had no idea. He found tears rolling down his cheeks. He didn't know why. Was it for himself? Was it for Ann, for what they had and what they'd never have? The tears kept coming. Was this how he'd die, weeping as he sang a song he didn't understand? He turned to the man beside him.

'I love her,' he said through his tears.

'No English,' the man said, smiling.

'I know,' said Will.

Dogface was close. He broke into the circle of singers muttering that Latin incantation. Will could see the mean, small eyes. If eyes were the window to the soul, his soul was yellow and bloodshot. His stare flicked from face to face and went past Will. Then it came back and fixed on him. Dogface grinned. He pulled something from his belt and stepped forward. There was a loud shout from up the stairs. It was Johnson calling.

Dogface turned and ran. The other two followed him. It must surely mean Ann had done it and brought the sentries. Perhaps Death didn't want him, he'd escaped it time and time again over the last few days.

He made his way warily towards the door and there was Ann coming the other way, swollen-faced, gasping, but alive.

'The sentries chased them,' she said, gulping in air. 'But they were too slow. The plotters got away.' Another wheezing gasp. 'They're sending horses to take us to Cecil.'

He held her tightly, then let go, fearful he would squeeze out the little breath she had left.

He looked at her, that knitted frown, her chapped lips and her rough hands, that sharp tongue and that quick mind, the woman who kept saving their lives.

He wanted to tell her what he'd told the drunken singer but he mustn't. She did speak English.

LIZZIE

She knocked on three doors before she found his. His face was grimy and in the dark corridor his teeth gleamed white like a chimney sweep at night. He looked startled to see her but started talking rapidly.

'I didn't send him to kill you. They were upstairs when you told me where you were staying and they heard through the floorboards.'

Something made her believe him, but was it the same something that had nearly got her killed?

'They're on to you,' she said. 'They know you're going to blow up Parliament.'

'Who is on to me?' he asked, not denying it.

'Cecil will know by now. You should run.'

'And why have you come here to tell me this?'

She didn't know the answer. She supposed she must think he was different from the others. But why did she think that? Because his teeth weren't filed to points? Because he was handsome?

'Did you invite me to St Paul's tower to throw me off?' she asked him.

He hesitated.

'Yes,' he said, 'but I couldn't bear to. I'd never hurt you.'

Now her eyes had got used to the gloom she could see there was dirt in his hair.

He went to take a step towards her but she held out the needle in her hand and he stopped.

'Why were you going to kill me?' she asked.

He hesitated again.

'I don't know. I was ordered to.'

Her rage rose and she wanted to stab him.

'So you and your mates kill children without knowing the reason why.'

He looked confused and shocked. Could someone act that well? Of course they could.

'What children?' he asked.

She told him. He closed his eyes for a moment and grimaced, but that made her more angry because it was as if he was the one in pain.

'I didn't know,' he said, 'I don't know why he'd do that.'

'Well, he did,' she said, and held up her left hand, still stained with blood from where she'd lifted the Widow off the floor, and waved it in his face.

'I'm sorry,' he said.

All his words seemed so useless.

'I haven't killed anyone, I swear,' he said. 'Well, not in London.'

'So you're not going to kill anyone when you blow up Parliament?'

'It's…' He was struggling.

If he said *you wouldn't understand*, she really was going to stab him.

'It's a war,' he said finally, 'there's tens of thousands dead already.'

'Including two children.'

'I'm sorry, I'm sorry.'

He looked pale and desperate.

'Everywhere it's the innocent who die,' he said. 'I saw it when I fought in the Netherlands. But this time it's going to be different. The great men who send us to our deaths, this time it's going to be their turn.'

'It's just more death,' she said. 'Anyway, it's not going to happen now.'

'No,' he said, staring at her and not moving.

'Hadn't you better flee?' she said.

Again, he hesitated.

'Cordelia, can I come and find you when this is over?' he said.

'Over? With men like you when will it ever be over?' she said.

In her head, she was running from the Spanish soldiers with her mother and brother, her house on fire, her town on fire. She could smell the smoke and hear the screaming. She touched her father's medal hanging around her neck and asked him the question she should have got an answer to a long time ago.

'Whose side did you fight on in the Netherlands? The Dutch or the Spanish?'

He opened his mouth to speak, said nothing, but she knew the answer to her question. She slammed the door and walked away.

ANN

She and Will had ridden on the same big dappled grey mare, her sitting behind with her arms around his middle. He'd told the soldiers he'd taken riding lessons but, going around a corner, one of the cavalrymen alongside them had to give him a shove so he didn't fall off.

She wondered what her father would have said seeing her escorted through the streets of London by a squadron of the king's cavalry to reveal a conspiracy to Lord Cecil. He'd just have told her, *No one likes a snitch*.

They were taken to a comfortable room, invited to sit on a bench covered in faded yellow cushions and told Lord Cecil was three minutes away. Her face was sore, but she could breathe. It came and went so fast, it was a strange thing.

'What do I look like?' she asked Will.

He ran his fingers gently over her mouth and eyes.

'You,' he said.

She'd sworn to God that she'd finally had enough of Will but it looked like God had called her bluff again, thrown them into danger and shown her she didn't want to lose him. She was tired of being wrong and God being right, but, oh well, that was God for you.

'I shouldn't have blamed you for what Dogface did,' she said to Will.

His smile faded.

'No, you should.'

At least he wouldn't suffer the guilt of killing a man as she had.

'Do you mind that I'm a murderer?' she asked.

'You could slaughter thousands and it would make no difference.'

Here they were close as close could be but she knew, when this crisis was over, that the dull everyday would leech all the joy out of everything and leave them apart again. He sat there in his hose and an undershirt with that yearning in his eyes again. She feared he was about to say something more about the two of them but now she knew what to do. Talk of murder.

'What did Spencer mean,' she said, 'when he told us he'd lent his carriage to someone more powerful than Cecil? Who is more powerful than Cecil? Apart from the king.'

Will was very still for a moment.

'Good God,' he said.

'What?'

'The stone in Kemp's mouth.'

'Go on.'

'When Kent did his impersonations of the king, he always put something in his mouth, a small apple or a bit of bread so he could mimic the way the king's tongue got in the way when he spoke.'

'So what are you saying?' she asked. He seemed reluctant to say it out loud so she did. 'That the king had Kemp killed?'

Will still seemed to be in shock at his own thought. He lowered his voice. 'The king can't be behind the conspirators though, I know he's not very bright, but he's not going to blow himself up. Perhaps Kemp's killing was nothing to do with the rest of it.'

They heard footsteps and voices outside and Will stopped quickly. She recognised Cecil. He was speaking with a loud, confident woman. It was Frances Strange.

'So is Sir William coming here?' she asked mockingly. Ann couldn't make out the answer but Frances went on in an exaggerated but uncanny impersonation of the West Midlands accent that Will now tried to hide. 'I've some tragedies for sale, some comedies, and some lovely lady's gloves. I've a remarkable offer just for you, buy a history play and I'll chuck in a pair of slippers.'

A couple of men laughed.

'I'm going to be a knight,' she went on, encouraged by the laughter. 'I can trace my lineage back through nearly five minutes to when I stumped up seventy pounds for it.'

The accent had got absurdly thick on 'stumped up' and the men laughed again.

Ann didn't want to look at Will and witness his shame, but she reached out and tried to squeeze his hand. He wrenched it away, that hand which had written Frances Strange those love poems, those things of beauty, which she repaid with mockery. She spoke again.

'Oh, what, he's here already. Oops.'

She came through the door with Cecil wearing a blood-red gown of spangled silk over a sea-green petticoat.

'Hello, Will,' she said, with no hint of shame. 'Have you come to hand yourself in?'

'I have some very important intelligence for His Lordship,' he said stiffly.

'Oh, my oh my,' she said, 'so important that you've turned up in your underwear.'

Will looked away and said nothing. Ann wanted to help but there was nothing she could say.

'Oh well, I better be getting along,' said Frances Strange.

'And who are you marrying today?' asked Cecil.

'Oh, there's talk of the king of Naples. He has the pox and likes boys, but at least Naples is warm in the winter.'

She headed towards the door.

'I always come here to find out from Your Lordship what's going on, and you tell me, and I leave and then I realise you've told me nothing.'

'It's a gift,' he said, and bowed.

She could see that bending down hurt him. Did Frances have him under her spell as well? She left without ever having acknowledged Ann in any way.

Cecil dismissed the two burly men standing at the door. Will still seemed rattled so Ann hurried to tell Lord Cecil that they'd had no idea that Bella was going to stray from the script when she was playing the witch. He waved this away, as if it was no longer important.

'Walk with me,' he said, and led them down to the courtyard full of rare beasts.

LORD CECIL

Walking sometimes helped allay the discomfort from his twisted spine. The yellow opium Bella had given him really did dull the pain but it dulled his mind too, and a dull mind couldn't run England. He thought how he bore this pain every day so England was well governed, while the king hunted and flirted and pretended to write books.

Fortunately, he had long ago abandoned the dangerous notion that the world was fair. The dungeons of the Tower were full of men who held that misconception.

He listened as they told him excitedly about the plot to blow up Parliament and nodded. He would let them keep talking for a few more moments. They walked past the giraffe lying on the ground, its big eyes blinking slowly. Its keepers had heaped rugs and blankets over it to protect it from the cold, but he doubted very much it would survive the winter.

In the courtyard of the Tower were these pampered animals the king could not keep alive. Outside its walls were four million neglected and half-starved subjects in dangerous good health. One day they would come for the king with their billhooks and cudgels – come for the king and him. He hoped, given his rotten health, that he might be dead by then.

Ann Marlowe had stopped to stare at the flying squirrels who no longer flew. It would be safest to kill her and Shakespeare. They didn't deserve to die. Shakespeare had stayed out of politics as he had promised – Judith, the maid with the hair lip who Cecil had paid to spy on him, had reported back regularly. No, they didn't deserve to die, but then the world wasn't fair.

The problem was he quite liked them, particularly Marlowe's sister. If only a few of the nobility had her intelligence and courage. Perhaps he should let the whole court get blown up and make her queen. He smiled at the thought. He would see if he could find a way of sparing them. It was time to tell them.

'You have indeed stumbled upon something,' he said, 'but it's a trap that is about to be sprung. Edgar Strange is my man.'

It was pleasing to see their surprise.

'Strange has followed my orders and encouraged a conspiracy to expose the traitors in our midst.'

He wondered if he should stop there, but they had worked out a great deal already.

'There is, as you have discovered, gunpowder beneath Westminster Palace, but you may rest easy because Strange has dampened it down so it can't explode. I have seen it with my own eyes.'

He was glad that he had chosen Edgar. Flawed men were easier to govern. He chose men as he chose apples. Most people looked for perfection but he looked for a wormhole because worms knew which apples were sweetest.

'We'll mention this to no one, my lord,' said Shakespeare anxiously.

'That would be wise,' he said. 'You make things up, don't you?'

'That's a part of what I do, yes.'

They were pernickety these playwrights, why could he not just say 'yes'?

'Make up the most prolonged and horrible death you can possibly think of,' said Cecil. 'If you ever tell anyone about this, yours will be much worse.'

Shakespeare looked relieved. He understood this meant they would live.

'Yes, my lord,' he said.

He turned to Ann Marlowe to be sure she had taken in his threat.

'Long and horrible, my lord, I understand.'

There was a flicker in her eyes. Was she mocking him? For a moment he wanted to make her afraid, but he let the thought pass. There were other things he wanted from Ann Marlowe.

Across the courtyard they were feeding the lion, throwing bloody chunks of meat through the bars. They had tried beef and venison but it seemed to prefer lamb. The king of beasts was a silent and straggly creature. The other king wanted him to get a new one that roared.

'Why are the conspirators trying to kill us, my lord?' Shakespeare asked.

'Well, you are very annoying,' said Cecil, which made Ann Marlowe smile. 'Perhaps it's revenge for getting involved in Marlowe's death, but it's not my concern.'

His back was hurting badly and he wanted to be rid of them.

'I'll get someone to take you to the gate.'

'Yes, my lord,' said Shakespeare, 'and was it them who killed Will Kemp?'

Did he not know it was stupid to annoy a man in pain?

'Enough,' he said walking away. 'How would I know?'

'You seem to know everything,' said Ann Marlowe.

Flattery. She had all the skills. He was fairly sure he knew what had happened to Kemp but there was no need for them to find out.

'All I can tell you,' he said as he walked away, 'is that it was nothing to do with me.'

He did not like events that had nothing to do with him but it was best to leave this one alone. He walked towards the wolves, who watched him the way he watched other men.

He would run through everything one more time before he made his final decision. He had thought Bella's brutal speech on the Isle of Dogs would have shaken James, but the next time he saw him, the king only had one question.

‘So, Cecil, my little cockroach,’ he’d said. ‘Who would win in a fight between a lion and a bear?’

He had pretended to think about it carefully.

‘I believe the lion, Your Majesty.’

‘But surely not if it was one of those big white bears you get up in, you know…’

‘You’re right, as ever, Your Majesty.’ It was always simpler to agree with him. ‘I think an ice bear would win.’

‘You must get me one at once so we can try it,’ said the king, and his bevy of young men had chanted their agreement.

Cecil had tried to explain that they were quite hard to catch, but some lickspittle had told James that the king of Norway had sent one to England as a gift in the thirteenth century, which was probably true, and that it had been dressed in a bonnet and taken on a lead to catch fish in the Thames, which was probably not.

Anyhow, the king waved away his objections and talked over him, calling him Lord Can’t and the Duke of Do-Nothing. The king’s young men – Proute and the others – laughed long and loud, glancing at each other, not wanting to be the first to stop. The laughter at some of his jokes went on for over a minute. It had led to the death of one lord who had collapsed in a paroxysm of coughing.

All this meant that England’s dwindling treasury would have to pay an enormous sum to secure an ice bear and transport it to the Tower where it would promptly die. He wondered if more traitors or exotic animals had died there during the king’s brief reign.

Servants were running towards him with his ceremonial robes for the state opening. It was time to leave and he still had not made his final decision. He had intended to reveal the conspiracy now – show James the barrels of gunpowder in the cellar, so the king could see how the witch’s prophecy had come true, but now Bella had failed him, would that be enough? The king’s mind could wander off so fast.

Cecil had to be sure he would write no more secret letters

to the pope offering to tolerate Catholicism in England. Edgar had been captured by the Dutch carrying it to Rome and Cecil, who was surprised by nothing, had been astonished – mostly that the king had concentrated long enough to write a letter. Besides, it was a foolish idea. If the Catholics were no longer persecuted there would be no one to blame for everything that went wrong and how could you run a kingdom without that? He watched the wolves watching him with those unblinking yellow eyes and decided.

He had everything under control. He would let James go to Parliament with his sons, let him sit above thirty-six barrels of gunpowder, then he, Cecil, would discover the plot in the middle of the ceremony and show James how close he had come to death. That would surely make a lasting impression even on him. Cecil looked forward to seeing his face. At least there were small pleasures in this thankless job. Who would win in a fight between a secretary of state and a king? Cecil knew the answer to that.

WILL

They went to the Widow's shop and found Lizzie there already. Putting yourself in the mind of others, seeing through their eyes, was not only what writers did, but how humans were kind to each other, but with the Widow he couldn't bear to try. Her loss was so unbearable.

She sobbed and shook, but still she was going through the accounts, sending messages to other merchants in the same business, gathering evidence against the murderers, all the while tears ran down her face between those big freckles.

They could have told her that there was no point, that Cecil wouldn't care about the fine details as long as their heads were stuck on pikes to greet everyone who crossed London Bridge, but the task seemed to divert her a little from her grief.

He thought he could just about make sense of it all... Cecil fears James is sympathetic to Catholicism, so he employs Edgar Strange, the charismatic son of one of the greatest Catholic lords to recruit persecuted and bitter Catholics to blow up the king and Parliament. Then, at the last moment, Cecil heroically discovers the plot and turns James against England's Catholics. Edgar is perfect because he is illegitimate therefore can't be their leader so when the trap is sprung he can just fade away.

Lizzie must have been running through the same thoughts in her head because she asked, 'So if Edgar Strange is working for Cecil what will happen to him?'

'He'll mysteriously escape when Cecil arrests the others,'

said Will. 'He'll turn up abroad somewhere with a lot of money.'

'Won't Cecil kill him because he knows too much?' asked Lizzie.

'It's unlikely. Cecil can't kill his double agents, because then it would be hard to recruit more.'

Ann, who was helping the Widow with the books, spoke to Lizzie without turning around. 'You went and warned him, didn't you?'

She gave a small, reluctant nod.

Will didn't suppose that would change anything. She had warned Edgar that Cecil was about to find out, but he already worked for Cecil. He would do nothing different.

Will's body ached and his head was thick with tiredness. He could have lain down on the floorboards and gone to sleep, but he couldn't leave the Widow to pursue her campaign on her own. A boy ran in with more information. A merchant in Catford had delivered sulphur to the Lambeth house and told them that it was owned by Robert Catesby. He must have been the man from the portrait who'd chased them. The shop door opened again and a figure peered cautiously around it. He took a moment to recognise her. It was Bella, wearing a black horseman's coat and a wide-brimmed hat. She took off the hat. Her head was shaven.

ANN

'Have you seen my dog?' Bella asked.

They had to tell her 'no'. Her legs gave way as she stepped forward and Ann got her a stool.

'Where have you been?' Will asked her.

'Hiding. Cecil may forgive you but he won't forgive me.'

Her face was hollow with tiredness and her bare scalp was criss-crossed with small cuts. She saw Ann staring.

'I sold my hair,' she said, 'to buy food and clothes. I got almost nothing for it.'

The prices for human hair and teeth had plummeted after the plague, when so much had been available.

'Why did you do what you did at the masque?' Will asked.

There was no anger in his voice so either he'd forgiven her or was just too tired.

'Why did I tell the truth?' Her gaunt face smiled. 'I'd always wanted to try it one day.'

That was all they were going to get out of her.

She gulped the glass of wine Lizzie gave her.

She had put them all in danger, but not as much as herself. Ann found her anger at Bella had gone. She had always been this dark, glamorous woman, poems written about her, characters in plays inspired by her, and yet in Cecil's London, she was just like them – another piece of bait wriggling on a hook.

Will had just started to tell Bella what they had discovered when the Widow suddenly slammed a jar on the counter.

'Why salt?' she said.

They all looked at her. Grim determination stiffened her pale and haunted face.

'Picks and shovels to dig under Westminster Hall, tarpaulins to hide the digging, sulphur, saltpetre and charcoal for the gunpowder, the faggots of wood to hide the barrels of gunpowder and make it look like a basement full of firewood.'

Ann listened to her, amazed her mind could function at all after what she'd been through, but she went on with a fierce concentration.

'Twelve barrels of salt.' She waved the order form. 'Why salt? Salt's a preservative. They're not pickling herrings.'

'How does salt preserve?' asked Will.

'It draws the water out of food,' said the Widow.

She and Will saw it at the same time and spoke over each other.

'It's to dry out the gunpowder.'

LIZZIE

'Was it Fawkes who put in the order for the salt?' Ann asked the Widow.

'Edgar Strange,' said Lizzie before she could answer. That was what he had been doing the day she had met him.

'Is he double-crossing Cecil?' asked Will.

Of course he was. She'd wondered when she went to warn him why he'd seemed so intent on justifying an outrage that would never happen. He'd been recruited by Cecil to organise a fake conspiracy but had double-crossed him and turned it into a real one. He'd shown Cecil the useless dampened gunpowder, then shipped the salt to the basement to dry it out. The explosives were set ready to light.

Ann and Will were about to rush off and warn Cecil again. Should she warn Edgar? Of course not, of course she shouldn't. She just had to tell that to her legs, which had taken a step towards the door.

The speech she loved to act out as she walked through the night spun though her head.

And when he shall die
Take him and cut him out in little stars,
And he will make the face of heaven so fine
That all the world will be in love with night
And pay no worship to the garish sun.

It wasn't true. Edgar would be dead and the nights ahead would be dark and terrible.

WILL

The king, Prince Henry, Prince Charles, Lord Cecil, the dukes, marquises, earls, viscounts, barons, baronets and bishops of England and Wales, the 467 members of Parliament who had gathered from every borough and county, were ready to parade rank by rank into the Palace of Westminster and stand on its ancient stone slabs in their silk and ermine above a basement packed with enough gunpowder to blow them and half of London to kingdom come.

Just for half a second, a voice in Will's head whispered, *Let it happen*. Let them blow up the rotten heart of England, destroy its greed and graft, its whispered sycophancy and fawning lies, smash it to smoke and dust. Let the poor sift through the charred bones looking for jewels.

He knew at once the thought was madness. A couple of days ago he had been trying to edge his way into the ruling class and now he was imagining its destruction. If the conspirators succeeded, the bad would be replaced with worse and England thrown into a bloody civil war. He went to speak but Bella got there first.

'You can't tell Cecil,' she said.

He had forgotten her for a moment, forgotten that everyone thought Edgar Strange was Bella's son. Of course she was going to try and stop them.

'So is it true?' Ann asked her. 'Is Edgar your boy?'

'Yes,' said Bella. She closed her eyes for a second and took a breath. 'I'm his mother and your brother Kit is his father.'

Ann stared dumbly at her. Will too. Was she just saying it to try to save her boy?

'Christopher?' Ann said incredulously.

But Will watched her face change as she put it together.

'Of course,' she said.

Yes, of course. How hadn't Will seen it before? Not just his face, but the arrogance, the charm, that wicked swagger.

Ann's exhausted face had come alive. She kept starting questions and giving up on them as the next leapt into her head.

'Cecil needed him to say he was Lord Strange's son to make the conspiracy work,' said Bella. 'He told me he would kill us both if I said anything.'

She seemed naked and vulnerable without that mass of dark hair.

'So,' she asked them, 'are you going to betray him so Cecil can have him executed? Are you going to kill the only thing that's left of Kit?'

EDGAR

They said bastards were infected with the sin of their parents. What rubbish. They said they were the children of Satan. Ridiculous. They said they just wanted to tear down society. Well, fair enough, they were right on that one. Why wouldn't bastards want to destroy an upside-down world which put the blind chance of legitimacy above character, intelligence and perseverance?

Bastards couldn't lie back in their fat feather beds and wait for wealth and advancement to be carried in on a silver tray. No, bastards had to make their own way, and here he was ready, a Catholic and a bastard, an outsider twice over, a sharp-toothed wolf in a pen of sheep. For years he'd waited, waited, waited, those teeth clamped into a subservient grin until his gums ached. Well, now the waiting was over.

He wondered what was it like being blown up? He'd seen it happen to enough men in Flanders, but what if you were one of them? Was it just a flash and instant blackness, or was there a half-second where you thought, *Oh, I'm being blown up*? He hoped there was. He just wanted Cecil to know for one tiny instant that he'd been outwitted. He'd been so full of himself when Edgar had been dragged before him.

'Now I know some of your Catholics have a taste for martyrdom,' he'd said, pausing to sip from his glass of red wine, 'but once it gets going, it really is very painful and I think you'll regret it.'

He'd poured a second glass of wine and offered it to Edgar. 'If I was you, I'd work for me.'

It had been an easy choice. They fed him some filthy infusion which was supposed to reveal if he was telling the truth but it just made him sick and confused. Still, whatever he said must have satisfied them as Cecil had taken him on.

Cecil gave him back King James's secret letter and told him to deliver it to the Vatican as if nothing had happened. He returned to England carrying with him the pope's promise of absolution, given in advance for any future acts of murder committed against England's Protestants. Cecil told him that he must stay away from his mother and put about the rumour that he was Lord Strange's bastard son. He was the perfect agent provocateur – Catholic enough to incite them but not noble enough to lead them. No, of course he couldn't lead them. Oh no, he didn't have the sluggish, complacent blood of the nobility running through his veins – just the brilliance of Bella and Kit.

Finding lost young men willing to die for a cause was easy – wasn't it always? The foul treatment of Catholics helped and the pope's letter promising heaven as a reward for murder was catnip to the pious and jaded sons of the gentry. It all went swimmingly until the day Fawkes followed him to a secret meeting with one of Cecil's men.

But the good thing about this line of work was once you were unmasked they didn't just slit your throat and chuck you in the Thames, they always tried to get you to betray your masters and change sides. And changing sides was something he was good at.

Fawkes told him that now Edgar worked for him and the others mustn't know, so here he was back on the side he'd started on. The others would see God's hand at work, but he wasn't sure about that. He wasn't really like them with their hidden rosaries and secret pilgrimages disguised as hunting trips. He doubted his eyes had that faraway look they had as they took the sacrament. The others would be murmuring their prayers as they did this work. He was thinking of Lizzie, her tongue stuck out to catch a snowflake. He didn't think God would mind, after all He'd created her, and what a job He'd done there.

There was a slow blackmatch leading to a quickmatch, Fawkes had taken him through it. The blackmatch he'd chosen burnt at three inches a minute and was eight foot long so that gave him just over half an hour to get away. The forty foot of quickmatch leading to the barrels of dried-out gunpowder was itself laced with gunpowder and burnt faster than a man could run. He and Catesby had tried it out in the woods up at Notting Hill, set it in a circle around them, and he hadn't been able to stifle a whoop of glee as the line of fire raced around them. He would light the blackmatch in twelve minutes' time when everyone was packed in upstairs. His heart was thumping and his neck and back were prickled with sweat. He lifted up another bundle of faggots to clear a path for the quickmatch. Fawkes had told him that once it was lit, nothing would stop it, but he wanted to be sure.

Someone banged on the locked cellar door. He froze. He wasn't going to open it. If the plot had been discovered, it would be best to light the quickmatch now and blow himself up with the rest of them. Even Cecil would draw the line at a triple-cross. A voice whispered his name.

'Edgar,' it called. It was Lizzie.

He went to the door. 'You must go away.'

'No, you must open the door.'

'I can't do that.'

'So what are you going to do? Light the gunpowder and blow both of us up?'

So she'd found out. Who else knew? He knew what he should do – open the door, invite her in, kill her, light the slow fuse and go. And he knew too that he wouldn't do it. He unbolted the door and opened it.

Lizzie stood there. Next to her were Will and Ann. They'd used Lizzie to get him to let them in. There was another woman there he remembered as the Widow, the woman whose partner and children Dogface had killed. He looked away from her quickly.

Someone else stepped into the square of light. 'Charlie,' she said.

It was his mother.

BELLA

There was no time to embrace him, but she could not help it. She put her arms around him and held her boy tight. She knew how she had missed this, but not how very, very much. Beneath the scent of cologne and whiff of sulphur, he still smelt the way he had when she last held him.

'You've cut off your hair,' he said, his voice breaking.

She had forgotten how she must look.

'I sold it.'

She finally let him go but he still held her hands in his. Ann was staring at him.

'So you're Christopher's boy,' she said.

'So it seems,' he said, and smiled at his aunt.

She could see him try to take control. He let go of her hands and stepped back.

'Now all of you, you need to get away from here at once.'

'You need to stop,' Bella told him.

She realised she sounded like she was telling the mud-smudged four-year-old to stop eating earwigs.

'No, Mama,' he said. She felt that word tearing at her heart. 'This will finally set you free from Cecil. Go, and tell them all to go with you.'

All of them tried to talk at once.

There was the sound of heavy footsteps and the rattle of armour from around the corner, probably the King's Guard they had seen patrolling the area on their way there.

'You must all go,' Charlie said.

'No,' she said. 'You must come with us.'

The footsteps were close.

'Quick,' he said, and gestured for them to come inside.

They hurried through the door and he closed it quietly behind them. He went to bolt it but stopped, realising the patrol would hear. The footsteps were outside. They all froze, waiting for the knock of an iron-gloved hand, but the footsteps kept moving and faded away. Bella realised she had been holding her breath and slowly exhaled. She heard the others do the same.

A whale-oil lantern hung from a beam, but it only made a small pool of light and they could not see how far the dark cellar extended. Will unhooked the lantern and held it up.

'No, put it down,' Charlie said quickly, trying not to shout.

She realised he was fearful of the flame so close to so much gunpowder.

There they were in a dark cavern packed with explosives that a spark could ignite at any moment. Oh well, much of her life had felt like that. Now she must save her only son.

'You must come with us,' she said to him.

His voice hardened. 'No, go and leave me here.'

He drew his sword but she could not get the four-year-old out of her head and wanted to laugh.

'We've sent a message to Cecil,' said Will. 'He should have got it about now, but if you come quickly you can escape.'

Even in the darkness, Bella could see he did not believe a word of this.

'I'm going to light the slow fuse now,' he said, 'so I suggest you leave as quickly as possible.'

He struck a match from the tinderbox, lit a taper and held that in one hand and his sword in the other.

Bella stepped towards him.

'Charlie, don't,' she said.

'No, I'm going to,' he said.

'What?' she said, taking another step. 'Would you kill your mother?'

'Oh, you're so dramatic,' he said.

Ann stepped alongside her.

'And would you kill your father's sister?'

'You might as well kill me,' said the Widow. 'Your friend killed the woman and children I love.'

He didn't waver, but then she knew he was a good bluffer.

'No,' he said, 'you won't stop me.'

The flame of the taper was nearly down to his fingers so he would have to make his mind up soon. She took another pace towards his sword and felt the point against her breastbone. She moved forward again and it pricked her. He didn't pull it back.

'Charlie,' she said pleadingly.

Now Lizzie was alongside her.

'Oh, so you're called Charlie, are you?' she said. 'I suppose that's an improvement on Edgar.'

She took another pace forward so he had to move his sword sideways and place it against her chest.

'Oh, now you're going to kill me,' said Lizzie. 'Make up your mind.' And she stepped boldly forward.

He let the sword drop.

She took another pace and kissed him swiftly on the lips.

'I think we've had enough murdering for a bit.'

He cried out in frustration, threw down the sword and blew out the taper. Bella felt a cool gust of relief. And a hot prick of jealousy that what had stopped him was a young woman's kiss and not a mother's entreaty. Children, eh? He stood there with his shoulders slumped and again she saw the petulant small boy who would not come in for dinner because he wanted to keep playing with the wolf cubs.

The door scraped open and she realised she should have bolted it after the patrol had passed. In walked Guy Fawkes, followed by Dogface, followed by someone else Bella took a moment to place. It was Frances Strange.

ANN

It was five against three, and God knows which side Charlie would join, but either way it was five civilians against two murderers and whatever Frances Strange was. Fawkes and Dogface had swords in their belts and the two of them and Frances Strange all held pistols in their hands so this was a fight that she, Will and the others could not win.

When she saw Dogface her hatred clenched into a tight knot and she wanted to run and claw at him. Will took her hand and at first she thought it was to hold her back, but he squeezed and squeezed and she realised that he too was struggling to contain his rage.

No one had thought to hold back the Widow and, as Dogface bolted the door behind them, she ran wildly at him, but he laughed, knocked her to the ground and kicked her when she tried to stand. Lizzie knelt over her and stopped her from getting up for another try. Frances Strange looked at them all, at the sword and tinderbox on the ground, and ended up staring at Charlie.

'Shouldn't you have lit it by now?'

'Just about to,' he said with his most charming smile. 'So, is it you Fawkes works for?'

She kept pointing her pistol at him as she spoke to Fawkes. 'Pick up his sword.'

'Don't you trust me after all I've done?' he said.

'No, of course not,' she said. 'You've changed sides so many times you must be dizzy.'

Her face was hard set, the giddy little girl gone. She stared at them – those razor-sharp blue eyes, those cheekbones you could cut yourself on – Ann realised she had hated her for the wrong reason.

Dogface swung his pistol around so he too was pointing it at Charlie. Ann saw Charlie consider reaching down to pick the sword up but Bella muttered, 'Don't.'

Frances looked her over. 'Better with hair,' she said as Fawkes went and picked up the sword.

'We know you've dried out the gunpowder and we sent a message to Cecil about an hour ago,' said Will.

'Is that so, Sir William?' she said, going into her impersonation of his Midlands accent. 'Well, we'll find out soon enough.'

He wasn't having much luck with that lie. Lizzie helped the Widow to her feet.

'Do you know,' said Frances, 'if only you'd let women act onstage, I do believe that would have occupied me and I wouldn't have been bothered about becoming queen?'

Ann couldn't help herself speaking.

'Queen?'

'Oh, I hadn't noticed you,' said Frances Strange.

The Widow slipped Lizzie's grasp and ran at Dogface again, but this time Fawkes struck her in the throat before she got there and she fell, winded, to the floor. Ann's rage tightened another notch but Frances went on as if she hadn't noticed what had just happened.

'Yes, someone has to inherit the throne after James gets blown up and the idea of Eugenia of Spain is plain silly. I met her once. She's a huffy bitch and besides this is England – we hate foreigners. So, yes, it's going to be Queen Me the First. I have as good a claim as anyone.'

'So you tried to kill us all to revenge your father?' said Will.

'Oh, Sir William, you would think that,' she said, putting on that voice again. 'No, revenge is so provincial. Grocers in

Luton seek revenge.' She was enjoying his confusion. 'You wouldn't understand, it's about reputation.'

'Reputation?' said Will. Ann could see he was exaggerating his bewilderment to keep her talking.

'Apart from Cecil, you are the only ones who know my father tried to depose Elizabeth. I can't be the daughter of a grubby conspirator. I have to be the poor, sweet innocent dragged unwillingly to the throne.'

She put on a little girl's voice.

'What? Make me queen?' She giggled. 'Oh well, if you really must. I'm just a silly woman who'll do exactly what you tell me.'

She was finally centre stage where she wanted to be – centre stage in her blood-red gown with a pistol in her hand.

'Well, thank God, you went for conspiracy,' said Will, 'because you'd have been a shit actress.'

Ann laughed and Frances smiled thinly. Was there nothing they could do apart from annoy her? Bella's hand was inside her doublet where she still had that little knife, but they were up against swords and guns.

'Use the swords to kill them,' said Frances. 'We don't want to set off an explosion. Yet.'

Lizzie must have picked up the tinderbox because she sparked a flame and lit a taper.

'Stay where you are or I'll light the fuse,' she said. She held that in her other hand.

'It's a slow fuse,' said Fawkes, weary at her incompetence.

'I think you'll find it's the quick fuse,' said Lizzie.

Ann stared at her hand. It was. Fawkes froze. She must have pulled the slow fuse towards her until she reached the blackmatch, for that's what she held. It was only a couple of inches from the taper so she could light it quickly.

Fawkes raised his pistol but Charlie saw what he was thinking – that he could shoot Lizzie before she could light it – and stepped quickly in front of her so he couldn't get a clear shot. Will and Bella caught on and did the same to block a shot from Dogface.

'Light that and we'll all die,' said Frances Strange.

'Good,' said Lizzie, 'that's better than just us dying.'

'You'll blow up the king and all the nobles,' said Frances Strange.

'Oh, well,' said Lizzie. 'They've never done anything for me.'

Charlie was smiling at her fondly. He couldn't help himself.

'Leave or I'll do it,' Lizzie said to Frances.

'She'll never light it,' said Frances Strange, and walked confidently forward.

Lizzie lit it.

Everyone ran. Frances, Fawkes and Dogface were much closer to the door and they unbolted it and threw themselves out. The rest of them had little hope of escaping the explosion.

'I love you,' Charlie shouted to Lizzie.

There was no explosion.

'Bolt the door,' yelled Lizzie, 'I cut the fuse earlier.'

Charlie bolted it.

'When?' asked Ann. 'How?'

'After I told the Widow to run at Dogface a second time.'

'Misdirection,' said Will, smiling.

'We should leave quickly,' said Charlie. He seemed to have abandoned the idea of blowing up half of England.

Ann looked down and saw a pistol one of the plotters must have dropped. She picked it up, wondering who would use it best, and chose Bella. Bella took it and handed Ann that little knife, Charlie had his sword, Will had picked up a length of wood. It would be a roughly even fight even if the three of them were waiting outside, but when they opened the door, no one was there.

'So do you?' Lizzie asked Charlie.

'What?' he said.

'Oh, I thought you said something just before you thought we were going to die.'

'I can't recall. Can you remind me?'

'Oh, for God's sake,' said Ann. 'Not now.'

They needed to find Cecil again and tell him what was happening.

There was a shot and Frances Strange, Fawkes and Dogface came running around the corner pursued by a patrol of the King's Guard, led by Sergeant-Major Colonel Proute. Fawkes fired over his shoulder as he ran and hit a soldier in the leg.

WILL

The Widow snatched the makeshift club Will held, stepped in front of Dogface and, when he swerved to go around her, she smashed him across the face with the fat lump of wood. There was a bony crunch and he fell and smacked into the cobblestones.

Ann, of course, went for Frances, that little knife she'd been given clenched in her hand. Frances Strange raised her pistol, but before she could fire Bella shot her in the leg and she yelped, more in outrage than pain, and went down.

That left Will without a weapon and up against Fawkes, whose enormous frame barrelled towards him. *I'm going to step aside and let him through*, he thought, but to his surprise, rage stiffened him and he threw himself at Fawkes's legs. A knee smacked him in the face and his head cracked hard into the cobbles but he glimpsed Fawkes go sprawling. Charlie jumped on him and a couple of the soldiers piled on top. He'd shot their mate, so they banged his head against the cobbles a few times – quite a few times. Will hauled his bruised body upright and picked up the sword Fawkes had dropped.

Fortunately, Sergeant-Major Colonel Proute's magnificent head was a handsome but largely empty chamber, and he accepted what he first saw that those running away were malefactors and those stopping them honest citizens. Frances Strange's ear was bleeding from when she'd hit the ground and one of her cream Italian calfskin boots had filled with blood from the bullet wound in her leg and now it dripped over the cuff and soaked into her red robe. Will couldn't help himself and put on his broadest Midlands accent.

'Oops-a-daisy, Queen Me's fallen over.'

A soldier yanked her roughly to her feet. The spangled silk shimmered as she flounced furiously in his grasp.

'Don't you dare touch me,' she said. 'Do you know who I am?'

'No idea,' said the soldier.

She tried to scratch the man with those brightly painted red nails, but he yanked her arms behind her back, and it snapped that necklace she always wore. The fat pearls clattered and bounced over the cobblestones.

ANN

Frances Strange tried to threaten Proute, who unfortunately did know who she was, but Bella told him that she was an agent for Cecil and that Frances Strange had led a plot to kill the king. It was the king who had knighted him and made him a sergeant-major colonel and Ann watched the steady progress of this thought taking shape in his head. He shouted at his soldiers to take Frances to the Tower.

She hissed at Will as they hauled her off.

'You know nothing will happen to me. Cecil won't dare and the king won't believe it. I shall walk free.'

She was right, of course. At least, she didn't look quite so hoity-toity as she was dragged away, hopping on one leg, but even now, it was as if Ann didn't exist. Ann stepped close to her and whispered in her bloody ear.

'I killed your father. I poisoned him.'

Frances's head spun round and she gawped. Ann identified herself helpfully.

'Christopher Marlowe's sister,' she said.

Ann finally saw doubt in her face as she was dragged hopping away.

Fawkes was too groggy to stand straight and a soldier held his collar to hold him upright, while another tied his hands behind his back. Proute pointed at two of the militia.

'Oi, Bogbreath and Lardbucket, you take him.'

They muttered, 'Yes, sir,' their faces set in grim hatred of their commander, and they walked him away.

Dogface was still on the ground, his face a bloody mess.

He rolled onto his knees and started picking something up from the cobbles. It was the pointy teeth that the Widow had knocked out of his mouth. He was muttering something in Latin and it finally hit Ann what it was – psalm fifty-one, the opening verse.

If you were up for a hanging offence, you claimed 'Benefit of Clergy', which meant you would be tried in a clerical court which wouldn't pass the death sentence. To prove you were clergy, all you had to do was show that you could read Latin, so they handed you a Latin Bible but they always asked you to read the same thing – the first verse from psalm fifty-one.

'Have mercy on me, O God, according to your great compassion blot out my transgressions.'

So criminals learnt the verse in Latin – the 'Neck Verse', because it saved your neck. In the Marlowe clan it was passed down to each new generation – taught in the cradle along with their ABCs – or more often instead of their ABCs. Her father had muttered it shortly before he died, as if Satan might spare him on a technicality.

She had an awful thought. Could it save Dogface? You could never tell with the courts. Or would he never get as far as a court? He was just the kind of thug who Cecil would enlist if he turned against the others. She pictured Dogface's sneer as he walked free.

Proute shouted at the two remaining soldiers to take Dogface away, and they yanked him to his feet, one hand still clutching his broken teeth. Ann caught a glimpse of the Widow picking something up. It was the dagger that Dogface had dropped, and she ran at him screaming. The scream was a mistake because the soldiers turned and saw her coming and one of them knocked the knife away with his metal gauntlet. Dogface laughed, spitting blood, and fixed those little red eyes on the Widow.

'You should have heard that little girl scream when I stuck her in the guts.'

Ann took two quick steps and stabbed him with Bella's

knife. She got two thrusts up under his ribs before one of the soldiers pushed her away. She staggered backwards and sat down hard on the cobbles, amazed at what she had just done, but there was Dogface bleeding on the ground in front of her.

No one moved for a second. Dogface's eyes were open but she'd seen enough men stabbed in Canterbury to know he wouldn't last long. His blood trickled between the cobblestones down the slope towards her.

'Arrest her,' shouted Proute to the two remaining soldiers.

What had she done – just when it was all over.

BELLA

'Go on, idiots, arrest her,' Proute repeated to the two soldiers, and they headed towards Ann.

'No,' said Will, and stepped in front of her.

He tried to explain to Proute what Dogface had done, how he deserved to die, but Proute was like all weak men given power – faced with contradiction he just grew louder and angrier. Finally he pulled a pistol from his waistband and pointed it at Will.

The pistol had five barrels and a mother-of-pearl inlay in its walnut handle. It was the pistol the king had brandished boastfully when he was Sir Stuart – a rare weapon handmade for him alone.

'Stand away, or I'll shoot,' bellowed Proute, flecks of spittle dropping on his absurd, made-up uniform. Will did not move.

'Do what he says,' said Ann and gave Will a shove, but still he stayed put.

'What a beautiful pistol, sergeant-major colonel,' said Bella. 'Where did you find such a rare weapon?'

Angry as he was, he was eager to tell her. He loved to boast.

'It was a gift from His Majesty the king himself.'

His fine jaw with its fluffy beard jutted out with pride.

'It must be worth the cost of a regiment,' said Bella. 'He must think the world of you.'

Proute's face flushed the same colour as his fancy-dress

tunic. He must have thought she was implying that it was a gift given for his sexual favours.

'His Majesty gave it to me for a service I carried out,' he said, self-importantly, then realising that this too could be misinterpreted, hastily added, 'A political service.'

WILL

For a moment, Will didn't see where Bella was leading, but then he did. Sir 'Rich' Spencer had lent his carriage to someone more important than Cecil, which surely could only be the king. Evan, the bottle boy, had seen the carriage sitting low on its hinges as if it was full – or as if a very large man sat inside.

'Did you kill Kemp?' he asked Proute.

Proute didn't even hesitate.

'He mocked His Majesty in pubs, and His Majesty heard of this vile insult.'

Will waited to see if he'd go on and he did.

'He demanded Cecil do something but the little cripple wouldn't murder him, wouldn't even cut off his ears and nose, so His Majesty enlisted someone he could trust.'

Yes, thought Will, *but not someone with the brains to keep quiet about it*.

'So you strung him up from the ceiling,' said Will.

'Don't think for one moment that I can be held responsible,' said Proute. 'His Majesty was with me.'

Ann spoke before Will could. She was as incredulous as him.

'The king murdered Kemp personally?'

'Oh, no, no, no,' said Proute. 'He's the king. No, he sat in the carriage during the execution. But afterwards, His Majesty thanked me and said what a beautiful adventure it had been.'

Will thought he was no longer capable of astonishment

but realised he was standing there with his mouth agape. One more thing surprised him.

'You knew how to make it look as if the door was locked from the inside?'

Proute was affronted.

'How would I know such a low actor's trick? No, his landlady, in her youth, had been some sort of player.' He spoke the word like it was 'whore'.

Will was going to prompt him to keep speaking but there was no need. He couldn't stop.

'It was fortunate His Majesty chose me, as I'm so strong that I could lift him with one arm, and had a free hand for the noose.' He was boasting like a five-year-old. 'I hoped Kemp might make one of his quips, but he just sobbed,' he said, with the petulance of a man who had been cheated and wanted his money back.

Proute waved a meaty arm at the two remaining soldiers.

'Come on, you sewage-eating clodpoles, take her away.'

Will tried to argue but the panic in his mind curdled his words and Proute boomed over him.

'Enough prattle. She killed a witness before he could be interrogated. She'll hang at Tyburn and that's an end to it.'

Will stepped forward and thrust the sword he was holding into Proute. He must have been very angry because it went through his ribs and came a good foot out of his back. Proute's mouth opened in surprise. He looked down at the sword and fell over. Again, everyone was still for a moment.

'Oh no,' said Ann.

The two of them were finally going to be together, only on a scaffold. Bella picked up the five-barrelled pistol.

'No need to shoot anyone, lady,' said the bigger of the two soldiers.

Bella kept hold of her pistol. The big soldier elbowed his mate.

'Me and him saw it all, didn't we? How our much beloved sergeant-major colonel got run through by the little pointy-toothed bastard, and how this good lady here managed to stab him to death with his own dagger before he could do any more harm.'

Now Will recognised him. It was the grizzled man who had been the first of the soldiers to disobey Proute and help fish Will out of the Thames. The scars on his baggy face looked like the seams on a much-mended pair of pantaloons.

'I've got that right, haven't I?' he said to his pal.

'You have indeed,' said the smaller one, glancing around to check there were no other witnesses.

He had the powerful shoulders and thin, stringy legs of a man who'd once been a sailor. At his feet, Proute had stopped moving, so perhaps Will had stabbed him through the heart. He'd been lucky to get the sword between his ribs. The little one now held the stage and was enjoying himself.

'You have it right, except in one small but important detail. I think you'll find our much beloved sergeant-major brigadier colonel was, in fact, run through twice.'

'Twice?'

'Yes, twice.'

The little one put his foot on Proute's chest, pulled out the sword and impaled him again with feeling.

'You sure it wasn't three times?' said the big one. He took the sword and did the same.

Proute's blood ran in channels between the cobbles, turning this way and that until it mixed with Dogface's blood. Proute would have been outraged to bleed to death with a commoner. The big soldier pointed at the five-barrelled pistol Bella had in her hand.

'That could fetch a lot of money.'

'It could,' said Bella, and handed it to him. He tucked it in his breeches and nudged Proute's body with his boot.

'Sad, our major corporal general never got to fight in a war but got killed all the same.' He looked at Will. 'It's a tragedy.'

The two soldiers picked up a leg each to drag him off.

Lizzie gave him a shove to get him started. The big one spoke between gasps of effort as he heaved.

'This was the noblest Roman of them all. Angels shall hymn him to his rest.'

This wasn't the time to tell him he'd mixed up two plays.

FRANCES STRANGE

Did she have to do everything herself? If she had stayed behind to light the fuse she would be queen by now. But, no, no, she had left it to a man.

God knows, she had done everything else. When Fawkes had told her of the plot to blow up King James – excellent idea – and the plan to install Eugenia of Spain as a puppet – less good idea – she had convinced him there was an English Catholic queen available and that said queen was standing in front of him. And when Fawkes had discovered that Edgar was an agent provocateur and wanted to kill him, well, sweet God in heaven, she had wanted him dead, but, no, no, she had told Fawkes that if they got Edgar to change sides then there was still a chance to outwit Cecil. She had done everything important and thought she could leave one small detail to a man – sparking a flame and holding it to a match. Something a child could have done – an idiot – even King James.

She would have been such a good queen, none of that male bluster and bravado, no starting wars because of small, silly slights. She would have put aside her personal feelings as a good monarch should, and got down to doing what was necessary – killing her enemies. No fooling around like Cecil with trials and made-up charges. She would do it properly, send murderers in darkness and make sure she wiped out whole families so their sons and daughters would not come looking for revenge.

People joked that when Elizabeth was queen, England was ruled by a man, and that now James was king, England was ruled by a woman. Rude. But if she had been queen they would have said England was ruled by a she-devil, though they would have said it very quietly because they would be terrified. She could have been Frances the Impaler – no, that was overly specific. Frances the Fearsome, that had a ring to it. Or just plain Frances the Terrible. Yes, that was the one. The weaker sex indeed. Why were all the female characters onstage such softlings? Someone should write a character like her.

There were footsteps outside and a key turned in the lock. They must be coming to release her, and about time. Now she could not kill them all she would have to find something else to keep her busy, something she was suited for – perhaps become a theatre producer.

TUESDAY

BELLA

Charles Clampitt and his new bride, Cordelia, arrived at Wapping in a cart to board the *Discovery*. They had been very late joining the expedition to found a colony in America, but they were making a generous contribution to the supplies – molasses, salted beef, even some gunpowder. The Widow had got a good price for the rings that had found their way off Proute's hands and into Lizzie's. Lizzie said the sergeant-major colonel had given them to her and Charlie as a wedding present, though there did not seem to have been a wedding.

Bella had found her son and now, what seemed only seconds later, she was losing him again. With kind winds he and Lizzie would arrive in America in ten weeks – with cruel storms they might never. Yet, what could she say, for when he was a boy she had told him tales of her voyages – of huge white fish with tusks as long as their bodies gliding ghost-like beneath the ice; of mile-long blue-black waves as high as hills rolling towards their tiny ship, each one weighing their fate like a God; of a vast flock of exhausted birds that had, in mid-ocean, rested on their rigging and turned it green and gold. She too had been forced to flee her country, though, unlike Charlie, she had not tried to blow up an entire ruling class. But, oh well, she supposed it showed ambition.

Charlie and Lizzie had said she should come with them, and as far as she could tell, they had meant it. She yearned to step away from this old world of tyranny and corruption into a New World where men would no longer be governed by a vain, bragging despot, but she had started again too many times with a new name and a new history. It was too late. She had set like molten metal in a mould – a dagger that could no longer be reshaped.

Besides, she still had hopes that Tamburlaine could be found. She had told herself that she had bought him for protection but now she knew that she had bought him because she needed a loyalty and devotion not found in men. She feared he had been eaten for he was the size of a small cow but she offered a generous reward and put out word in all the small villages east of London, in every tavern in Limehouse, Shadwell, Ratcliff, Poplar and Bow.

She was still exhausted from her time on the run and she sat on the cart with Charlie while Lizzie led the oxen and Will and Ann walked behind. Above them a heron flew down the river, its wide wings flapping so slowly it didn't seem enough to keep it in the air.

After Proute was killed, Will and Ann had hurried to find Lord Cecil and she calculated that, rather than flee, she stood a better chance of survival if she came with them to ask his forgiveness.

When Cecil met them, he ignored her. Ann and Will told him of how Edgar had double-crossed him and Cecil made it very clear that history would record that it was he who had sent his men into the crypt, discovered the gunpowder and saved England.

Sure enough, he was going to release Frances Strange. He required a conspiracy which was going to install a foreign Catholic as queen. It was only as he left that he turned to Bella.

'As you've cut off your hair,' he said, 'I won't cut off your head as well.'

It was all that she could have hoped for.

They turned a corner and there were soldiers guarding the dock, huddled around a brazier, roasting what could have been a rabbit but was probably a cat. Charlie was being hunted but he was well disguised with pale make-up, his hair dyed and cut short and the high crowned hat and plain grey doublet of a Calvinist. He must have been London's most handsome Puritan.

Bella tensed nervously as they reached the soldiers, but Lizzie did a sudden cartwheel and grinned at them as she picked the reins back up and they just grinned back.

If Bella had had a daughter she would have wanted her to be like Cordelia Clampitt. And her son – would she want him to be like Charles Clampitt? Well, he was and she loved him dearly. She wondered again if she should step aboard the ship with them, but no, America was for Lizzie and Charlie – what a race they would make!

WILL

'Proute deserved to die,' Ann said to him as they helped to unload the cart. 'You don't need to feel bad.'

'But I do,' he said.

'That means you're a good man.'

He didn't feel like a good man.

'It'll get better,' she said, 'you need to distract yourself.'

He would. He'd write. He'd seen evil in men – and in a woman. He'd seen a family murdered. He'd write about that. He'd write about a world sunk deep in darkness where men threw away reason and turned to superstition and witchcraft. Now he could see how the stories from Holinshed, the tales of King Llyr and Makbeth would take shape.

He'd write about the barbarity before civilisation and the different barbarity when civilisation failed. And he'd write a fool worthy of Kemp though Kemp could never play him. Will had been a bad friend, abandoned him in his foolish quest to become a gentleman. Well, he wasn't one and never would be.

Ann was pointing.

He turned to see Mr Charles Clampitt carry his new bride up the gangplank onto the ship, grinning that wolfish grin. For a moment he was fearful for Lizzie, but thinking about her he wondered if he should be fearful for Charlie. Or perhaps America. Charlie put her down and Cordelia picked him up, slung him over her shoulder and carried him across the deck past some surprised sailors. Had he and Ann ever been like that? Not really. He wondered if they ever could be.

BELLA

A small voice called her name, and when she turned she saw a gang of children beyond the soldiers waving at her. On a rope they held a very large dog.

'Tamburlaine,' she cried, and he heard her.

He looked this way and that, saw her, yanked the rope out of the children's hands, bounded towards her, bowled over a soldier and jumped a pile of barrels. She braced as he leapt up, but he knocked her over anyway. She felt the hot, comforting stink of dog breath as he licked her face. He jumped up and pranced in excitement, his bottom in the air, tail thrashing, knocking over everything in reach. He was back, the dog that had changed her, the weapon that had become a conscience. The children ran past the soldiers and all tried to tell her at once how they had found him in Whitechapel, hungry and howling. Of course, everyone knew whom he belonged to, and they had been looking for her.

She got to her feet, thanked them and asked them what treats she could buy them from the vendors and they said marchpane, honey cakes, jellied eels, griddled pigs' trotters, fried chicken feet and roast chestnuts and she promised to buy all of these. They patted and petted him as he rubbed his great, grizzled head against her legs. He was very smelly for a conscience.

LIZZIE

The longest side of their cabin was shorter than she was and the bunk where she was curled up smelt of tar and sweat but she didn't care.

When Lizzie had run through the dark streets of London performing the speeches she loved from *Romeo and Juliet*, she barely thought about how it was the story of two lovers from opposing sides in a war, two lovers who ended up dead. Perhaps real life would have a happier ending. There was a knock on the door.

'It's Charlie,' said Charlie.

'You don't have to knock. You're my husband.'

He came in.

'Us Puritans are very proper.'

He looked at her and unusually seemed lost for words.

'My bounty is as boundless as the sea,' she said. 'My love as deep; the more I give to thee, the more I have, for both are infinite.'

'Mine too,' said Charlie, then closed the door and lifted the sheet that covered her. She wore only Frances Strange's restrung pearl necklace. He looked at her with a kind of wonder.

'Oh my America, my new-found land,' he said.

'Have you stolen those words from someone, Mr Clampitt?'

'I'm not the thief, Mrs Clampitt,' said Charlie, as he got into the bunk beside her. 'Now I do hope you like turkeys and tobacco.'

'Potatoes are my particular joy.'

She'd heard that the first expedition that had gone looking for sites to build settlements had only survived the winter because the local tribes had taken pity on them and brought them food. She didn't know if she'd survive the New World, she just knew she couldn't endure the old one.

The ship had been resting on the mud but the tide was coming in and, as she wrapped her arms around Charlie, she could feel it start to move, just a quiver and creak at first, but then it wobbled afloat. She liked feeling no solid ground beneath her feet.

ANN

Evan had come to say goodbye. He'd found Glendower wandering lost in a bog and he, Glendower and the monkey were going to take the magic show to Wales. Evan claimed the monkey understood Welsh. Everyone was leaving and it was time she went back to Kent.

Ann was squeezed together with Will, sitting on a capstan on the dock. He'd wrapped his fur cloak around both of them and she lay her own cloak over their knees for extra warmth. Here they were parcelled up together again, but nothing had really changed. Whatever it was between them had gone on for half a lifetime and they'd never been able to make it work. They blamed it on the world but she suspected it was just them.

Underneath the bundle of clothing, he tried to take her hand. Underneath, of course, so no one could see.

'No,' she said.

He looked at her startled. It had come out louder than she had meant. But she was the practical one and she needed to be practical.

'I can't manage without you,' he said.

What was he talking about?

The Widow had lost her lover and the children that she adored. They had tried to get her to come and see off Charlie and Lizzie, but 'no', she'd said. 'I've too many things to do at the shop.' Ann knew she was trying to find a way to shut out grief, and the Widow knew it too, and they both knew it wasn't going to work, yet still she got on with it, still she managed. Well, if she could manage so could Will.

'Ann,' he said to her.

He must have said 'Ann' to her so many thousand times over the years, angry, sad, weary, excited, happy or just asking her to pass the butter, but this felt like a new 'Ann' that she couldn't quite fathom. He said it again.

WILL

Why was he trying? He doubted he had ever persuaded her to do anything.

A bitter gust blew down the Thames. He looked at Ann, that strand of grey hair among the black as it blew across her forehead, cheeks red with cold, those brown eyes that had refused to fade away back when he tried to forget everything about her.

'We've wasted too much time,' he said. 'We're married to people who we don't love, who we don't even like. We should be together.'

She shook her head violently but its ferocity made him think she was struggling with herself and it gave him hope.

Over long years of separation, against all logic, despite the misery it had brought them, they still held each other in their hearts. Wasn't that love? She had risked her life to pull him from an icy river and he had killed a man to save her from the gallows. If that wasn't love, what was? She infuriated him, she mocked and derided him, drove away his friends, turned his life upside down and he didn't know how he could live without her. That was love.

ANN

It didn't surprise her that he kissed her but it surprised her that she kissed him back. She kissed him back for a long time, so long that his lips, chilled by the cold wind, grew warm. Oh, why did he have to make it so hard? Why couldn't he walk away, leave her to busy herself with one thing after another, and year by year forget him? She broke away. He was breathing hard, those giveaway eyes of his full of yearning and fear.

'I love you,' he said.

She didn't doubt it, but to her, love wasn't being struck by an arrow from Cupid's bow. Love was being stuck in the guts by a broadsword that was thrust up under your ribs and sliced your heart in two. She mustn't be tempted, fall into the same trap, believe love could conquer all. Love could conquer sod all.

'Nothing's changed,' she said. 'I'm a married woman. You know the rules. You can't walk around London with me and I'm not going to be the mistress you keep in an attic.'

'Damn the rules,' he said, but he'd said that before and it didn't change anything. 'Come live in my house,' he said, 'come live with me.'

He hadn't said that before, but saying it and doing it were two different things.

'What will people think?' she said.

'People can go whistle.'

'Listen to you, Sir William.'

'You're never going to let that one go, are you?'

'No,' she said, but she liked the 'never' because it spoke of them being together for many years.

Death had tried to grab her but came away clutching only thin air. Now was love stretching out a hand, careful fingers hovering fearfully? Should she reach out and grasp it or would it just drag her back down into misery like before?

'What do we do when everyone turns on us?' she asked.

'We'll stay at home, we two alone will sing like birds in a cage and laugh and tell each other tales.'

'Oh, poetic,' she said, but her doubts took hold again as she remembered how he had poured out his heart to another woman in those sonnets.

'Shouldn't you save that for one of your sonnets to the raven-haired Frances Strange?'

'Oh, come on,' he said. 'Surely you know.'

She didn't.

'What do you mean?' she asked.

'The dark lady, she's you.'

'Me?'

'Of course she's you! Who else could I write love poems to?'

She thought he was lying, then she knew he wasn't.

'It's not at all clear,' she said, hearing the peevishness in her voice. 'She sounds like an aristocrat.'

'What do you want me to write?' he asked. 'Sonnet to the dark-haired landlady of the Flying Horse?'

She didn't see why not, but she let it pass for now, their faces close, their breath mixed together, white vapour in the cold air. She put her arms around him.

She still wondered how would they survive the ordinary. It wasn't tragedy and death which had battered her but the slow grind of all those days, not the storms of life, but the never-ending grey drizzle, the chill gloom of early dusks. Was she even still capable of joy?

No, she was talking rubbish again. Damn it, he was right, they'd wasted enough time. What did she always do? She got on with things, got on with things and laughed at disaster. Well, if she could laugh at that, she could laugh with happiness, with joy, with love.

Her body was shaking and she felt tears in her eyes. She hadn't cried for the dead, for any of the dead, and here she was sobbing. Will wiped her tears away with a kerchief that needed a good wash.

WILL

Was Ann crying tears of happiness? He wasn't quite sure. Happiness and sadness got all mixed up. That was the trouble with life – it couldn't make up its mind if it was a comedy or a tragedy.

Lizzie and Charlie came on deck and waved. The tide was in and the sailors unhitched the ropes and wound them in coils on the deck. Perhaps new beginnings were possible. The three ships hoisted topsails, and out into the brown torrent of the Thames sailed the *Constant*, *Godspeed* and *Discovery*.

AUTHOR NOTE

At the end of the first book I said there were a few deliberate historical mistakes to help the story, but I was sure there would be many accidental ones. There were.

The Historical Novel Society was very nice about the book but they got me bang to rights on a few errors. There were no telescopes, no house numbers, and potato pies were a luxury.

There's one where I kick myself. A reviewer on Amazon pointed out that the diminutive for Christopher Marlowe was Kit not Chris. Of course it was! I've changed it this time.

So, what is true? There's not that much that we can be absolutely sure about, which of course is very helpful for a writer.

There are as many conspiracy theories about the gunpowder plot as there are about 9/11. I would say that it probably did happen and it's possible Cecil knew about it. It's also conceivable that Cecil encouraged it, though fantastically unlikely that Shakespeare uncovered it.

I have probably been unfair to Guy Fawkes, who was always described as brave, though he was willing to kill hundreds if not thousands of people. It is true that he used the pseudonym John Johnson and that, after his arrest, the authorities took two days to discover his real name.

I have also libelled King James the First. His poor reputation has recently been reassessed though, of course, you can't write a book agreeing with what has been said before. Those around him described him as witty and clever but then he was King so they had to. It's true he did write books, but then so did Sarah Ferguson.

He is probably best judged by his actions. While King of Scotland he personally interrogated witches and had Agnes Sampson both burned and hung. It is also true that before he became King of England he did write a secret letter to the Pope. Anyhow, I have gone with the lazy, thin-skinned, pompous, misogynist – any resemblance to modern-day rulers is purely coincidental.

Turning to other characters John Webster was indeed the son of a rich coachmaker and his first play really was called *Christmas Comes But Once a Year*. Oh that it had survived.

The date of Kemp's death is unclear but he probably died in poverty around this time.

Ben Jonson did kill a man in a sword fight, and was imprisoned for insulting the King, but was released before November the fifth and was reported to have attended a dinner held by the gunpowder plot conspirators though now some dispute this.

Frances Strange is loosely based on Anne Stanley, Lord Stanley's eldest daughter. I changed her name to Strange for consistency, then struggled so much with two Annes that I gave her the name of Frances, her youngest sister. Anne Stanley led a fascinating and difficult life, but was not involved in the gunpowder plot unless history missed that.

Bella, Lizzie, Proute, Edmund Strange, the Friar, Evan and Glendower are all fictional – that is, even more fictional than the rest of the characters. There was, however, a conjurer in London who made the severed head of John the Baptist speak to the crowd.

Many small details are probably true. The plague of 1603 to 1604 killed around sixteen per cent of Londoners and I did read somewhere of schoolboys flogged for not smoking.

King Haakon IV of Norway did give Henry the Third a polar bear, which supposedly wore a bonnet and was taken by its handler to fish in the Thames on its lead. It's not reported how many handlers it got through.

Entry to see the menagerie of exotic beasts in the Tower of London – including lions and leopards – cost one penny, though it was free if you bought a dog or cat to feed the lions. However there were no giraffes in London until 1827.

Three ships did leave London to found the colony of Jamestown in Virginia though not until 1606. Saint Paul's tower did have a rotten balcony, and lovers carved their name initials in the lead.

The Dark Lady sonnets are hard to date but most likely written in the last years of the 16th century. Numerous scholars say they have worked out with certainty who the dark lady is and there must be at least two dozen names. None of them are Ann Marlowe.

Ann's mother and father most likely died in 1605. Not a great deal is known about her husband, John Crawford, but he did become Sergeant at Mace in Canterbury and probably died before 1610. Ann was a feisty widow arrested three times in her fifties for fighting neighbours with a sword. She probably outlived just about everyone in this book and is believed to have died aged eighty-one. She had twelve children, so she almost certainly had living children in 1605.

There was a mention of a Shakespeare play called *Love's Labour's Won* but it is uncertain whether this was a lost companion piece to *Love's Labour's Lost* or a misprint.

1605 is just before Shakespeare's most extraordinary period of creativity when he wrote *Macbeth* and *King Lear*. Macbeth was clearly influenced by the craze for witchcraft and the gunpowder plot.

I've owned up to a few deliberate inaccuracies where I've changed things to make a better story. I'm sure there are many more where I've just got it wrong. I hope you enjoyed the book enough to overlook them.

ACKNOWLEDGEMENTS

First and foremost I would like to thank Cari Rosen who is a wise and sharp editor and whose enthusiasm launched me into the wonderful world of writing fiction.

Also huge thanks are due to my publishers, Tom Chalmers, Fiona Wilkinson, Lisa Paderes, Sam Rennie and everyone else who does such a brilliant job at the Book Social.

Rose Cooper has done her second extremely classy cover and thank you to Ross Dickinson who came out of retirement to copy edit it. I hope he didn't regret it when he saw my grammar again. Any mistakes are mine not his.

Thank you to my agent Marc Berlin and my assistant agent Julia Wyatt. Marc has been my agent for longer than I can remember, though given his vice-like grip on everything, I'm sure he remembers perfectly.

Again I should mention the Lockdown Bakehouse, where everyone tolerated the many hours my dog and I occupied a table while I wrote it.

Thanks to Lara, Louis and Jack who again helped me grapple with technology and everything else in life.

Above all thanks to my wife and fellow writer Bernadette Davis who probably read it more times than she would have liked, who told it how it was and always made it so much better.